Matched in Seoul, Found in Love

ALEX ALVIN

SASHKINA

ISBN:(Paperback) 979-8-9923881-8-3
(eBook) 979-8-9923881-3-8
Author: Alex Alvin
Cover Design: Damonza and Diego Catto Val
Editor: Kirsten Rees, Editor, Coach

• Website: sashkina.com
• Instagram: @alexalvinauthor
• Facebook: @AlexAlvinAuthor
• Email: alex@alexalvin.com

PART
One

CHAPTER

One

"Can you hold the elevator, please?"

Her voice reached Jason's ears while he frantically pressed the 'close' button. A manicured hand shot between the sliding doors, that immediately opened back up with an ominous squeak. As the elevator shook, Jason let out a barely perceptible groan. Climbing stairs all the way to his eighth-floor apartment would have put a nail in the coffin of his long day.

Having just gotten off the metro, Jason wiped beads of sweat off his forehead and adjusted his scrub top. Summer of '22, everyone agreed, was beating heat records, even for the Washington, DC area.

"Thanks!"

Teeth clenched and desperate to get home, and yet her voice drew his eyes upwards. A young woman had stepped into the elevator, now staring directly at him. Jason swallowed hard. He didn't expect her to be so attractive.

"Could you press eight for me, please?" The woman looked at him expectantly.

Realizing the stranger would be going to his floor, Jason gestured at the control panel, where the number eight had already been hit. The woman glanced over and smiled. As she did this, he studied her.

She had a nice, open face and large brown, almost black, eyes. Her reddish-brown hair was pulled up into a ponytail, a loose strand dangling to her shoulder.

He forced a polite smile, but then noticed the telltale swimming bag she was carrying. It was a large one from 'The Container Store,' with blue and white stripes. He'd been seeing it at the pool a lot that summer. Immediately, his smile faded.

Jason's apartment building had the nicest pool in the neighborhood: large, deep, shaded. When looking for a new place, he had made sure of that. Only to discover right after moving in, however, that the pool was always overcrowded, which made it nearly impossible to enjoy. He strongly suspected outsiders somehow snuck in, and now wondered if the attractive stranger was one of them.

The elevator doors opened, and they walked out, the woman stepping out first. Jason dragged his tired legs along the corridor, while she marched on, confidently at first, then paused abruptly to look at her watch, so that he almost bumped into her. She turned around, her large dark eyes looking directly at him. They were unsettling.

"Excuse me, do you know where 805 is?"

"805?" Jason's voice cracked. He threw a sideways glance at his own door, just down the corridor. This uncomfortably attractive woman was standing between him and a quiet evening.

"I am cat-sitting," she said, as if that explained anything. "My friend, Charlie, she's gone to her parents' in L.A. Family emergency. But she got this kitten two weeks ago. She asked me to cat-sit. I've never been to her new place though."

Jason felt sorry for her. Well, almost, but then she adjusted the straps of her swim bag, and he remembered the crowded pool.

"805 is right this way," Jason squeezed out. "Just follow me. I'm in 807."

He winced at the overshare but kept walking.

Too late now. But of course, what did it matter? I'll never see her again.

One good thing about living in a large apartment complex was the high turnover of residents and the anonymity. They came and went, and Jason could keep to himself. Which was just how he liked it. Soon, though, his plans would roll out for his future. Married, settled down, and living a completely different life.

Jason thought about his upcoming trip to Korea. In just three weeks, he would be in Seoul, where he would meet several women, matched by the algorithm of the dating app, Kayeon. It was the best dating app in Korea, powerful and thorough. Thanks to Kayeon, Jason had three matches already lined up.

Just a matter of meeting them in person, and then, Jason hoped, he would find his perfect match and future wife.

"Thank you so much. You know, the cat's name is Percy." The woman adjusted the strap of her swim bag that had slid down her shoulder again. "Isn't that adorable? If I ever get a cat, I'd also name it Percy."

"Percy? That's so old-school." Despite himself, Jason felt the corners of his mouth turn upwards.

"I know. That's what makes it adorable. She's orange."

"She? I thought Percy was a boy's name."

"It is. But Charlie thought the kitten was a boy at first, then just decided to keep the name. So now Percy is short for Persimmon, not Percival."

"That's cool."

"You wanna meet her? The kitten." The woman scanned

Jason's face for a reaction, then narrowed her eyes. "You aren't an axe murderer, are you?"

"Of course not." Jason shook his head. "Far from it. I'm a podiatrist."

She didn't react, and Jason suspected she didn't know what a podiatrist was. Most people under fifty didn't and this woman looked considerably younger. He'd guess she was in her early thirties.

But the next moment, her face brightened.

"You're a foot doctor? But that's fantastic. Feet are like wings."

"Like wings?"

"Yes, they help us move. They're like the human equivalent of wings."

"Never heard that one before." Jason raised his eyebrows. What the woman was saying sounded very strange, but she seemed friendly enough. "805 is right here." He pointed to the door and stepped back to let her through.

"Thank you."

"You got it," Jason said and walked up to his door, his keys jangling.

What is the matter with me? Why did I tell her I was a podiatrist?

Fumbling with the keys, he heard her open the door to 805. A series of loud, almost aggressive meows followed.

"There you are, Percy! Come here, little girl. Come here."

Out of the corner of his eye, Jason could see the woman squatting at the threshold, while a bright orange paw extended to touch her.

And then, it was too late.

"Look at this girl." She picked up the kitten and brought her towards Jason, seemingly oblivious to anything else in the world. The kitten wasn't just orange; it was a bright color, almost glowing. A veritable fireball.

Percy's eyes were closed, while she purred like a Porsche

engine. So loudly, Jason suspected it could be heard at the other end of the hall. The dark-eyed stranger's hand swept gently back and forth between the kitten's ears. "Little Percy, you must be so lonely. You're just a little baby, aren't you? Aren't you?" An even louder purr was heard in response. "Want to pet her?" The woman asked, and Jason nodded.

The door to his apartment stood ajar. The three of them, Jason, the woman and the kitten, had created a strange configuration, with the corridor between them connecting the two neighboring apartments. It was an odd sense of belonging that struck him. As if the walls of the apartment did not exist and he was now a part of something bigger. He had joined a purpose, and it was thanks to this kitten and this bizarre woman. She lifted the tiny creature closer to him. Jason reached out to press his finger gently between Percy's ears. Sensing his touch, the kitten opened her eyes. They were unlike anything Jason had ever seen before. Bright, clear, greenish yellow. Percy stared at Jason for a moment, as if to ascertain if he could be trusted, then closed her eyes and returned to purring, comforted by the touch. Jason wanted to pick the little cat up and hold her, but at that moment the woman announced:

"I gotta check on Percy's food. The poor thing must be starving."

"Yes, of course. I'm Jason, by the way." He reached out his hand, but realized she wouldn't be able to shake it, being fully occupied with Percy. So, he pulled back and stuck it in his pocket.

"I'm Kiana."

"Kiana? That's a cool name."

"Yeah. Everyone says that. My dad's Persian." She shrugged. "He picked it."

"Oh, neat."

"And my mom's Russian."

"That's a great combination!" Jason exclaimed and turned

beet-red. Why was he complimenting this stranger on her heritage? Her voice, her demeanor sounded flirtatious, and that threw him off.

"I know, right? Only in DC!" Kiana rolled her eyes. "I mean, where else could this happen? A Russian-Persian. And I speak fluent Russian, not that I ever get to use it."

"That's so cool," Jason gushed, forgetting all about a relaxing evening he'd been planning. "I'm nowhere near as interesting as you."

"Come on! I bet you're fluent in Korean."

"What?" Jason's mouth gaped open. "How did you know?"

"I went to George Mason. We had a ton of Korean students." As she spoke, her hand returned to petting Percy, who kept purring loudly.

"No, seriously? No one ever guesses I'm Korean."

Jason didn't have the typical Korean looks. At least he didn't look like any of the BTS boy band members or K-drama actors, with their striking features and swoon-worthy faces. Jason had never had any misconceptions about his appearance: he was average-looking, at best. He knew his face was unmemorable with its flat nose, prominent cheek-bones, deep-set eyes, bushy eyebrows. It was the kind of face you ignored, and most women did exactly just that. The only thing he liked about his appearance was his height: standing at 6'2. He was also fit, having spent years doing taekwondo. Though he'd given up the martial art after spraining his ankle, the habit of exercising never left him.

"I can just tell. And you look Korean."

"I do?"

"Yeah. You're Korean, right?" Now it was her turn to blush. "Just making sure."

"I am."

Jason was about to say something else, just so he could continue the conversation, but the kitten stopped purring, and meowed loudly, opening her mouth wide and revealing tiny sharp teeth.

"Percy is hungry," Kiana yelped. "I better go feed her."

"It was nice meeting you," Jason managed to say, but his new acquaintance was already rushing into the apartment, whisking Percy away. The door to 805 slammed shut, and he was left standing alone in the corridor.

Without Kiana and Percy, the hallway was back to its normal appearance – dimly lit, worn-out carpet, walls painted a neutral soul-sucking gray to conceal dirt. Jason hesitated for only a brief moment before going into his apartment.

CHAPTER

Two

THE SECOND HE GOT INSIDE, his phone pinged. A text from his mother.

Jason always suspected she had that 'mom sense' and knew when she could get his full attention. No point in trying to ignore the text, because if he did, she would call. And if he didn't pick up, she would call back until he answered. The thirteen-hour time difference with Korea did not stop his mother from speaking with her son twice a week to check on him and keep him updated on the latest news from Seoul.

A quick glance at the notifications confirmed it.

> Jun, call me.

She always called him by his Korean name, which, of course, had to be changed the second he had landed in America.

Fortunately, Jason's uncle Suk-jin, who'd been living in New Jersey since the early 1980s, explained to his parents that a name like 'Jun' would be a problem for a boy, and everyone agreed Jun should pick an American name instead. He chose his name because of the actor, Jason Lee. It made sense with their family name, which was also 'Lee', and his uncle, who went by the name Henry in America, approved.

"Smart boy," uncle Henry shouted on the phone, "Good choice. Good thinking. And with your last name, no one can tell if you're white or Asian, or whatever. Excellent choice."

Jason didn't know why that was important at the time, though it became evident shortly thereafter. And so, Jun Lee became Jason Lee, which was supposed to guarantee him a relatively normal social life in America upon arrival. That didn't exactly happen but moving to a new country at the age of fourteen without speaking a word of English wasn't supposed to be easy.

Jason's mother had always been a morning person with no problem getting up at five to call her son right when he got home from work. Just as she was getting ready to go on her morning walk in Namsan Park.

So, he picked up the phone and called her, preempting additional texts and calls.

"Jun, are you alright? Have you had dinner?"

"Eomma, please, don't worry." Jason tried to keep his voice steady. "I just got in, so I'm about to make dinner."

"My poor son!" His mother exclaimed so loudly, Jason pulled the phone away from his ear and started to frantically search for his headphones, so he could free up his hands. "It's all because you're single. You need a wife to make you dinner, to wait on you. What man cooks his own food?"

The question was rhetorical, of course. He stayed silent. There was no use in saying anything to his mother on the topic. So, he waited. Usually, his mother would move straight to how Jason needed to continue the family bloodline, how many of her friends already had grandkids in elementary school, and how, at age thirty-seven, he was nearly past his prime and would likely be too old for his children if he ever managed to reproduce.

"Jun! Are you listening to me?"

"Yes, Eomma." Jason put his headphones in just in time to hear shrill notes in his mother's voice. He tensed. His mom never lost her temper. "Jun, this is important. How is the search going?"

"It's going well." Now it was his turn to sound shrill.

"Well, I am glad we enrolled you in the app. It works so well. Just so well. My neighbor, Mrs. Moon, her daughter got married last year, all thanks to the app. It's a modern-day miracle." Jason's mother gushed about the matching service, Kayeon. This was nothing new. It was Jason's mother who had recommended the dating app to him, had enrolled him, submitted all the documents on his behalf. Now, thanks to her, he had installed the app on his phone and was scrolling through the matches daily. All of them pre-screened by the dating service and its powerful algorithm, and meeting his requirements, one of which was a readiness to move to the United States if the relationship were to lead to marriage.

"Eomma, I'm not arriving in Seoul for another three weeks." Jason raised his hands in meek protest, forgetting his mother couldn't see him.

"Planning is important, Jun, especially in the summer months. Have you made sure they will be in Seoul when you are there? I don't want any of the matches to be on vacation. That would just be bad luck." His mother paused. "But of course, if one was not available during your visit, then it just wasn't meant to be." His mother, despite her insistence Jason use the dating algorithm and leave nothing to chance, was a strong believer in fate and destiny when it came to love.

"Don't worry, Eomma, I got three dates lined up already. And that's all they let you do in a week. And then for the following week, in case I need it, I'll find a few others. And I'll be all set."

"Great, great, Jun. You have to make the most of your time in Seoul."

"Of course."

He'd already cooled down in the apartment. Though the building was old, the AC worked very well, and Jason kept it running all day, with the thermostat set to 73F. But he could still feel the metro, the grime of the commute, which felt as if it had seeped into his bones. Jason needed to get out of his scrubs.

To his relief, he heard his mother say: "Well, I've gotta go on my walk before it gets too hot out. It's been raining a lot, but this morning is lovely."

And so, the conversation ended. Now Jason was truly free for the night. He put his phone on the charger, had a shower, then sat on the couch, a navy blue Arhaus piece he'd carefully selected after researching for hours, and stared mindlessly at the TV. Shortly after settling into his new apartment, he'd bought a 75' Samsung, and it dominated the living room. The second he'd brought it into the apartment, Jason knew he'd made a mistake.

But returning it to Best Buy was too much of a hassle, and he'd gotten a great deal on Black Friday. Jason consoled himself that pretty soon he'd be moving into a house, and the TV would finally get the space it deserved. For now, it took up almost the whole living room wall, and made him feel guilty if he didn't turn it on.

And so, he did, flipping through the channels, as he settled on a movie about a wealthy socialite in love with a young man. Immediately, Jason thought of Gwen, his last serious girlfriend. They were together for four blissful years and would have gotten married, but her family was old money from Philadelphia's Main Line and expected Gwen to never work a day in her life and eventually marry someone who'd grown up playing lacrosse.

But Gwen and Jason were in love and existed in their own little world. It had been a bubble, as they learned, as soon as

Gwen introduced him to her family. It took just one dinner to break them up.

The family patriarch, Grandfather Strickland, a tall, gray-haired man with a paunch, had served in Korea in the Marines. Grandfather Strickland took one look at Jason, banged his fist on the table, and announced he 'never expected to have a Gook sit at his table.'

Jason stood staring at Gwen, waiting for her to confront her grandfather, but she'd frozen in place. The rest of her family did the same until Gwen's mother, the first to recover, took Jason aside and asked him to 'come back later'.

Jason left the restaurant and went back to his apartment, where he waited for Gwen to call him.

The call never came. Not that night, not a week later.

There was no explanation, no apology, no closure. Nothing. Jason blamed himself and agonized over how he should have reacted to Grandfather Strickland. Whether he should have resisted or should have grabbed Gwen and run out of the restaurant. Whether he should have confronted Gwen's family. The worst of it was that Jason missed Gwen.

He missed her for far too long, and for many years the thought of Gwen made him feel a familiar, sickening mix of longing and dejection. Now, it felt more like an old scar that occasionally twinged.

By the time Jason was ready to date again, he was busy studying for the MCATs and then he'd started podiatry school. No one dated in podiatry school. Everyone was too busy. There were a few hook-ups, but no one ever came close to how he felt with Gwen, though their relationship had been so long ago, sometimes Jason wondered if it ever happened. The thought he'd dreamed it up crept into his mind more and more often, as time went on, separating him from his only meaningful relationship with a woman.

In the back of his mind, Jason had always assumed he'd find someone as soon as he'd finished his studies, but what he didn't take into account was that he'd have to do several rotations and a residency, all in different hospitals across the country. There was no sense in finding someone only to move away several months later.

The transient lifestyle suited Jason – it provided an easy explanation for why he was still single in his late thirties.

CHAPTER
Three

JASON FLIPPED to an episode of *Law & Order*, as he did whenever he wanted comfort.

Upon moving to America, his uncle Henry had recommended they watch TV 'to improve their English,' and so, the Lee family had the TV on at all times. In high school, if Jason had a minute to spare, he would dutifully sit in front of the TV and watch whatever was on. He'd been addicted to television ever since.

His favorite show quickly became *Law & Order*. There was something about its formula that worked: the storyline, the mystery, the detective work, all tightly wrapped into a forty-five-minute episode with an ending that made sense and offered a resolution. Jason could always count on it to make him feel good. He paused the show for just a moment to make himself a bowl of ramen, of which he knew his mother wouldn't approve. And then sat down in front of the TV while slurping his noodles. It was Thursday night, and on Friday he'd have the early schedule. The head podiatrist at the practice, Dr. McGrath, a confirmed bachelor in his early fifties, went out dancing salsa and bachata on Thursday nights, so on Friday mornings it was Jason who had to start at 7am, while Dr. McGrath showed up at noon.

"I love those thirsty Thursdays," Dr. McGrath would chuckle. The same thing happened on Mondays, because, according to Dr. McGrath, the best salsa and bachata gathering was on Sunday nights in Adams Morgan.

The TV episode finished just after seven. To get to work on time, Jason would have to get up at five the following morning. At first, he thought of hitting the gym, but then he remembered the pool, which closed at eight. The image of Kiana with her 'Container Store' bag flashed in his mind. Normally he avoided the pool because it was so crowded, but not that evening.

I should really make use of it more, he thought, as he changed into his swim trunks, pulled on a pair of shorts and a t-shirt, grabbed a towel, and rushed to the third floor.

It was crowded, with not one lounge chair available. *This is crazy, who are all these people?* He let out a deep breath, resigning himself to hanging his towel on the railing and jumping right in.

"Hey, Jason!" he heard a woman's voice but didn't turn. He had no friends in the building, always keeping to himself. And there were plenty of guys named Jason.

There was also no point in socializing. The main reason he chose this building was because he'd gotten a good deal on the rent and the building was right by the metro. And he was too busy, anyway. Soon, he'd meet his future wife and move out when they bought their new home. That had been the plan since his mother had shared her idea about the dating apps and how well they worked in Korea, convincing him Kayeon's algorithm was the best and the most powerful ever created.

And why not? Jason thought.

People have used matchmaking services for ages. He

didn't trust himself to make the decision in love. Not since Gwen.

"Hey! Jason! Wanna put your stuff down on my chair?" The voice insisted, making Jason turn in its the direction. It was Kiana. Waving to him from the middle of the pool. Her hair in the setting sun had turned a golden hue, her eyes were sparkling, and she looked like an Egyptian goddess.

"Thanks." Jason nodded, trying to keep his cool. His heart leaped, and he was suddenly incredibly happy to see a familiar face in the building. Though technically, Kiana didn't even live in the building and represented the invaders who had taken over the pool. Making it impossible for honest, rent-paying residents like himself to get a spot. And yet, none of that mattered. It was so much better to feel, for once, like he belonged. Like someone actually cared about his well-being, even something as mundane as getting a lounge chair.

"It's the one with the pink towel." Kiana pointed, and Jason saw a huge Hello Kitty emblazoned on her towel. It wasn't just pink; it was hot pink, but it was too late at that point. So, he set his dark blue, neatly folded towel next to hers and jumped right in.

Another thing about his building pool was that no one swam. People just sat around the pool and drank from bottles that Jason suspected contained something stronger than just water. It was just the two of them swimming.

Kiana in her lane, and Jason in the one right next to hers. She pulled on her swim goggles, gave him a smile and swam off. Jason started doing laps. His usual swim was forty laps, but this time he went for fifty. He wasn't exactly showing off, but maybe just a little. Something about Kiana made him want to impress her.

"You're so lucky to have a pool in the building!" Kiana noted after Jason got out. She was sitting on the lounge chair, their lounge chair, he realized, wrapped in her Hello Kitty towel. Her neck and shoulders were exposed, and so were her feet.

With his years of experience as a podiatrist, his eyes were always on the job. Or, rather, on people's choice of footwear and their feet. People's feet were a story waiting to be told. He noticed her beautiful pedicure, intricate flowers drawn on toenails painted bright purple, and then he winced. He could see a bunion forming on her left foot. In its early stages, but he could tell in a couple of years she'd end up with a problem. He looked away.

"Thank you. It's nice," Jason said, standing next to her. "I'm gonna move out pretty soon, though."

"Really? When?"

"I don't really know for sure, but I'll likely be getting married next year." He crossed his arms.

"You have a fiancée?" Kiana opened her eyes wide.

"Yeah. She's back in Korea." Jason bit his lower lip.

It wasn't technically a lie. In a few weeks, he'd meet a good match in Korea. Only a matter of time before he proposed and she joined him in the US.

His mother was sure he needed to marry a 'real Korean,' not a Korean-American. According to his mother, the issue with Korean-American women was that they had different expectations from their husbands and were, for the most part, incredibly spoiled. At least that was the conclusion Jason's mother had reached after moving back to Korea. And his father followed along with it, as he always did with matters of the heart.

"Oh, that must be hard." Kiana gave Jason a pointed stare.

"What?"

"The long distance, I mean." Kiana shuffled to the side, to make room on the lounger, but Jason continued standing. The possibility of such close proximity to his new acquaintance challenging him to his very core.

"Yeah. But we'll be together soon," Jason noted, looking

away. The lie was sucking him in deeper and deeper, but at that point he couldn't admit his future wife was a phantom of his imagination. Or, worse, a collective dream he shared with his mother.

"I totally get it." Kiana swallowed hard. "I'm in a long-distance relationship myself."

"For real?"

"Yeah. That's a strange coincidence, both of us being in long-distance relationships."

"Yeah, kinda weird."

"And we're gonna get married probably next year, too, my fiancé and I."

Jason glanced at her left hand. There was no ring. She followed his eyes and clarified:

"We've talked about marriage, but Ross hasn't proposed yet. Maybe in a year or two. But first, we'll get a house, spend some time together."

"Oh, wow, you guys are getting a house together?"

"Yeah." Kiana nodded vigorously. "I'm gonna go look at one tomorrow, actually. Ross wants to buy it, but he doesn't wanna do it sight unseen. So, he asked me to go there with the real estate agent. Check it out, make sure I like it, too."

"That's very considerate. Where are you guys looking to buy?"

"Arlington, right around this area."

"But aren't these houses very expensive?" Jason drew a wide circle to encompass all of Arlington, which included plenty of single-family homes.

"I guess, but Ross saved up a ton of money. He's in the special forces and was a contractor over in Afghanistan. He's put away, like, $300K or some crazy amount. It's because he doesn't really spend it on anything. He lives abroad now. But he's moving over here." She smiled a happy, satisfied smile. "To be with me."

"Nice." Jason swallowed hard. $300K was exactly the amount he'd borrowed for podiatry school, and the debt was crushing him. Between paying that off and his living expenses, he hadn't been able to save much for a down payment. That was one of the issues with the idea of moving out quickly soon after marriage. Although he resisted mentioning it to his mother.

"So, how did you guys meet?" Kiana asked, and Jason looked at the ground.

"Long story." He rubbed his neck.

Jason didn't want to continue lying to this stranger. He shivered and remembered his towel, which was still sitting on the edge of the lounger. He picked it up and wrapped it around his torso, suddenly very self-conscious. He'd been working out regularly at the building gym, but for some reason the image in his mind was of Ross with a six-pack and his own body lacking in every way.

"Have a seat." Kiana pointed to a spot right next to her. Jason had no choice but to sit down, millimeters away from her. The proximity to Kiana unsettled him. The moment he sat down next to her, he felt his breath catch. He avoided eye contact the best he could to get away from that feeling.

"Umm, so, your fiancé," he croaked, trying his best to ignore the feeling of intimacy, "have you been together for a long time?"

"About six months," Kiana noted casually, brushing her hair to the side. He could feel her staring at him, and Jason turned to face her. The moment he caught her gaze, he could have sworn there was a spark. He felt it, and immediately it was as if his whole body was on fire. The feeling was so strong, he found it terrifying, so he jerked back and shifted on the lounger.

"Six months," Jason repeated. His heart beat fast; he felt as if any moment he would betray himself and his feelings. *What is going on?*

"Yeah." Kiana shifted slightly and put her feet down on the ground.

"Did you know him before you started dating?" Jason asked, surprising himself at his ability to think rationally.

"Oh, no, we met online."

"Online? So, like, a dating website?"

"Yep. I know some people are embarrassed to admit it, but we did. It really works. Ross and I are so compatible. Like, it's really crazy."

"Compatible how?"

"Well, he's everything I want in a guy. I like the strong, military types. And he's good-looking." She held up her fingers, folding them one after another, "And he's smart. He's a provider. Wants to have a family."

"But aren't there a lot of guys like that?"

"Are you kidding me? Not in DC! DC is terrible for dating. The worst place ever. And since Covid, it's only gotten worse." Kiana raised her voice, and Jason noticed one of the lifeguards looking over at them.

"I had no idea."

"If you're a single guy, you can have any girl you want. Literally. And if you have a decent job, you'll have a line forming at your door."

"Well, not me." Jason chuckled. "Not that I'd want that." In that moment, he didn't want a line of girls, only this woman sitting in front of him. Then he wondered where that thought had come from.

"Anyway, we met online and really hit it off. So once Ross is back here, stateside, we'll move in together and start our new life."

"Nice."

"Yep!"

"He must be something special," Jason said.

"I think so, too. I can't wait to meet him."

"What?" Jason gaped at his new friend.

"I mean, in person. We FaceTime literally every day. Ross doesn't want to take any leave, 'cause he needs to save for the house. But we speak all the time, sometimes twice a day even. I really feel like I've gotten to know him really well already."

"I see what you mean. I guess real estate is important." Jason sighed. There was no point in this conversation anymore. What was he even doing, talking to this unavailable woman, and him, about to meet his future wife and start their life together? "Anyway, I've gotta go. Have an early shift tomorrow, so I have to get up at five."

"It was nice talking to you," Kiana said. "By the way, have you noticed the woman?"

"Which woman?"

"The one with the ankle monitor. Isn't it crazy? My friend, Charlie, told me about her. She's on house arrest." Kiana lowered her voice, her eyes darting to the opposite side of the pool.

Jason followed the direction of her gaze and noticed a tall blonde in a yellow bikini, an ankle monitor attached to her left leg. The blonde was reading 'People' magazine, oblivious to the world.

"That is the craziest thing I've ever seen." he turned to whisper, only to find Kiana already leaning close. He breathed in, feeling the spark again.

"Yeah, so Charlie said she's there every day. She never goes into the water, just sits at the pool all day."

"People are so weird."

"They really are. What do you think she did?"

"Probably some white-collar crime. Like embezzlement."

"I think she was a madam," Kiana said, the expression on her face deadpan, and rose to leave.

Jason threw on his t-shirt and shorts and followed. Walking out of the pool area, Jason pondered Kiana's words. She didn't live in the building, and yet she had already plugged into its world, whereas he had remained an outsider, despite living there for nearly a year. They took the elevator to the eight floor together and walked down the corridor, chatting, as if they had known each other forever.

The new sensation of being with Kiana, of this newfound connection, felt good. It filled Jason with hope, illogical as it was, as if by being around someone like Kiana, everything would turn out for the best. They reached the door to apartment 805 first.

"Have a good evening," Jason said.

"You, too."

She opened the door, and immediately Jason heard a loud meow. An orange paw appeared, and Kiana leaned in to pick up the kitten. "Aren't you a good girl?" she cooed. "Bye, nice chatting with you."

Before he could respond, Kiana disappeared.

THE FRONT DOORS slid open and Jason stepped inside the shiny, outpatient podiatry clinic. In the morning sunlight, the bright orange couches and sleek marketing posters on the walls looked even newer. Its interior never ceased to impress him.

He thought back to his first day at the clinic, the stark contrast of this place compared to Queens Sacred Heart Hospital, where he did his fellowship in wound care prior to moving to DC. His final year there coincided with Covid, and Jason had spent a good portion of it witnessing death.

He was no stranger to fatal outcomes, but as a podiatrist he hadn't dealt with death directly, not the same way a surgeon would. Diabetic feet, calluses, inflammation, ulcers, amputations. But then, the pandemic hit and the patients started coming in.

Located in an underserved area of Queens, the hospital bordered two large nursing homes. Once one resident got infected, it was just a matter of time before the rest of the residents got sick. Defibrillators, exhausted nurses, extra shifts quickly became his new reality. The year nearly broke him.

Until then, he was sure he would work as an inpatient podiatrist at a large hospital.

Just at the right time, he got the offer from the new outpatient clinic in Northern Virginia, right outside of Washington DC. With nothing keeping him in Queens, Jason set out for Arlington, VA, in the summer of 2021, accepting the opportunity.

Jason looked over his schedule for the day, and his heart leaped when he saw the name of his first client that morning.

Audrey Simmons.

The first time she came in, Audrey announced, "I've never been to a podiatrist before. I just liked your photo on the website. You look like a decent guy. You have a nice face." She was in her seventies but sounded almost naïve.

Her comment completely disarmed him, and now he smiled fondly, looking over her file.

She arrived promptly.

"How are you, Audrey?" Jason asked. She insisted he call her by her first name, and not Mrs. Simmons, though he had tried.

"I am doing quite well. I suppose I'll be able to go back to getting pedicures now? Now that you've taken care of my ingrown toenail, I should be fine, right?"

"It depends on how you're healing," Jason noted. He had performed her matrixectomy, a permanent removal of the problematic part of the nail, two weeks prior. The procedure would save her from the monthly treatments, and this was Audrey's check-up appointment.

Unless there were complications, this would be it.

Audrey was very chatty. Over the course of the year she'd been his patient, Jason had learned quite a few details about her life: she'd been married longer than he'd been alive, which was exactly how she'd put it.

Audrey often mentioned he reminded her of her son. Also single, it seemed. Her daughter had provided two grandchildren at least. The topic came up frequently in the time he had been treating her.

Today was no exception.

Audrey settled into the chair and he began the examination.

"I bet your mother can't wait for you to get married and have kids of your own," she noted.

"She tells me that all the time," Jason admitted. "I am going to Korea next month and will see her soon."

"I hope you have a nice break." Audrey smiled at him. "And listen to your mother," she added softly.

"I will, of course." Jason nodded absentmindedly. He'd just taken the instruments out of the freezer and ripped open the plastic.

"I hope you meet someone amazing soon." Audrey shifted in her seat. "Everyone should experience great love in their life. At least once. That's what I believe. Have you ever been in love?"

"In love?" Jason grunted. "Now, let's see what we've got here. Place your right foot on the stool, please. We'll see how it's healing."

Once Audrey lifted her foot, Jason rolled his chair to examine her toe. It was her second toe causing issues. Always the same one.

"It's so tiny now." Audrey sighed. "But at least it won't be digging into my skin."

"Yes, unfortunately, we didn't have many options. It looks like it's healing nicely. Any pain?" he asked, while gently pressing on the skin around the nail.

"No, it's fine," Audrey said. "But you haven't answered my question."

Jason could feel his patient staring at him, and he looked up to meet her gaze. He expected to see the usual kind smile, but the expression on Audrey's face was grave.

Jason pulled back in surprise.

"I am not sure I believe in love. I mean, I know people talk about it, there are books, all that, but it's mostly just this romance stuff. For marriage, things have to be calculated; you can't really be too emotional." He shrugged. "There are so many factors to consider."

"Well, that's a rather cold-hearted approach to life." Audrey narrowed her eyes. "I am surprised you feel that way. Did someone break your heart?"

"Me? No." Jason hummed. The image of Gwen popped into his head, and Jason felt the old but familiar knot form in the pit of his stomach. "I just don't believe in love. As a doctor, I mean. It's just a chemical brain reaction." He bit his lip and rolled his chair back, getting up.

The instruments landed in the sink with a loud clink, and he noticed Audrey flinch. "Now, you're all set. You should be fine. If there are any issues, you know where to find me." Jason turned to his patient and gave his face the usual reassuring expression.

"Thank you, Dr. Lee. You're a great doctor. I hope you know that." Audrey slid her right foot into her sandal and fastened it up.

"I'm glad I could help you, Audrey. Looks like you'll be able to go back to those pedicures."

"I had a great love once, until I lost him," Audrey noted casually as she got up from the chair. Jason was about to escort her out of the room, but something in her voice made him pause. "A Russian defector. And he was taken away from me."

"What?" Jason's mouth gaped open. "That sounds like something out of a movie."

"Oh, yes. You could say that. His name was Anton. Beautiful man, inside and out. Anton Konovalov," she said the name with adulation, as if it were a prayer. "He was tall, handsome. I'm just 5'1 and he stood at 6'3, or maybe even taller. A real bear. Broad shoulders. Just, wow."

"A defector?" Jason had seen several episodes of *The Americans* and immediately added, "Was he a spy?"

"Funny you should say that. Some people have hinted he may have been a spy, but he'd been cleared by the FBI. Both of us were so young. Just an incredible love story. I had planned on introducing him to my parents, but my father served at a secret base in North Carolina. Anton wasn't allowed to go."

"So where is he now? This man?" Jason raised his eyebrows, hesitant to leave this intriguing conversation. "Did you marry him?

"No." Audrey shook her head ruefully. "He's dead."

"I'm so sorry," Jason said, looking at Audrey with compassion.

"The most awful thing is he was taken from me so suddenly. We said goodbye right before Christmas. Next thing I heard, he had died from a gunshot."

"That's terrible. How did it happen?" Discussing the death of a loved one was something Jason knew well. He'd gotten good at consoling relatives at Sacred Heart Hospital. But this was something entirely different.

"No one knows for sure. Though there is a lot of information online about it," Audrey noted with a sigh. She brushed back her bangs. "I must be going now. I don't normally talk about it. The whole story is too traumatic. Even my husband didn't know about it until a few years back. When this awful woman produced a documentary about my Anton and his life."

"There's a documentary?"

"Oh, yes. Anton became a celebrity. He converted to Christianity, you see. His faith in the Lord propelled him to fame. A Soviet defector becoming a Christian was big news then. And he wrote a memoir, which got published right after he died. So, his memory lives on. I just wish I had closure."

"Thank you for sharing your story with me," Jason said,

subtly glancing at his watch. As if on cue, the assistant knocked, indicating it was time for his next appointment.

"You know, maybe you can look into it." Audrey darted her eyes at Jason, as she was walking out of his office. "It might help to get a fresh perspective on it."

"You mean, investigate what happened to the Russian defector?" Jason stared at her. He found the idea tempting. Audrey would no longer be his patient, and he'd always liked watching crime shows. *Would this be just like that?*

"Yes. Would you? It would mean a lot to me, and, Dr. Lee, I just have this great feeling about you. I've told you, haven't I, it's like you've got this ability to fix things."

"To fix things?" Jason shook his head. "I do fix feet."

"Dr. Lee, I mean, things in life. As soon as I had my first appointment with you, I got good news. We couldn't sell our apartment in DC, the tenants refused to move out, it was this terrible ordeal, but then, the day after my appointment, they left. Just moved out." Audrey snapped her fingers. "Imagine, a year of struggle, and then, something changed. What's more, after my third appointment, I learned my daughter was expecting."

"It's probably just a coincidence," Jason said. The conversation with Audrey was bordering on absurd. *First, Kiana and the comparison of feet to wings, and now this.* The strange thought crossed Jason's mind, and then he had an idea.

"You know what? I just met someone who speaks Russian. So actually, I might be able to help you with the investigation," Jason promised absentmindedly. "I'll see what I can do."

WHILE WELCOMING his last patient of the day, Jason noticed the head physical therapist's own client. An older, grumpy man, who constantly grumbled, complained to Cassie about his pain and was rather unpleasant. The man came in with his son. An overweight, tortured-looking, young man, who sat in the waiting room, scrolling on his phone, with a look of extreme boredom. Right before the pair left, when Cassie tried to convince the young man to help his father, the son dismissed her rudely, which Jason overheard.

As he passed through the physical therapy area, Jason reached over to high-five Cassie. She was always in a good mood. Not once had Jason seen her perturbed. It was as if nothing bothered her, not the weather, the challenging patients or any staffing or billing issues.

"Cassie, how do you do this?" Jason now asked.

"Do what?" Cassie raised her eyebrows.

"Stay so calm."

"I know I'm doing what I'm meant to do. Helping people."

Jason's eyes lit up. "Thank you for the reminder." This was the reason he'd become a podiatrist in the first place, to make a difference. "I sometimes forget." Jason helped Cassie straighten out the PT equipment.

Ever since he was little, Jason had wanted to become a doctor. He just didn't know what kind until his mother's accident. Shortly after they had moved to America, and it became clear the money his father would make working alongside Uncle Henry would not be enough, his mother got a job at a restaurant. A hole-in-the-wall establishment not far from their apartment in Palisades Park, New Jersey. She didn't speak any English, but most of the clients were Korean. The money was good, helping the family stay afloat.

Until, one day, they got a panicked call from the restaurant owner telling them, 'there'd been an accident.' His mother was brought home in tears, her ankle swollen, crying out in pain. It was the first time Jason had seen his mother in tears, and it deeply unsettled him.

"I tripped on the steps," she repeated, frantically rubbing her leg. A neighbor suggested they sue the restaurant owner, but the owner was a respected member of the Korean community. He was kind about the accident and gave Jason's mother $300 to help with her recovery.

Now Jason realized how fortunate they were to have had health insurance. Something they got at his uncle's insistence, after he shared how life in America without health insurance was a death sentence waiting to happen. It was thanks to this very health insurance, his mother was able to see several doctors. Jason accompanied her to every appointment, so he could translate.

For several months, she explored different types of treatment, but her pain didn't go away until she saw Dr. Brick, who was a podiatrist. The second Jason saw what the doctor did, he made up his mind: he, too, would one day become a podiatrist. Keenly, he watched how the doctor appraised his mother's condition, how he skillfully established what needed to be done. How firm yet gentle his touch was. And how the visits to Dr. Brick restored hope in his mother, who started getting better and fully recovered within months.

"So yeah it really motivates me. Otherwise, it's easy to forget." Cassie adjusted the weights. "I also do a gratitude practice in the morning."

"What's that?"

"I write down all the things I'm grateful for. All the good things that happened the day before. For example, if a patient got better. If I got a good review, or, the other day, the cashier at Target gave me a free sample. Some new energy drink. It was so nice of him." Cassie glanced at her clipboard. "I got another patient coming in," she noted and stretched. "But you should try it. It really helps. I've been doing it for almost a year."

"Sure, I might give it a try." Jason agreed and walked to the exit. "Have a great weekend, Cassie."

"You too, Jason." Cassie gave him her usual, broad smile.

The receptionist, Betsy, was sitting at her computer, and waved as he walked out the door. He waved back.

The summer heat slapped him the minute he got outside. The air was thick and muggy, the sky ominously gray. On the horizon, Jason could see a storm cloud forming, and he sped up his pace so he could get on the metro before the rain.

I guess, no pool today, Jason decided, descending the escalator steps.

The thought was unpleasant. He realized, somewhere in his mind, he'd assumed he would see Kiana that afternoon. Not only that, had been looking forward to seeing her. Jason rolled his eyes at this reaction. He preferred staying in control of his feelings and quickly reeled back his enthusiasm. Besides, there was no sense in getting to know Kiana, who had a boyfriend, while he, Jason, felt hopeful about meeting his future wife soon.

But by the time he got out of the metro, the clouds had

passed. The concrete was wet, and a few passersby wore shellshocked expressions on their faces.

"What a weird storm!" he overheard someone say, and noticed the person wringing water out of his t-shirt. "Rained so hard, but over in five minutes, tops."

The air was still hot and muggy, but not as oppressive as before, which improved Jason's mood. Thinking of doing the gratitude practice as soon as he got home, he decided to write out the list of things he was grateful for on his phone. That seemed like a faster, more efficient way to do it than writing by hand. The first on the gratitude list would be his upcoming trip to Seoul, as well as the powerful matchmaking app.

As Jason passed by apartment 805, he heard a loud meow. *Percy.* Jason stopped in his tracks, picturing the adorable orange kitten. He walked up to the door.

"Percy," Jason called softly. The meow repeated. "Poor kitten, are you okay?" The meow grew louder, more insistent. It sounded urgent. "You must be hungry, little girl." Jason tried to stick his fingers under the door, but it was fitted tightly. "Don't worry, Percy, Kiana will be back soon." Jason tried to keep his voice calm and collected, just like he would with an anxious patient.

Although he had never had a pet, he assumed Percy would be soothed by the sound of his voice. It seemed to work, and the meows subsided. *I should have gotten Kiana's number,* Jason thought.

Suddenly, the image of sitting next to her, the spark that flew between them, flashed in his mind. He immediately dismissed it.

For the cat. For Percy, he mumbled to himself. *I wonder how often Kiana comes by to check on the kitten.*

Jason furrowed his brow. He remembered how small Percy was, how the kitten had rushed to Kiana the previous day and shook his head. *I should have offered to help.*

Standing in the corridor and speaking through a locked

door wasn't going to help matters. With a sigh, Jason walked to his apartment. He'd just gotten his keys out, when a loud meow made him turn. Jason returned to 805. He spent the next five minutes squatting next to the closed door, speaking to Percy. It wasn't until a resident had walked by and had given him a curious stare that Jason went to his own apartment.

What if Kiana misses a day? What if she isn't coming tonight? How will Percy do all on her own? The terrible thoughts pierced Jason's imagination. He barely paid attention as he boiled water and made himself a bowl of ramen, remembering too late he'd be eating the same thing as the day prior, then plopped down in front of his TV to watch an episode of *Law & Order*. But he couldn't focus. He slurped his noodles in silence, turned the TV off and decided to go to the pool, half-hoping to see Kiana there.

It was better than inaction and the uncertainty, and Jason embraced it.

The pool was unusually empty that afternoon, likely because of the storm. Without giving it another thought, Jason placed his towel on the same lounger where he and Kiana had sat the previous evening. The lifeguard, busy scrolling on his phone, barely acknowledged his presence, and Jason dove right in.

There was no motivation this time for him to swim extra laps, but Jason pushed himself anyway. After the fortieth lap, he lost count, and just kept going. The lifeguard's whistle pulled him out of the water.

"Break time," the guy announced.

Jason had been the only one in the water, but the guard made him get out anyway. Jason obliged.

"I don't know why they do that," came the now familiar voice. As he pulled himself out of the water, he saw Kiana, with her huge 'Container Store' bag, walk up to the edge of the pool. "I didn't realize they closed down."

"They don't do it every hour." Jason shrugged. "Depends on the lifeguard, I guess."

"Oh, I see." She ran her hand through her hair.

"How is Percy?"

"Did you hear her?" Kiana opened her eyes wide. "She was meowing so hard when I got in."

"I did." Jason nodded. "I was worried about her."

"I don't know what to do." Kiana placed her swim bag down on the concrete with a sigh. "Charlie, I mean, Charlotte, we just call her Charlie, her father is really sick, and it's all so sudden. But I can't keep cats in my apartment. So, I can only come after work, because I have to go in every day. Percy is so little though. Charlie was working from home, so it would have been perfect, but now I don't even know when she'll come back. She's my best friend, we've been friends for almost twenty years. We met our freshman year in college." She sat and reached for her towel.

Jason's thoughts immediately flashed back to his own oldest friend, Hyun-woo. The only person from elementary school with whom Jason had kept in touch. Before moving to America, they had lived in the same building and were best friends. Their friendship survived Jason's emigration. Through Hyun-woo, Jason got a glimpse of what his own life could have been like, had he stayed in Korea. Hyun-woo had completed military service, finished his degree and worked as a software engineer at Kakao. He was now married and had a young daughter.

Kiana finished sorting her stuff and looked up at him.

"I was thinking, maybe I can help?" Jason offered, edging to the lounger.

"Help? How?" Kiana tilted her head.

"Maybe I can check on Percy?" Jason reached for his towel.

"But I'll have to give you Charlie's key."

"Yeah, that's not a great idea."

"Or, I mean," Kiana moved her bag and placed it on the chair next to Jason's, "it's probably kind of crazy, 'cause I just met you, but would you mind taking Percy for a few days? So, she stays with you?"

"With me? I've never had a cat." Jason carefully wrapped the towel around his torso.

"It's not a big deal. I'll show you what to do. So, she doesn't feel so alone. And then Charlie will come back, I think in a week. Is that okay?" Kiana looked at him as Jason sat next to her. She began speaking faster, trying to get all the information out. "Cats are so easy. I had a cat when I was younger, Assiya. She lived until age eighteen. My current landlord doesn't accept pets. But after Ross and I get married, I'll probably adopt a cat. I really want a British shorthair."

"Oh, nice."

While Kiana spoke, he'd made up his mind. "I can keep Percy. But only until I go to Korea. I am leaving in exactly three weeks."

"Oh, really? Three weeks is plenty. Charlie will definitely be back by then. She's actually supposed to be back next week. Thank you so much! I'll just call Charlie to check but thank you. You're so awesome. Thank you, Jason." Kiana's face lit up and she looked even more beautiful.

"Not a big deal. I've always wanted to have a cat," Jason noted, pleased with himself. "So, this will be a way to try it out."

"So is your family allergic or something? Is that why you'd never had a cat before?" Kiana looked at him with compassion.

There was a time, when he was five years old, when he dreamed of a pet cat. Begged his parents to get one. But they refused. Their apartment in Seoul was too small, he wasn't old enough to take care of a pet, and his mother found cats to be distasteful and their smell offensive. When they'd moved to America, Jason hoped getting a cat would be easier, but that didn't happen either. As an adult, Jason had simply forgotten he ever wanted a cat.

"No, but my parents were never really into it. And then we moved here, to the US, when I was fourteen, so things were hectic."

Hectic was an understatement, but Jason rarely spoke about immigration. He remembered little from his first years in the United States. If pressed, he called that time 'survival,' or 'trying to stay afloat,' and would sometimes add he was lucky to 'have made it out alive.' Everyone would usually laugh at that statement, but Jason was only half-joking. He'd blanked most of high school out, because it had been too traumatic.

As he said this, Jason scanned her face for a reaction, but Kiana was busy, typing furiously on her phone.

"I'm just letting Charlie know what's up." Kiana swept the hair away from her face. "I decided I'm not going to ask for her permission, 'cause, like, this is really important. It's not good for Percy to be alone for so many hours at a time. And I'm not gonna move in here, you know?" Kiana pointed back at the building. "So this is basically the only solution we've got at this point. Thank you, Jason!" She smiled.

Jason wondered if she'd heard what he had said about moving to America and his parents and decided she hadn't.

"Alright, so when will Percy get moved to my place? Right away?" Jason raised his eyebrows. The idea of a joint project with Kiana was exciting, despite the impossibility of being with her.

"Yes, is that okay?" Her phone pinged, and she looked down at it. "Oh, wait, I gotta respond right away. It's Ross!" Her whole face lit up.

This is what love is, Jason thought ruefully, as he watched Kiana type on her phone. *I hope I meet a woman who feels about me this way soon.*

"Ross was just asking me about a place I went to see with

his real estate agent. He got this woman; she's a real shark," Kiana noted with approval. "The real estate market is so competitive in this area. Especially now. But his agent's great. Ross wrote a whole letter describing why he wants the house, how he's always dreamed of living in the area. I didn't see the letter, but his offer was accepted on the spot."

"You have to write a letter? To buy a house? I've never heard of that."

"Yes, if there are multiple offers. It might make a difference. I guess for Ross, it did. He put how he and I would be living in it, and how the two of us are in love." Dreamy notes appeared in Kiana's voice and Jason, despite himself, felt a knot form in the pit of his stomach. Yet another reminder of his own inadequacy. "I went by to check it out for him just the other day. Ross said he wanted someone he trusted to be there. And the real estate agent was there; she kept talking about 'the kids running around.' It was kinda creepy, but kinda cute, too."

"Like, your kids?"

"I guess, once Ross and I have kids together. A bit premature, I would say." Kiana giggled. "But I definitely want to have kids. I think Ross is going to make such a great father."

"Umm…so…"

The conversation was going way off topic, and Jason wondered what else Kiana would tell him about her relationship. A part of him was curious, but another part felt embarrassed at being privy to these details of someone else's life. Someone he found, despite himself, very attractive.

The lifeguard blew the whistle, and Kiana shifted in her seat. "I think we can go in now. And, by the way, I owe you a favor. So, if you need anything…" Kiana looked at him expectantly. As she did, Jason remembered the Russian man and his promise to Audrey.

"Actually, there might be something." Jason scratched his chin. "The weirdest thing happened today at work. Someone asked me to investigate a cold case, involving a Russian spy. She used a different word, though. Not a spy."

"What?" Kiana opened her eyes wide. "Don't tell me you think I'm one."

"No, of course not." Jason let out a laugh. "But the woman who asked said she was once in love with a Russian spy, and he died a mysterious death. There was a documentary made, and most of it is in Russian. Didn't you say you're part Russian?" Jason fidgeted in his seat.

"I am." Kiana bit her lower lip. "You have a good memory." She narrowed her eyes at Jason.

"So, I would like to help her look things up. You speak Russian, right?"

"I do." Kiana nodded. "My mom always speaks Russian to me."

"Will you, maybe, help me look him up and investigate what happened?"

"You're talking about a Russian spy?" Kiana stared right at him, and it made Jason uneasy.

"Not a spy, sorry, he was a defector. That's the word she used," Jason corrected himself.

"A defector is very different. Not every Russian is a spy!" Kiana threw her hands up in the air.

"Of course. You know, the woman, she asked me to help her, that's all." Jason kept stumbling on the word, and had almost revealed Audrey had been his client. Even though she would not be coming back, Jason didn't want to reveal their connection.

"I see. And you agreed to help her?"

"I did. I'm really curious. I've never investigated anything before. Though I've watched lots of *Law & Order* episodes." Jason noticed Kiana nodding and continued, encouraged, "And I read lots of Agatha Christie novels when I was young. All of them, actually."

"I see. I think the two of us make a great match, then,"

Kiana said, and Jason breathed out in relief, "because I happen to absolutely love Sherlock Holmes."

"Great, so we're well qualified then." Jason bobbed his head, grateful Kiana was 'in' on the joke.

"Alright. Let me do a few laps, then we can move Percy. Oh, we can also watch the documentary together." Without warning, Kiana took off her shirt, so Jason averted his eyes. "I'm happy to put my Russian skills to use, and to return the favor."

"You mean, tonight?" Jason glanced at his watch.

"Unless you have other plans."

"I don't."

CHAPTER
Six

WHILE KIANA DID LAPS, Jason considered going into the pool again, but decided against it. He sat and pondered the situation, the peculiar turn of events in his life. He was always like that. Jason let things evolve naturally only up to a point, and then he took a step back. Just so he could review whether he'd made the right move.

Moving Percy to his apartment was the right thing to do, of that Jason was sure. The meows were heartbreaking, and he wanted to help. And as far as investigating the story of a Russian defector, Jason knew why he'd asked Kiana to help. Though it hurt to admit it, spending time with her felt good.

"Hey! Ready?" Kiana stepped out of the pool. "I'll tell you all about having a kitten, don't worry."

Jason got up from the lounge chair and handed Kiana her towel: a paler shade of pink than the day prior, but still with the Hello Kitty logo on it. It wasn't until Kiana had thanked him that he realized the gesture was almost too intimate, as if they were a couple.

"Did you see her?" Kiana asked as they walked out of the pool.

"Who?"

"The house arrest woman. I think I heard her ankle monitor beep."

"There's no way." Jason turned to surreptitiously survey the woman, who was sitting in the corner of the pool, flipping through a 'US News and World Report' magazine.

"I really wanna know what she did."

"Well, maybe we can investigate her as well," Jason said, emboldened.

"We'd need to know her name," Kiana noted. And immediately stopped and faced Jason. "Wait, do you know the name of the Russian defector?"

"I, I think so." Jason scratched his forehead. "It was Antoine. I think."

"That's not a Russian name. Not Antoine." Kiana shook her head.

"Umm, I don't know then. And I don't remember the last name. I think it had a V at the end?"

"So there's no way we'll find him then, that's pretty much half of the Russian last names." Kiana frowned. "Can you ask the woman? Like, call her?"

"I guess." Jason bit his lower lip. He'd called Audrey once before to check on her. It was after her first visit. But now, faced with this possibility, he was unsure. "Should I actually tell her? That we're planning to look up the documentary?"

"Yeah, why not? I mean, you'd tell her if you found anything afterwards, right? So better to let her know now, before we get started." Kiana cleared her throat. "I believe in transparency." She glanced at her phone. "Speaking of which, Charlie says it's cool to move Percy, so we're all set."

"Sounds good. Listen, I just wanna take a shower. So how about we move Percy in, say, fifteen minutes?" Jason checked the time. It was almost six pm.

"That works. Charlie lets me shower at her place, so I can do the same. I'll knock on your door when Percy and I are ready." Kiana looked happy and somehow very hopeful. Jason wondered how old she was.

His mother had always insisted Jason's bride needed to be at least four or five years younger than him. "Even ten years younger than you is fine, Jun," she'd recently told Jason. "That would mean the girl is in her late twenties, the perfect age for child bearing."

Jason disagreed, and, despite his mother's efforts, the matches Jason was about to meet in Seoul corresponded to his criteria: they were in their mid-thirties. The thought that Kiana could be much younger than him disappointed Jason. He wanted her to be closer to his age, wanted to have more in common with her.

————

After taking a shower and changing, Jason took out his phone and looked up Audrey's number. *I guess I'm actually doing this,* he told himself, dialing her number. He wanted to reassure himself that what he was doing was right, and Audrey had, indeed, given him the permission to investigate the death of the Russian defector. She picked up on the first ring.

"Audrey?" Jason hesitated for a moment. "This is Jason Lee, your podiatrist."

"Oh, hello," Audrey said. "Honey, could you please turn the TV down?" Her voice was muffled for a moment, and then, louder, as she spoke into the receiver, "Is everything alright?"

"Yes, it is. I'm calling because of what you'd asked me to do," Jason said. "I wanted to check whether it was okay for me to watch the documentary about the Russian defector."

"About Anton? Of course."

"Anton, that's right. I couldn't remember his name. I would have to look him up."

"Thank you. I knew you would take it seriously." Audrey's voice brightened. "I really appreciate it."

"Would you mind spelling his name for me? I'll write it down."

"Of course, of course." Audrey proceeded to spell the name. "Anton Konovalov."

"Got it!" Jason said, having typed the name into his phone, and at that very moment he heard a knock on the door. "I have to go. I'll let you know if I find anything out."

"I appreciate it."

As soon as Jason hung up, he heard a loud meow. He opened the door and watched, as if in slow motion, how Percy wriggled herself out of Kiana's hands, slid to the floor and within seconds disappeared under his Arhaus couch, slithering underneath the gap between the cushions and the floor.

"Wait, what just happened?" Jason gasped, following the kitten with his eyes.

"Don't worry, she'll be fine. Cats are so intelligent. Hold on for just a moment." Kiana retreated into the hallway, and returned moments later, dragging in a huge bag with the 'Fresh Direct' logo on it. It was filled to the brim with different sized cans and containers.

"Let me help you." As he reached for the bag, their hands brushed for a second. "What's all this?" Jason asked, trying to ignore the spark. It was there, he couldn't deny it. For himself, at least.

"This is Percy's stuff." Kiana surveyed the items, seemingly oblivious to the feeling. "Her food, the toys. And I'll be back with her litter box and filler. I didn't want to put it in with the food."

"I'll help you get it," Jason offered, and the two of them left the apartment together.

"I had no idea cats needed so much stuff," Jason noted

several minutes later, as he was dragging a fifteen-pound bag with litter box filler into his apartment.

"I guess it's quite a bit." Kiana, who had followed him inside, surveyed the bags. "Here, I wanted to show you this." Kiana reached deep into the Fresh Direct bag and produced a piece of fluff on a stick. "This one," she shook it, "is the best. So simple, but Percy loves it."

"Nice," Jason nodded, trying to hide his surprise. He'd seen kittens play in commercials, but the idea of actively playing with one was new to him. "So, how much do I have to play with her?"

"What do you mean?" Kiana raised her eyebrows.

"Like, how much time each day? Is it important for her development?"

"Oh, probably, like, thirty minutes?" Kiana waved her hand indefinitely in the air. "But, I mean, kittens play. Like little kids, you know?"

"Yeah." Jason averted his eyes, so as not to reveal his similarly lacking knowledge of little children. "And with the litter box, does she know how to use it?" Right away, Jason pictured his mother's face twisted in disgust, mentioning how cats were dirty creatures, and how the smell of their litter box was absolutely appalling.

"Yes, Percy is potty trained. She's been using the litter box since before Charlie got her. She's really a clean little girl, isn't she?" Kiana kneeled and reached her hand under the couch. "Come here, Percy, come here.

Jason also got on his knees next to Kiana and looked under the couch. Bright green eyes glowed in the dark, staring at him from the very back. The eyes did not blink.

Taking care of a kitten suddenly seemed way more complicated than Jason had ever imagined. Whenever he thought of getting a cat, he always pictured the same thing: the cat purring next to him, as he ran his hand through the animal's fur. The cat would tilt its head, giving him a meaningful stare, and the image would end there. Now, with the kitten hiding under the couch, Jason wondered what he was to do.

How will I make sure Percy eats? How do I introduce play time? And what about using the litter box? Though Kiana had reassured Jason everything was fine and Percy was potty trained, Jason had his doubts.

"Here, kitty, kitty, ksksksks." Kiana made a kissy noise, which sounded almost primal. The green eyes blinked twice, but Percy remained in her hiding spot. "I guess she's scared." Kiana pulled her hand back and got off her knees. "I tried calling her the Russian way. My mom taught me."

"There's a Russian way to call a cat?" Jason also rose from his knees.

"Yes, absolutely. And it works," Kiana said, sounding less certain. "Well, most of the time."

"I never knew there was so much to cats. I kind of assumed having one would be easy," Jason gave Kiana a look full of doubt.

"I see. So, I guess I have to tell you everything there is to know about cats?"

"Pretty much."

"Alright, then. Here comes the crash course."

They spent the next hour going over how to take care of Percy. Jason learned that the little cat had to have water accessible to her at all times, that there were two types of cat food, wet and dry, and how to make sure Percy had the most nutritious meals. According to Kiana, it was normal for Percy to sleep most of the day, and it would take time for her to get used to his apartment. As she explained everything, Kiana moved expertly throughout his place, setting up Percy's things, opening food containers, arranging the litter box.

"So she might stay under the couch until tomorrow?" Jason asked after Kiana had finished talking and sat on the couch, arms folded on her lap.

"She might," Kiana said. "You never know with cats. You just set everything up, the food, the litter box, just like we did. And you wait."

"I see. I'm great at waiting." Jason laughed. "You have to be, as a doctor."

"I'm not patient at all." Kiana sighed.

"Maybe it's a cultural thing. In Korea, we always think in terms of centuries, generations, things like that."

"Yeah, that's not the American way."

Jason bent down and looked under the couch. Again, he saw the same two green eyes staring back at him, unblinking.

"I'm patient." Jason grunted, getting off his knees. "But I'm just worried about Percy. That's all."

"Percy will be fine. I'm sure she's very grateful you've temporarily adopted her. She'll be so much better off here. Now, do you want to look up that guy?"

"Sure!" Jason produced his laptop. "And this is his name." He showed Kiana the defector's name he'd typed into his Notes app.

"I see, Anton Konovalov." She pronounced the name with a Russian accent, stressing the last syllable of the first name and the third syllable of the last name. The man's name sounded completely different, somehow dangerous and appealing at the same time. "That's a unique name. I'm sure we'll find him right away."

Jason nodded, as he typed the defector's name into Google.

CHAPTER
Seven

RIGHT AWAY, results populated on the screen.

Jason had put Anton Konovalov's name in quotation marks and double-checked the spelling, expecting a mix of results that would need to be further reviewed and narrowed down. Instead, the very first entry led to a Wikipedia article.

"A self-described former KGB agent and Soviet Navy officer, who had carried out missions against Christians and defected to Canada in 1970," Jason read out loud. The image accompanying the article was of a young, handsome man, grinning, as he pointed at a map. The man sported a seventies haircut reminiscent of the Beatles, with soft dark curls covering his ears.

"You think that's him?" Jason asked, pointing at the screen.

"It's gotta be." Kiana gasped. "Wow. I guess the guy was a big deal."

"Let's see what else there is."

"Alright," Kiana leaned closer, and Jason caught a whiff of her perfume. It was something citrusy and also sweet, but not overly so, pleasant. Jason opened his mouth to ask Kiana what it was, but then remembered that they'd only met the day prior. The realization hit him – he had known Kiana for a little over twenty-four hours, and yet, here they were, sitting in his living room, researching something together. And a cat, the tiny kitten named Percy, had somehow made her way into his apartment and would settle there for a whole week ahead.

What if Kiana is some kind of swindler? What if this is something she does? And the mention of the woman with the ankle monitor?

Suspicion crept into Jason's mind. With a sinking feeling, Jason examined Kiana out of the corner of his eye.

Her hair was pulled back in a bun, and for the first time he noticed her clothes: she was wearing a black tank top and a long jean skirt. Kiana had taken her shoes off when entering his apartment and he saw her platform sandals sitting by the door. He frowned. Platform footwear was his pet peeve. Not as bad as pointy heels, of course, but too many of his patients assumed platforms were good for their feet, disregarding the distortion they introduced into the ideal foot positioning, eventually atrophying the muscles, leading to problems.

Jason started going through a list of potential issues Kiana would have because of her platforms, but then caught himself. Somehow, this train of thought led him to the conclusion that Kiana was a regular human being. *She's fine, definitely not a conwoman,* he reassured himself and only then realized Kiana had been speaking.

"I think he must have been very impressive. Look at how much information there is. It's kind of incredible my mom never mentioned this guy."

"Your mom? What do you mean?"

"Well, I mean, there weren't that many Russians in Washington, DC back then, so they all knew of each other. But I guess he'd moved here earlier." Kiana stared at the laptop. "Look, it says here this guy has written a memoir. And he was what, twenty years old? Who writes a whole book at that age?"

"Oh, that's right. Audrey did say something about a memoir." Jason cleared his throat.

"Yes, look." Kiana clicked, and Jason saw the image of a book cover. Again, the same young man was staring at him, only now his face had been torn in half and he looked forlorn. The title read, *I Am Sorry, Dasha.*

Jason and Kiana read the title out loud in unison and exchanged a look.

"Jinx!" Kiana yelped, while Jason yelled out, "Jjijjibbong."

"What's that?" she asked, surprised.

"It's like jinx, but in Korean," he explained. "For some expressions, I still use the Korean terms."

"Ah okay. My mom moved here in her twenties, so I know the drill. There are so many things she prefers to say in Russian." Kiana gave him a reassuring smile. "So, who's Dasha? Is that the woman's name? The one who'd asked you to help her?"

"No. It must be someone else. Should we buy the book, you think?"

"No way. Here, I bet there's a summary." Kiana had taken over his laptop so quickly that Jason didn't realize what had happened, but she was now clicking away. "It sounds kind of strange for a title."

"Look." Jason pointed at the screen. "Anton Konovalov's autobiography, *I Am Sorry, Dasha* or 'The Oppressor,' was released posthumously," Jason read out loud. "The memoir details Anton's life in the Soviet Union, tracking his early years at an orphanage, to his quick rise through the ranks of the KGB and then as a naval officer, who made a daring escape off the coast of Nova Scotia and asked for asylum in Canada before making his way to the United States. Dasha is the nickname of the woman, Daria Akimova, who was a Christian Anton supposedly abused during his time at the KGB."

"That sounds awful." Kiana frowned. "But also, a bit far-fetched. The guy was how old, exactly? Twenty? Twenty-one? And he'd done all that?"

"Here's more." Jason breathed out, staring intently at the screen. "Anton Konovalov became a Christian convert and preacher during his time in the United States, reaching millions on TV and radio."

"Wow." Kiana leaned closer and stared at the screen. "That's impressive. The guy must have learned how to speak English really fast. He was in the US for how long?"

"A year or two, I guess."

"There's no way. How did he become a preacher in *one* year? My mom moved here forty years ago, and she still has an accent when she speaks English. And she studied at one of those English schools in Russia."

"Same with me, I've got an accent, don't I?" Jason had worked hard to sound as American as possible. Now, over twenty years after moving to the U.S., he had managed to get rid of most of his accent, but always doubted himself.

"You barely have one." Kiana reassured him, placing the laptop back on the coffee table.

Jason stretched. "Do you want to stop? I'm not sure what else we can find out tonight."

"But that woman asked you to help her, right?" Kiana raised her eyebrows. Jason noticed her eyes looked different, depending on the light. This time they were chestnut brown.

"Yes, but this just raises so many questions. And what can we possibly find out from Googling this guy?"

"I always think things happen for a reason." Kiana swallowed hard. "Like us meeting, it was to help Percy. Or the woman asked you to help her, and this guy is Russian, and I'm half-Russian. It's all somehow connected. Don't you think?"

"I guess." Jason shrugged. He didn't believe in the supernatural. Not in the very least. Life was just life. And in his profession, everything worked based on logic and science.

That's what he'd learned. But Kiana spoke with such passion, Jason didn't have the heart to contradict her.

"Here, let's keep on going. Maybe we'll see something else," Kiana clicked on another link. It also started with 'I'm sorry…"

Jason was about to say that it was likely another link to Anton Konovalov's book, but the link opened a YouTube page.

"I Am Sorry, Anton," Jason read slowly.

"What's this?" Kiana pointed at the page, showing Anton's face, with the same haircut, the same smile, his handsome face looking at the two of them.

"It's the documentary." Jason exhaled, "This must be the one. Audrey, she told me about a documentary."

"Let's see how long it is," Kiana said, and pointed the cursor to the screen. "Forty-five minutes. That's not bad; we can watch it on 2x."

"Sure." Jason nodded. He'd never done that before, but Kiana confidently changed the settings and clicked play.

The documentary had been made by a woman, who'd been fascinated by Anton's story and had traveled to Russia to investigate his life and achievements, to find out more about a great man like Anton Konovalov. She received a grant and, over the course of several months, she'd met with his friends, his former colleagues in the Soviet Navy, even the KGB, and interviewed staff and former wards of the orphanage where Anton had grown up. The woman referred to Anton's book several times and mentioned at the beginning of the documentary how much she admired the defector.

And then, the inconsistencies began.

None of the man's friends from the orphanage shared the same version of the awful, hungry upbringing Anton described in his memoir. The staff at the orphanage were all kind and caring, everyone repeated. Anton's friend, whom he mentioned by name in his memoir, went as far as to accuse

Anton of being a traitor and a liar for complaining about the orphanage. But the woman didn't give up on her quest to get answers.

She went to several Christians whom, according to Anton and his confession, he'd abused during his time in the KGB. And she even met Daria Akimova, the very Dasha to whom Anton apologized in his memoir. At the time of the filming of the documentary, Daria was an older woman; she looked to be in her seventies, and she showed no recollection of any abuse. She was surprised to learn about Anton and what he had presented in his memoir.

"Let's slow this down," Jason asked after they watched Daria Akimova repeat her assertion and stare at the camera with her eyes open wide.

Kiana adjusted the settings and they continued watching, as the documentary, methodically, bit by bit, discredited Anton's story.

The last interview was with a KGB officer, a man who remembered Anton, and who said with a smile, 'Anton must have gotten himself into some trouble. He probably lied to make some money.'

"So, what would you say to him if you saw him now?" The documentary woman asked the KGB officer.

"I would hug him like a son. I'd tell him, I understand he must have fallen on hard times, but he shouldn't lie for profit."

"Wow, this is powerful." Kiana looked over at Jason. He noticed her eyes were glistening. "So, is she asking you to find out more? Beyond the documentary?"

"I don't know," Jason shook his head. "She called the documentary 'awful'. So, maybe she wants to know if there is something else. Listen, let's maybe grab a bite to eat?"

As soon as he said those words, he realized it sounded as if he'd just asked Kiana on a date. But that wasn't possible, because she had a serious boyfriend and he, Jason, was about to travel to another part of the world to meet his future wife.

"Sure!" Kiana perked up. "I was just thinking, life is so weird. I mean, who would have thought we'd be researching some Russian defector together?" She rose from the couch and stretched, but then froze mid-movement, and whispered, pressing her finger to her lips. "Look over there, but quietly. I don't wanna scare her off." She pointed to the corner of the living room.

The kitten was perched on the windowsill, staring outside. She looked completely at ease, as if she'd been living in Jason's apartment all her life.

"Isn't it awesome? I guess Percy's comfortable enough to come out of her hiding." Kiana clapped.

"That's great." Jason nodded and moved to pet Percy, but Kiana stopped him. "Don't. You've gotta give her a bit more time."

"I see." Jason tried not to let his disappointment show. He'd been keen to play with Percy and to finally pet the kitten.

"Soon, but let her come to you. Cats are kind of like women that way." Kiana smiled.

"Ha, that's funny. I guess I'm not an expert," Jason said and immediately turned red.

There's no way she likes me, Jason immediately told himself. But the idea was too tempting, too perfect. It would have been so wonderful to actually find a match this way. Rather than fly across the world and meet AI algorithm-generated matches in Korea, then, within a week's time, make the decision on which one of the women to pursue, all under the watchful eye of his mother. Jason let out a barely perceptible sigh.

But Kiana was in a serious relationship, and Jason had tickets to Korea, had already sifted through the matches, having already set everything in motion. At the thought, he bolted upright.

It was eight in the evening in DC, and already Saturday morning in Korea, when he usually responded to his messages on the Kayeon app.

"I gotta check something real quick," Jason mumbled and retreated to his bedroom, squeezing through the half-closed door.

Before Kiana had gotten to the apartment, Jason had left the door open just a crack. His room was, by Jason's standards, messy, but he didn't want it to look like he was hiding something. He hadn't made the bed that morning, and his workout clothes were still hanging on the chair. Though the dating app was in Korean, Jason didn't want Kiana to see the phone interface, which featured the tell-tale image of two pink hearts, intertwined.

As soon as Jason opened the app, he saw a message from one of his matches, Min-jung. So far, of the matches the algorithm had provided, Jason liked Min-jung the best. She worked as a daycare teacher and spoke great English. She taught expatriate children at one of the elite schools in Seoul. Eager to move to the U.S., she had mentioned she would be quick to get her teacher's license in Virginia. Min-jung said her dream was to become a mother herself, and she was already great with children. Jason liked that, too. He'd always wanted to have kids. A boy and a girl. Having grown up without a sibling, Jason thought it was important to have at least two children, to somehow dilute the parental influence.

Though he'd never admitted, even to himself, his mother's influence over him was over the top, he wished for his children to have a different experience in life. The message from Min-jung was sweet:

> Wishing you a great weekend, can't wait to
> meet you.

Jason smiled. He was about to respond, but then he saw Percy.

Sitting by the door of his bedroom, the kitten stared at Jason intently.

"Hey there, Percy." Jason reached to pet the cat, and Percy leaned into his touch. "I love the color of your fur. It's such a pretty shade of orange." Her purr got louder, as if responding to the compliment.

"I see, you guys are bonding. How great is that?" Kiana had walked up to the door and was looking at the two of them in approval. Percy moved away from Jason and rubbed against Kiana's legs.

"Sorry, my room is kind of messy," Jason said, freezing in place. He'd barely had enough time to shut off the dating app and looked up at Kiana's face to make sure she hadn't seen it. She was surveying his bedroom, and he let out a sigh of relief.

"You're so tidy," Kiana noted in admiration. "Your whole place looks spotless."

"Thanks."

"This cat just melts my heart," Kiana said, practically purring herself. "I wish I could take her with me; she's the most adorable little girl." She nuzzled into Percy's nose.

"She really is. I'm so glad she'll be living here for a few days."

"Did you know that most orange cats are boys?" Kiana asked. "It's because the orange color is transmitted through the X chromosome. So for a female cat to be orange, there would have to be two, and it's very rare. So, Percy is unique."

"Oh, wow, what a cool fact." Jason looked at Kiana in amazement, impressed by her knowledge. Immediately, he reminded himself she had a boyfriend, the muscular Ross, and swallowed hard, following Kiana out of the bedroom.

CHAPTER
Eight

AS THEY GOT into the elevator, Jason braced himself. They were about to go out in his neighborhood, which was known for its plethora of bars. But Jason didn't digest alcohol well and shunned bars, which eliminated quite a few options.

On the ride down, his thoughts flashed to his father.

"Good thing you aren't living in Korea. Imagine if your boss invited you to go out drinking and you couldn't even handle one single beer." Jason's father would often reminisce, though not too fondly, of the Korean tradition of drinking with one's colleagues after working hours, which was still strong to this day.

"That's a good thing, Abeoji, but drinking a lot isn't good for you anyway," Jason would note. "Alcohol is a huge stress on the liver. All of your systems."

Refusing to drink hadn't been an option for his father, but it was for Jason.

Outside, the weather had cooled down, and it no longer felt stiflingly hot. Though it was still too much for Jason's taste, he didn't mind walking outside, since it was with Kiana. Being around her made everything better.

"So, where do you want to go? There are so many choices

here." She pointed to the left, in the direction of Clarendon, to indicate the range of options in that part of Arlington.

"You choose," Jason said, ready to explain to Kiana that he didn't drink.

"Well, there's the Serbian place. It's kinda like Russian food, and I could always go for some Russian food." Kiana looked at him hopefully.

"That's cool. I've never had either."

"We might not be able to get a table. It gets really busy. So, we might need to eat at the bar, and I have to tell you, I don't drink."

"You don't drink?" Jason gaped at her, unable to hide his surprise. He'd almost always been the only person in a crowd to refuse a drink.

"I stopped drinking last year." Kiana bit her lip. "I mean, I don't think I had a problem, but during Covid there was so much marketing of alcohol, have you noticed?" Without waiting for an answer, she continued, "And so I fell for it, and then one week, I caught myself drinking every night, by myself, and I got really scared. So, I stopped completely, and then I realized how much better I felt without alcohol. Now I just don't drink at all, and, besides, I have an early workout tomorrow."

Right away, Jason remembered his taekwondo training days, but then reminded himself the sport was too risky on the lower extremities, his own ankle sprain after which he'd quit the sport, a case in point.

"Really? I didn't think, well, I guess I should never assume."

"Did you think I was some kind of party girl?" Kiana flipped her hair and shrugged. "It's okay, lots of people think that about me. But I'm not. I'm the opposite."

"What's the opposite of a party girl? I mean, I didn't think you looked like a party girl. I just didn't realize about all the marketing, that's all."

"Oh, yeah. But I guess I'm the type of girl who stays at home and reads books. 'Cause that's what I like to do. I'm not really that outgoing; I just put on a front."

"Why?"

They were walking down Clarendon Boulevard without a clear goal, but both of them were too enthralled in conversation to care.

"Well, people don't always like introverts. Or maybe introverts don't really like being around people. But for my job, I have to be around people. So, it's a chicken and egg situation."

"What do you do?"

"I thought you'd never ask." Kiana giggled. "I mean, that's like the first question everyone asks you around here. But anyway, I'm a program manager for a commercial real estate company."

"Oh, wow."

"I really love it. I enjoy my work."

"That's really great. So do I."

"Wait, where are we going?" Kiana asked and stopped cold in the middle of the sidewalk. "Do you want to just grab a sandwich somewhere and sit outside? It's not insanely hot out, so it might be nice."

"That's a good idea. What about this food truck?" Jason pointed at a black truck parked on the corner block. "I've definitely seen it around but have never tried it."

"Yes! I love El Pollo Loco, the 'Crazy Chicken.' Their burritos are insane."

"Alright, we've got a plan," Jason said, as the two of them approached their destination.

"It's a shame Percy has to miss out. I'm guessing cats don't eat spicy chicken," Jason said after they had placed their orders and waited at a nearby picnic table.

"Yeah, better not. But some people make their cats homemade food. I used to boil chicken bones for my cat. Like, I was hardcore into making home-cooked meals for her. I even made her bone broth. The stuff everyone raves about, you know, I made it in an Instant Pot. It's ridiculously easy. But anyway, you could do the same thing."

"I don't have an Instant Pot. Should I get one? For Percy?" Jason swallowed hard. He barely cooked for himself. *Will I have to change my habits to cook for the kitten? Percy is only staying with me for just a few days.*

"No, no, not at all, especially since Percy won't be with you for much longer. I'll bring some bone broth for her this week. If that's okay with you, of course." As she said this, Kiana's phone pinged, and she reached for it.

"It's Ross," Kiana announced, immediately typing a text in response.

Jason noticed several heart emojis and looked away, feeling a pang of jealousy. He frowned at his reaction. A couple holding hands passed them by, and then another one with the man pushing a stroller. Jason let out a sigh.

Soon, soon, he reassured himself.

But seeing the display of affection around him, it was hard not to feel like perhaps he'd focused too hard on his career and not enough on finding 'the one', assuming she would just walk into his life one day. As his birthdays crept closer to his late thirties, and the dates he'd gone on were less than inspiring, he was starting to lose hope. This was another reason why his mother's suggestion of the matchmaking service in Korea suddenly made sense.

"Ross likes to wish me goodnight. It's late at night for him, but he checks in with me, anyway. It's sweet," Kiana said, putting her phone away.

"Yeah, that's nice." Jason said, trying to keep his voice steady. The food truck operator motioned, and Jason got up to get their orders. Kiana stood to follow him, but he stopped her. "Don't worry, I'll bring it over."

"That's a nice lady you got over there." The vendor clicked his tongue in approval. "Sweet lady, I can tell."

Jason turned back at Kiana. She looked beautiful resting on the bench. She'd let her hair down, the expression on her face relaxed and sweet.

"Oh, we're just friends," Jason responded. *Are we even friends?*

"Friends, amigos, yes, yes, very good. Beautiful lady." The man either didn't understand what Jason had said, or being friends with a woman existed outside of his realm of possibilities. But Jason knew that nothing romantic would ever happen between him and Kiana, and, in a way, that was fine.

In just a few weeks, his life as a single man would hopefully be over.

"You know what's weird about that dude?" Jason said as he placed the containers on the picnic table.

"The food truck guy?"

"No, Anton. I can't stop thinking about him," Jason admitted, taking a seat.

"I mean, other than lying about everything for money?"

"Well, we're not sure he actually lied. The guy accusing him of it is, after all, a KGB agent. But also, you know what's weird? Audrey said he was *killed*. 'Taken away from her' is what she actually said."

"Oh yeah? Killed? Like who killed him? The Soviets?"

"I don't know. It wasn't in the documentary, though, which is strange. I mean, if they were going to expose the guy for being a liar, wouldn't you think they would at least mention his death, too? And shouldn't you speak only good things about the dead, anyway?" Jason furrowed his brow.

Kiana froze, as Jason was speaking. "It's actually quite strange. You're right," she said after a pause.

Then, she pulled the two boxes out of the plastic bag.

"Let's eat," she said. She nudged the first box to Jason, and the gesture struck him. *This is what it's like to have a woman who cares about you*, Jason thought. *I can't wait.* That very second, his phone buzzed with a notification from the dating app, and he glanced at his screen. It was a chat message from Yuna, another one of his matches.

"Is that her?" he heard Kiana ask.

"Who?"

"Your fiancée?" Kiana looked at Jason expectantly.

"Listen, I don't actually have anyone. At least, not officially."

"You don't? But I swear I saw your face light up when you got that message." Kiana froze with her fork half-lifted over her burrito.

"Well, I haven't met her yet. We're only arranging for the date, but it'll be in Korea."

"So, you've already spoken to her? Like Ross and I?"

"No, we haven't done FaceTime or anything like that. I've set up a few dates, and then I'll meet them when I'm in Seoul. And then, ideally, one of them will be a perfect match and we'll get married."

"But why are you going all the way to Korea to do it?" Kiana gave him a puzzled look. "Have you tried looking here?"

"Of course. I've been on a few dates, none of them got really serious. No one ever felt like 'the one', you know? I think it's time to try harder, to try something different. Maybe it's a cultural thing."

"It sounds like me ten years ago. I was actually married before, to a Russian guy. That did not go well. He'd turned out to be a total mama's boy."

"You were married before? So, you're divorced?" Jason gave Kiana a curious look. He'd never heard anyone willingly admit they were divorced.

"Yes. I got married at twenty-eight. I was married for, like, two years. The worst thing ever. It turned out to be, kind of like, almost an arranged marriage. We were compatible on paper. You know, culturally, our backgrounds, all that. We had a huge wedding, all these guests, it was epic. I think I got married only to please my family. But I learned a lot."

"So, what happened?"

"Here, don't let your food get cold." She took another bite of her burrito. "It's really good. I love this food truck." Kiana chewed, then continued speaking. "Well, his mom kept coming to stay with us. His parents lived in Texas, and she would come and stay in our apartment, and she always demanded we give her our bedroom. And then, she started rearranging things. I'd come home, and there would be a new painting hanging on the wall. Or the furniture would be moved around. Or she'd throw out my dishes and replace them with something she liked."

"And he let his mother do all that?"

"We kind of had to." Kiana reached for a napkin. "You can't say no to a Russian mother-in-law. Plus, my ex would gaslight me. So, if I ever got mad, it was all my fault or I was imagining things. But at a certain point, my mom got involved. She didn't know how bad things were, but once she found out, she told me I had to get out of the marriage and she'd support me. And then my dad got on board, so I got divorced. I'd only been married for two years, and the divorce wasn't a big deal. We didn't have kids, or it would have been awful."

"You don't want to have kids?"

"I do. Just not with my ex. If we'd ended up having kids, we would have stayed connected forever. And that awful woman would have been their grandmother. But now, I'm free, and thanks to that, I met Ross. I would never have been able to appreciate someone as wonderful if I hadn't been through my marriage and divorce. So, this is what I believe. You've gotta go through these experiences. But anyway. So, have you always dated only Korean women?"

"No." Jason swallowed hard, remembering Gwen. "I've

dated non-Korean women. And I was in a longterm relationship with one, we were together for four years."

"That's longer than my actual marriage. It must have been serious." Kiana's mouth gaped open.

Jason hadn't spoken about Gwen in ages. "Yeah, we almost got married. It was painful when things ended," he said and put his fork down. Speaking about the experience was a sure way to make him feel nauseous.

"Sorry," Kiana said. "That sucks. I shouldn't have asked."

"It's okay. It was a long time ago. But I guess it was my character-building experience."

"Well, see, if we drank, I would have toasted to finding love. But I hope you meet a wonderful future wife in Korea," Kiana said emphatically.

"Thank you. And I hope once you and Ross meet in person, you will have found 'the one.'"

Something about the conversation felt bittersweet. Did he want Kiana to have found 'the one'? She'd just told him she'd gone through a divorce. As far as his mother was concerned, that alone would disqualify Kiana as a possible match. Not to mention the fact that Kiana wasn't Korean. But he had come to learn over the years that while his mother meant well, she wasn't always right.

What am I even thinking?

And yet, Jason felt as if, after confiding in each other, their conversation had opened the door to the possibility that their friendship could become something more.

He looked up at Kiana and heard her say:

"I am sure it'll be like that for me. I just have a great feeling about Ross."

"Yeah." Jason's heart sank. *Enough of this nonsense,* he told himself and dug his fork into the burrito so hard, the plastic snapped.

CHAPTER
Nine

THE PAIR WAS quiet for a few moments, and then a police siren broke their silence.

"Must be the Clarendon bros, getting drunk. Every Friday night, like clockwork." She rolled her eyes as the flashing police car drove past them.

"So, do you live nearby?" Jason asked.

They had just finished their meal, and he stuffed the empty containers back into the plastic bag, preparing to throw them out.

"I do, not far from your building, actually. I live in the garden style apartments, over in Dominion Village." Kiana rose from her seat, and Jason did the same.

"Would you like me to walk you back?"

"Thank you, that would be great. I mean, it's safe, but you never know." Kiana smirked. "And since we've established you aren't an axe murderer."

"Yes, and I've got Percy's seal of approval," Jason added, with a wink.

He felt good. Meeting Kiana, their conversation, the way the evening had unfolded, everything about it was perfect, if he were to ignore the impossibility of a romantic relationship with this attractive woman. They walked uphill, passed Jason's apartment building, then turned onto a narrow side street. It was chock full of parked cars, all arranged at a slanted angle to save space. They crossed the street, walked past several nearly identical two-story buildings, and stood before a door with the number 2023C on it.

"So, this is me," Kiana said.

"Your apartment number is 2023? That's kind of neat, like next year, right?" Jason said.

"I guess so. I keep thinking next year will be special for me. But I moved here after getting divorced, so, maybe, my time has finally come." Kiana ran her hand through her hair. "It was nice spending time together. Have a great night."

"You, too."

"And thanks for walking me home! You're such a gentleman, Jason. Your future wife is a lucky woman." Kiana waved at him and unlocked the door to her apartment. It made a screeching sound as she pushed it open, and then, she disappeared.

He walked back to his building in quiet contemplation. The kitten greeted him at the door, and Jason picked her up and gave her a kiss on the nose. As soon as he put Percy down, she sauntered to the food bowl, which stood empty, looked up at him expectantly and meowed.

Jason couldn't remember Kiana's instructions regarding the number of times a day to feed Percy and whether he needed to give her dry food or wet food in the evening. One more important than the other, he recalled, as kittens needed good routine. When Kiana spoke to him, it all seemed to make sense. But now, staring at the kitten, Jason felt nervous. Was Percy genuinely hungry or asking for food simply because he had come back?

He reached for his phone to text Kiana only to realize they hadn't exchanged numbers. Jason shook his head at his own carelessness. Not having had the foresight to get the woman's number after spending a whole evening together and walking her home wasn't normal for him.

He let out a groan.

There can't be that many people named Kiana in Arlington. What did she say she did for a living? Jason scratched his head. *Something in real estate!* He typed her first name into Google, added the location and the search term 'real estate'. Right away, the page populated with several hits.

Kiana Nasiri, Jason mouthed. *This must be her.*

The first hit was to Kiana's LinkedIn page, and he checked out her photo. She was wearing a navy-blue suit and a white shirt, her hair pulled back, with a focused expression on her face. She looked more serious and closer to his age in her headshot. Jason read through Kiana's credentials. In addition to a bachelor's from George Mason, Kiana had earned a Master's degree in Real Estate Finance from Georgetown and a PMP. Jason looked up what a PMP was and learned it stood for a project management professional certificate, which required hours of training and passing a difficult exam.

That's really something, he thought, *meeting someone like her in an elevator.* Percy crept up to him and meowed, reminding Jason it was time to eat.

What have I gotten myself into? He googled 'feeding a young kitten,' hoping for a detailed explanation of how much dry and wet food to give, but the instructions were mixed and varied depending on the cat's age, which, Jason realized, was another thing he hadn't had the foresight to ask.

Another loud meow got Jason out of his contemplation, and he rushed to give Percy wet food, which the cat devoured in mere seconds, then walked over to the bowl with water and drank greedily.

This is a good sign, Jason thought and sat in his favorite spot, on the couch in front of the TV. He was about to switch it on, but then remembered Audrey and the documentary. And the reference to Anton Konovalov's death.

Jason entered the man's full name and 'cause of death' into Google. What seemed like thousands of results appeared. There were newspaper article clippings scanned and uploaded into Google, all referencing an FBI investigation.

There's no way, Jason thought, clicking on the top result. *If the FBI looked into it, why is Audrey still asking questions?*

The article detailed the mysterious death of a Soviet defector, who, at age twenty-two, was shot at a California ski resort over Christmas vacation in the company of his seventeen-year-old fiancée.

Poor Audrey, Jason thought. *What a story? No wonder she is so traumatized. But seventeen is so young.* Jason kept on reading. A photo, now familiar, of Anton Konovalov, followed. The same smile, the same seventies suit, and the same haircut.

And then, time stood still.

Jason saw the name of the young fiancée. Mary Ward. There was even a photo. A young blonde woman with large curls smiled at him. She looked nothing like Audrey Simmons, even discounting for a fifty-year difference. Seventeen-year-old Mary Ward, who was tall and had a Hollywood appearance, could not have transformed into the tiny Audrey Simmons. He remembered clearly Audrey's own words, she was 5'1.

SAN BERNARDINO, Calif., Jan. 3 (UPI)—A young Russian defector, found dead in a rented mountain cabin, apparently shot himself to death accidentally with a gun he carried because threats had been made against his life, the authorities said yesterday.

The body of Anton Konovalov, 22 years old, was found on Monday in a one-room cabin near Bear Mountain Ski Resort with a single bullet wound in his head from a .38-caliber Smith and Wesson revolver.

His death was reported by Mary Ward, 17, of Brentwood, Calif., who had rented the cabin with the former Soviet sailor for the New Year's holiday. The couple were engaged and were to be married the following summer.

Mr. Konovalov was apparently examining the gun, when it went off, a police spokesman said.

Jason stared at the article in astonishment. Nothing about it made sense, and its contents did not align one bit with Audrey's version of the story. The defector, whoever he was, could not have been Audrey's 'great love', if he died next to another young girl over Christmas. Unless Audrey had been that person and somehow changed her appearance, but Jason discarded the idea as preposterous. He looked up several other articles about Anton Konovalov's death, and all reported the same thing. In some, his death had been judged to be accidental; some referenced a suicide investigation, but none mentioned Audrey Simmons. Not even once.

Did she make this up? Jason wondered. He'd seen enough *Law & Order* episodes and knew some people processed trauma in different ways. *Is there a chance Audrey met the Russian defector, fell in love with him, but her feelings were unrequited?*

But Audrey, at least from how she presented herself to Jason, was a calm and collected person, well meaning, organized, with a successful marriage, children and grandchildren.

Why would someone like her come up with such an outrageous story and call some man her great love fifty years later?

But Jason knew this for sure: people never ceased to surprise him. He'd seen it with some of his other patients. Some, who came off as completely careless, were very focused on their health and serious about treatment. And some, though they seemed as the type of person that would follow instructions to a 't', ended up not following them.

"You should never assume anything," his mentor at podiatry school, Professor Herman, a burly man in his seventies, had told him. "Only one thing will be for sure. Your patients will surprise you."

And so, Jason never assumed. Or at least he tried not to. He tried not to assume a patient with poor hygiene would let his infection get worse, or a woman, who washed her hands three times while sitting in his office, would take the same kind of care on her foot wound.

Jason would have kept on googling Anton Konovalov's story, but Percy jumped onto the couch, curled into a little ball, purring right next to him. Jason checked the time. It was past midnight. As soon as he realized how late it was, he felt his eyelids were about to close of their own accord. He rubbed his eyes to try to wake up, just so he could get ready for bed, then picked up the kitten and placed her on his pillow. Percy didn't wake up and continued her slumber. Jason settled on the bed next to the cat and let the rhythm of her breathing lull him to sleep.

———

Jason woke up to a strange sensation. Something brushed against his hand. He jerked it back and felt a pull. Jason opened his eyes to see Percy, who had extended her paw, with one claw gently, but firmly attached to Jason's skin.

"Percy, good morning," Jason said, slowly, so as to avoid a scratch, taking Percy's claw out. "Were you trying to wake me up? You're adorable, did you know that?"

Percy meowed in response, and Jason got up right away, eager to feed the kitten. He found himself in the kitchen, opening a can of wet food for Percy and refilling the water dish, completely reversing his usual morning routine, which, on weekends, involved an elaborate ritual of lounging in bed and drinking a morning espresso, then, sitting on the balcony and reading the news.

Jason rarely left his apartment before noon on weekends,

and only to go to H-Mart to get his grocery shopping done. That was the great thing about living in Northern Virginia – access to the best Korean grocery stores and restaurants. He loved stocking up on just about anything he ever wanted and more: kimchi, ramen, rice cakes, moon cakes, japchai, frozen squid. Jason didn't need to cook, because the stores boasted an incredible fast-food hot bar, where he usually bought enough prepared food to last him through the week. Korean food was his comfort food. And he sought it out.

But that morning, after fixing Percy her breakfast and cleaning her litter box, a much less pleasant task, Jason found himself energized and ready for a change. He made his usual espresso shot and downed it in one go. He pet Percy, who had curled herself into a ball on the couch, right in the middle of Jason's favorite spot.

"Hey, Percy, so, you like to wake me up, is that what you do? You're so cute. Such an adorable little cat." Jason squeezed in next to Percy, careful not to disturb the kitten. His eyes darted to her toys, but Percy was slumbering so peacefully.

It was only eight in the morning. Jason considered going back to bed, but by then the shot of espresso was pumping through his veins, and he quickly dismissed the idea. And then he remembered Kiana and her 'early morning workout.'

I should probably do the same thing, Jason thought and recalled hearing about a running group that met at Roosevelt Island, which was not far from his building. He'd been meaning to try it, hoping it would be a nice substitute to taekwondo, which Jason still missed.

He looked it up and found the running group website.

'Saturday mornings at Roosevelt Island,' it said. No need to sign up in advance; just be there by 9:00. The group had different running levels and, according to reviews, offered 'a great, collegial atmosphere.'

He could make it to the location in thirty minutes or less if he walked. The decision was instantaneous. Jason grabbed a bagel, spread some butter on it, refilled his water bottle, and was ready in five minutes. As he closed the door behind him, he heard Percy's meow, which Jason took for approval.

The leisurely walk down Clarendon Boulevard was pleasant. Overnight, it had gotten even cooler, and Jason felt refreshed and relaxed as he chewed on his bagel. A homeless man was stretching on a bench. Normally, Jason would simply hurriedly toss a coin and avoid eye contact, but not that morning. Even the homeless man had a story, Jason was sure of that. He smiled at the man, and the man waved at him.

"Hey there, hey, hey," the homeless man said, and Jason felt pity for the guy. *Who knows what he's been through? Maybe he lost everything during Covid?*

Jason knew people like this man. Some had hit rock bottom because of hospital bills, because they'd lost a family member who had been their support network. It happened more often than people realized. At Sacred Heart Hospital, Jason felt, he'd seen it all. He wasn't burned out, exactly, but he'd definitely seen the dark and hopeless side of humanity. And Jason wasn't sure how long it would take him to erase that vision. Or whether it would ever happen.

Occupied with these thoughts, he passed the Arlington farmers' market. A woman pushed a stroller with an active toddler uphill, the look in her eyes focused. To Jason's surprise, he overheard the two of them, the woman and the toddler, having an engaged conversation about a car wash. The toddler insisted on going back to watch the cars being washed, while the woman patiently explained to the little boy, they needed to get 'some fresh vegetables at the market.' Jason smiled to himself, passing the pair.

The realization that he'd been spending his weekend mornings locked in his apartment, and was missing out on witnessing things like this, hit him.

By nine, Jason was at the entrance to Roosevelt Island. He'd been there only once since moving to the area. The parking lot was full, despite the early hour. He saw people pulling kayaks into the water, a group of bikers, and then, after crossing the bridge, several runners, who had assembled by the statue of Theodore Roosevelt.

Jason surveyed the crowd. Three volunteers, all wearing baby blue vests, were greeting the newcomers. The serious runners, easily recognizable by the focused expressions on their faces, stretched, chatting gingerly with each other. A group of older women stood next to them, all engaged in multiple overlapping conversations. There were several couples, some with children, some with dogs, some with both. By the process of elimination, Jason approached the group of the serious runners.

"Don't worry, buddy, if it's your first time and you fall behind, someone from the group is right behind you." One of the men, who was wearing sleek running gear, gave Jason a somewhat patronizing look.

The run through the peaceful, shady island felt refreshing, but by the time he headed back, Jason wished he'd taken the car. The 5K took longer than expected and when he emerged onto the concrete sidewalk, about an hour later, the sun beat down hard. Already sweating from the run, as he walked up the steep hill back to his apartment, Jason felt weak and exhausted. The light, energized mood of the morning vanished completely.

Percy greeted Jason by the door and surveyed him, meowing.

"You poor thing, I know, I know. You want company, don't you?" Relief flooded him, as he stepped into the cool of his apartment.

Jason petted Percy between the ears and asked, "Are you hungry? Well, let's get you something to eat, then."

Percy meowed, and Jason gushed, "Are you answering

me, Percy? Well, that's what happens when you live alone, ha? You start speaking with a cat."

Meowing repeatedly, Percy headed to the kitchen, her tail raised high. There was something regal in the way the cat moved. Jason followed Percy to the kitchen, where he found the kitten sitting in front of her bowl with an expectant expression on her face.

"You're so little, and yet, so smart already. I can't wait to see what you'll be like as a grown cat," Jason said.

Only then to remember he would have to give Percy back to her owner in just a few days. Jason sighed and got out sliced turkey for a sandwich. This wasn't his usual lunch, but even heating up a frozen meal seemed to be an ordeal, so it would have to be a sandwich.

Placing a slice of turkey on a piece of bread, Jason heard a loud meow. The next moment, he felt Percy's claw gently, yet firmly, pressing into his foot.

"Ouch!" Jason exclaimed and looked down. Percy meowed again, moving the claw just a little further down. "Is that because of the turkey? Alright, please stop, Percy." He ripped off a piece of turkey and, unable to move his foot, placed it right by Percy. The claw retreated, and Percy chowed down the food. Preempting another claw, Jason gave Percy more turkey, and finished his sandwich as quickly as he could.

"You're so little, Percy, but you have a great appetite," Jason noted, as the cat gave him an expectant look. "But all the turkey is gone."

He watched as Percy headed to his bed and jumped up on it, curling into a ball. "A nap? Is that what you want to do?" Following, Jason sat on the bed, and as soon as he did that, the kitten started purring.

"You know what? A nap isn't a bad idea at all," Jason said and climbed into bed.

CHAPTER

Ten

BEFORE HEADING to work on Monday, Jason fed Percy, made himself an espresso and sat to down scroll on his phone to read a bit more about Anton Konovalov, hoping for a clue. He hadn't stopped thinking about the defector all weekend. Percy's meow pulled Jason out of his thoughts.

"Now, Percy," Jason told the cat, "I'll be back as soon as my shift is done. Please don't worry." The cat blinked in response. "So, it won't be too late, alright?"

Jason was sure he and Percy had an understanding, but he still wondered how the kitten would cope alone in the apartment in his absence.

He liked Mondays. He liked getting an early start to his week, liked commuting to work in the wee hours of the day, when the metro was nearly empty. The patients who came in on Monday mornings were usually the conscientious types, eager to 'start the week off on the right foot'. This was another of Dr. Herman's sayings, and as corny as it was, Jason liked to repeat it from time to time.

Why wasn't Kiana checking on Percy? Jason wondered on his way to the office. It had been two days since they last saw each other. He could contact her, now that he'd located her

LinkedIn, but Jason wanted Kiana to make the first move, since Percy, was, after all, her responsibility.

"Good morning, Dr. Lee. Some woman left a message for you over the weekend," Betsy greeted him, handing Jason a piece of paper with a number written on it. Betsy was in her late fifties, and, in stark contrast to the carefree attitude of the PT, Cassie, inclined to dark moods.

"She said you would know what it was about." Betsy huffed. "Some people. They just think they're the center of the universe. Name's Kiana Nasiri."

"That's my neighbor." Jason's heart leaped at the mention of Kiana's name. "Well, kind of. I'm watching her cat." He clarified, catching a surprised look from Betsy. "Her friend's cat."

"You're watching someone's cat? Wow, I didn't take you for a cat person." Betsy gave him a glance over, as if seeing Jason for the first time.

"A cat? You're cat-sitting? But that's so adorable!" Cassie had overheard their conversation and walked to the reception area, a huge smile on her face. All three of them, Betsy, Cassie and Jason joked they were the 'nightmare morning people', after discovering how perky and upbeat they were during the early shift. "But you're right, Betsy, I wouldn't have thought Jason was the type."

"Why not?" Jason crossed his arms.

"Because you're not a creep," Cassie said categorically.

"Thank you. I guess," Jason responded. "What does any of this have to do with being a creep?"

"It's because all those single dudes with puppies, they only get pets to pick up women. And you're not the type," Betsy noted with authority. Betsy had just remarried, having reconnected with her new husband through Facebook. They had gone to the same high school, and Betsy was a firm believer she'd gotten 'the last good man in the DMV.'

Jason had by then learned that in the DC area, 'the DMV'

didn't mean the Department of Motor Vehicles, but stood for DC, Maryland and Virginia.

"Oh, is that right?" Jason had stayed away from the subject of dating at work, but his colleagues knew the basics about him: he was single. Now, the conversation was bordering on dangerous, the possibility of divulging personal information pressing on him hard. Jason took a subtle step back.

"Yes, all these dudes get puppies just so they can go to the dog park and get the chicks. And the women think they are wholesome because they're taking care of a dog." Cassie shook her head indignantly.

"I had no idea," Jason said. He had taken another step back and was almost half-way to the safety of his office.

"See, you're not one of them. And taking care of a cat while the owner's away is a nice and honorable thing. You should put that on your dating profile." Betsy covered her mouth. "If you ever make one, Dr. Lee." She exchanged a barely perceptible look with Cassie.

"So, who's this Kiana? Is she cute?" Cassie winked at him.

"Leave him alone, Cassie." Betsy put her hands on her hips. "Can't you see he's ready to run away? But that woman sounded like trouble, I can tell you that much."

"Oooh, trouble! Sounds exciting!" Cassie breathed out and then noticed a client walking into the waiting room. "Alright, my first appointment is here. Keep me posted on the updates!" Cassie sauntered into the PT space.

"So, is it just cat-sitting?" Betsy gave him a curious stare, then added, "Now, you be careful with those ladies, Jason." The receptionist liked to alternate between calling him Dr. Lee and Jason, though he could never predict when she would use one or the other. "You're quite a catch, and those girls, who knows, they will do anything to score a great guy like you."

"Thank you, Betsy," Jason noted. "I'll keep that in mind." It wasn't the first time Betsy had offered him motherly advice, but Jason didn't buy into Betsy's view of the universe. And not just because of how dark it was: Jason believed whatever advice Betsy had shared didn't apply to him, because he was Korean. There were simply too many family expectations on both sides.

Jason's relationship with Gwen was a case in point. If Jason had a chance at building a relationship that would lead to marriage, he had to date a Korean woman and not waste his time on the likes of Kiana, who was already, Jason reminded himself, attached.

The quick reality check had served its purpose, and his mood soured. Jason checked the schedule. He had fifteen minutes before his first appointment. He unfolded the paper with Kiana's number and saved it into his phone, then started typing:

> Hey, this is Jason Lee. I got your number.

Then stopped himself. *Of course, she knows where I got her number.* Jason erased the last part of the sentence.

> Hey, this is Jason. What's up?

This sounds too dry. He erased the "What's up?" When he finally sent the message, it read,

> Hey, this is Jason. Thanks for finding me.
> Percy is doing well.

Jason hit 'send' before he could change his mind and edit the message again. He was still looking at his phone, when three dots appeared. A response came within seconds.

All is well. I am glad I found you. Charlie looked up your name in the resident directory, and the work number was the only one listed. Will you be home after six? Can I stop by? I miss Percy.

Sure. See you then.

Jason felt his heart rate accelerate at the thought of his reunion with Kiana. He noticed his first client walk in, arriving for his appointment early, and was grateful for the distraction.

It was a patient, who suffered from diabetes and had a bad infection in his foot. The man always came in with one of his children, either a son or a daughter. While the son never paid much attention to what Jason said, the daughter usually gasped, in a futile attempt to warn her father of the terrible things that could happen to him if he didn't follow Jason's instructions.

Jason preferred the son, simply because he was calmer.

But today wasn't his day, and he saw the man walk in with his daughter. Preparing for a doomsday conversation, Jason steeled himself.

"Hello, Dr. Lee," the daughter breathed out, her eyes already moist. Her father followed behind her with a cane, a grim expression on his face. "Dr. Lee, my father doesn't seem to be responding to the antibiotics. His sore is getting worse. Dad, show Dr. Lee what's going on." The daughter's voice sounded urgent.

"Sure." The man groaned as he positioned himself in the examination chair. The sore that had developed on the man's foot had been growing steadily since Jason first saw it, and Jason had already told the family the foot might need to be amputated.

"Dad, please tell Dr. Lee about the antibiotics."

"I can't keep taking them. My PCP says my liver is shot, and it's either the liver or the foot at this point." The man sniggered. "I'll take the liver, 'cause I only got one of those."

"Daddy, that's not funny," the daughter shrieked, on the verge of tears, and Jason scanned the office to make sure he had tissues available.

"Let's see what's going on," Jason said.

From the man's speech, he couldn't tell whether his patient had been taking the antibiotics, or whether he had stopped midway. With the man's attitude, it was almost impossible to determine whether his health outcomes mattered. Jason put the rubber gloves on and carefully lifted the man's foot up.

"Actually, it looks like it's improving," Jason blurted out in surprise after looking at the ulcer. He normally tried to conceal emotion from his patients. Dr. Herman had told him, 'A doctor has to remain calm, and never be overly optimistic or pessimistic'. But this time, Jason broke the rules. He was genuinely happy for the patient. The ulcer was starting to heal, with the tissue repairing itself.

"Really?" The daughter jumped up. "But it looks terrible." She furrowed her brow, standing behind Jason and staring at her father's foot. "Daddy, this doesn't look good."

"See right here?" Jason gently pointed to the edge of the ulcer. "The tissue is healing. That's a great sign. Exactly what we want to see."

"Well, Doc, thanks for all your help." The patient gave Jason a high-five. "I guess I still got it."

———

As soon as Jason opened the door to his apartment, he saw the little cat sitting by the front door, as if expecting him.

Percy meowed. It sounded normal, as if the cat was

simply saying hello to Jason. There was no sense of urgency in it. Jason knelt down.

"How are you doing, Percy? Were you okay? Did you miss me?"

For dinner, Jason heated scallion pancakes, his other favorite go-to meal on weekday evenings, after ramen. As he was stuffing the second scallion pancake into his mouth, he heard a knock on the door. Jason's heart leaped, and he jumped, letting Kiana in.

"Hey, how are you?" His new friend walked in, smiling. "And there's my little cat!" She reached to pet the kitten, who licked her hand. "Did you miss me? How are you, Percy?" Kiana picked the kitten up and cuddled her. "Hey, Jason!" She smiled, a big, open smile, and his heart melted.

At that moment, he would have given anything to have Kiana tell him she liked him. Just a mere hint, a small chance, the tiniest possibility of something romantic happening between them would have made him try to make the first move. But Jason quickly reminded himself that Kiana was as good as engaged to some superior human being, a military hero, who was about to come back from Afghanistan with a huge amount of money, buy a home, and Kiana could finally settle down. And he would find his perfect match in Korea. Jason shut off his thoughts.

"Percy has been great. I love having her around. I'm so glad you left a message with the office," Jason noted after watching Kiana pet Percy, while the kitten's purrs got louder and louder.

"Yeah, is that okay? I should have just gotten your number, but I totally forgot, and I didn't want to bother you over the weekend," Kiana explained.

"It would have been fine," Jason chuckled. "I actually found you on LinkedIn."

"You did? How?"

"Well, it looks like you're the only Kiana in Arlington. And what you told me about yourself, I mean, George Mason, matched. I didn't know you had a Master's as well. And a PMP? I had to look that up, but it sounds very impressive."

"Yeah." Kiana shrugged. "I mean, in DC, you pretty much have to have a master's if you want a decent job. But wow, I thought only girls were into stalking."

"Stalking?" Jason balked at the characterization.

"I'm just joking." Kiana waved her hand. "And I'm grateful you're taking care of Percy."

"Speaking of which, I wanted to check, when is your friend coming back?"

"I actually spoke to Charlie last night, and there's kind of an issue. Well, so Charlie's dad isn't doing well, and she had this whole big problem with her situationship right before leaving."

"With what?" Jason frowned.

"Like, this guy Charlie was seeing, we call it, you know, a situationship. It's not a relationship because the guy isn't committing, but they were together, somewhat. It went on for, like, a year, or almost, and Charlie was hoping the guy would finally decide to commit and make her his girlfriend."

"A year is a long time."

"I know. That's what I told her. If you're with a guy for that long and he isn't committing, it's not going to happen," Kiana rambled. Her cheeks had flushed red, and she was gesticulating, with Percy having jumped down on the floor. "But as a guy, don't you know right away if you like a girl or not?" Kiana asked and stared directly at Jason.

"Umm, it depends," he averted his eyes.

"Either you do or you don't, right? I read that a guy either immediately knows you're the one, or it's never going to happen." Kiana opened her arms wide. "And with me and Ross, it was clear from the beginning. He told me the second he saw my profile, he knew it was meant to be for the two of us."

"Oh, wow." Jason bit his lower lip. "I think all people are different, men, women, you know. There are just so many factors. You were going to tell me something about Percy?" Jason tried to steer the conversation away from the topic of Ross, whom he started to despise.

"Oh, yeah, I almost forgot. It's just, umm, I get really protective of Charlie. I mean, she's my best friend. I was never a fan of the guy, the situationship one, and now that it's over, she's very sad, but the guy was a total jerk and told her he wasn't going to stick around while she was in California with her sick dad."

"How awful. It's really cruel."

"I know! That is exactly what I told Charlie, but she still keeps defending this dude. You know what I read?" Kiana swallowed hard. Without waiting for an answer, she continued speaking, "in a situationship, the only thing the two of you agree on is that you don't like yourself very much."

Jason's mouth gaped open.

"Wow, that's rough. But I guess it's true. I could never be with someone who's dating other people. I'm just not into games like that."

"See, it's because you're not from DC!"

"Maybe." Jason sighed. "But what were you saying about Percy?"

"Oh, yeah, I gotta take Percy to the vet."

"The vet?"

"Yeah, Charlie isn't coming back for another two weeks now, and Percy's got a vet appointment this coming weekend. She is getting spayed."

"I see."

"You won't need to do anything. I have the pet carrier, Charlie told me where to find it, it's been in storage, anyway, the only thing is, I'll just have to come and get Percy that morning, and then she'll have her surgery and then I'll bring her back."

"Alright. And Charlie will be back before I'm off to Korea, right?"

"Yes, absolutely!"

CHAPTER
Eleven

"SO SORRY. It'll be over quickly, alright? You don't worry about a thing. You'll come back as good as new," Jason repeated over and over again. Percy was sitting next to him, cleaning herself, after having had a full bowl of wet food, followed by two slices of turkey, which Jason ended up buying specifically for her.

A part of him felt terrible about what Percy would experience, but, of course, Jason knew spaying the cat was the right thing to do. Percy couldn't contribute to the growing population of cats in Arlington, which, if he were to believe his research, was getting out of control. Kiana had reassured him that Charlie had made the appointment with the best vet in Arlington, and all of Percy's expenses would be covered, but Jason couldn't help, but feel pity for the kitten every time he looked at her.

On Saturday morning, as agreed with Kiana, Jason had gotten Percy ready early. He made himself an espresso and tried his best to ignore the increasingly loud meows. But the vet's instructions were clear: Percy had to fast to avoid vomiting under anesthesia. So Jason tried his best to reassure Percy that everything was fine, and she would eat soon.

"Kiana will be here any minute, alright? And then you'll go to this place. It'll be nice…"

Percy gave him a look full of disapproval and turned her head away.

"It's going to be okay." He said, although he didn't feel like what he was saying was true. To take his mind off Percy's procedure, Jason tried scrolling through the news, but it didn't help.

At exactly eight, Kiana knocked on his door. She was wearing shorts. Her legs looked tanned, strong, and Jason immediately averted his eyes.

"Hey, how are you?" Kiana asked, placing the pet carrier on the floor and opening its door. "You look pale." She reached out to touch his cheek, fixing her gaze on him for just a moment. "Where's Percy?"

"Hi," Jason croaked. "Percy's right here." He turned to the couch, where Percy had been sitting next to him for the last hour. The cat was nowhere to be found. "I guess she went to the kitchen." Jason walked to Percy's bowl. Percy wasn't there either. "Maybe she's in the bathroom?"

But Percy wasn't in the bathroom, either.

The kitten was missing.

"Do you think she ran out of the apartment when I walked in?" Kiana asked, her eyes wide open.

"I don't think so," Jason said, but a shadow of doubt had crept in. "She must know we are planning something. I feel bad doing this."

"Come on, it needs to be done, it'll be quick, no reason to worry," Kiana said, her voice shaky, almost as if she were reassuring herself. "Come on, Percy, it's not a big deal; please come out." Kiana opened the door of the cat carrier wider.

"I guess Percy is smarter than we think," Jason noted, staring at the cage. "I wouldn't go into that thing voluntarily either."

"Did you look under the bed? I bet that's where she's hiding. Cats love those kinds of spaces."

"Good idea." Jason kneeled on the floor, peering under his bed. A second later, he realized Kiana was right there, next to him. The proximity to her was almost too much, and his heart raced. Jason gulped, and at that very moment heard Kiana let out an excited cry.

"There she is!" Jason noticed Percy's bright green eyes staring at him.

"Come on, Jason, help me get her out," Kiana said. "I'll just cajole her out, and maybe you can catch her on the other side when she runs out?"

"Alright, let's try," Jason said, his voice uncertain. The kitten hissed. "Percy, I'm sorry, I am really sorry."

It took Jason and Kiana several attempts to get Percy to leave her hiding spot. By the time they were done, and Percy was safely locked in the pet carrier, both were sweating.

"Wow, she's a feisty little girl." Kiana ran her hand through her hair. "With my cat, when we had to go to the vet, it wasn't easy, but not as crazy as this. I guess it's because she's very young."

A loud meow reached their ears. Then another one.

"This is just too much," Jason said, and put his finger into the cage, trying to pet Percy between the ears. But the kitten stuck out her claws. Jason pulled back his hand just in time.

"I didn't expect the chase to take so long." Kiana threw a skeptical look at the pet carrier. "Percy's so stressed out."

"Listen, how about I come along with you to the vet? Would that help?"

"Are you sure? I don't want to impose. I mean, it would be great, of course. Thank you so much for offering." Kiana checked the time.

"Great, let me just get ready." Jason retreated to his bedroom, where he quickly shed his workout clothes he'd put on earlier, so he could change into his regular weekend attire:

jeans and a t-shirt. He slipped on his jeans, and hurriedly pulled on his t-shirt, as he walked out of the bedroom.

"Ready?" he asked, noticing Kiana's eyes darting up from his torso.

"I am." She nodded, looking away.

Several minutes later, Jason followed Kiana out of the apartment, carrying the cage with the angrily meowing Percy.

Jason had always believed you can tell a lot about a person from their car. It wasn't the model of the car, not really, but more so how clean it was and what they kept in it. But all he could tell from Kiana's car, a Mazda CX3, was that she loved fitness. The passenger side had several water bottles, a set of weights, a yoga mat and a pair of tennis shoes.

"I like to keep workout gear in the car, in case I end up going straight after work," Kiana explained, as she moved the yoga mat out of the passenger seat to the back. "During the lockdown, I worked out at home, but it got so boring. So now that the studios have reopened, I try to go as much as possible."

"Oh, wow, what kind of workouts do you do?"

"I go to barre," Kiana said. "Also yoga, and then I go to this place called Hard Base."

"Wait, bar? What bar?" Jason threw a confused look at her.

"Not that kind of bar." She shook her head. "It's ballet-based fitness, actually." Both of them were trying hard to ignore Percy's meows that had no indication of subsiding. They were coming at a frequency of approximately three per minute, were evenly spaced and sounded ominous. "Barre is actually really good for core and for muscle fitness."

"I see."

"It's just a short drive." Kiana made a right onto Arlington Boulevard. "Fortunately for all of us."

"So, what's Hard Base?"

"It's actually really great. So it's kind of like Pilates, but on crack. I think that's the only way to describe it. Every time I go, I feel like I'm going to collapse and die. I really do."

"Wow, and you like that kind of stuff?"

"Yes, at least I know I'm working out, you know? It's almost like a cult." There were dreamy notes in Kiana's voice.

"I see," Jason said, "but it's not dangerous, is it?"

"Dangerous? How?"

"Like, you won't hurt yourself?"

"No." Kiana waved her hand in the air.

"I used to be really into taekwondo, but I quit, because it was hard on my feet and ankles. I can't be a podiatrist with foot problems." Jason chuckled.

"You got a point there. Taekwondo sounds really great, I guess you know how to fight."

"I do." Jason bit his lip, wistful for the rush of confidence martial arts had given him in the past. Though he tried, he hadn't been able to recapture the feeling with other types of exercise.

Kiana steered right and took the exit onto N. George Mason Drive, then made a quick turn and they pulled into a parking lot. "Here's the place. I used to bring my cat here. It's really great; this vet has been practicing for, like, thirty years. Old school."

They both reached into the back seat at the same time to take the pet carrier out, and almost bumped noses. A current ran through Jason's body. He glanced sideways to see Kiana blush.

"Is it okay if I help?" Jason breathed out. Being next to Kiana, while ignoring how attractive he found her, was a constant quest, challenging his whole being.

"Yes, thank you." Kiana gave him a careful stare. "I'm just not used to anyone helping. So used to doing things on my own all the time."

Jason didn't respond. He reached for the pet carrier.

"Now, Percy, please don't worry," he said, lifting it out of the car. "What a good little girl you are."

Kiana locked the car, and they walked to the clinic together. Jason placed the carrier in the waiting room, and immediately noticed a huge black cat sprawled in the window. The cat was staring at Jason, its eyes fixed firmly on his face.

"Oh, that's Simon." Kiana smiled at the cat. "He's been here forever. He's probably twenty years old. Simon runs the show around here."

"I can tell." Jason looked at the cat with respect. As if satisfied by the impression he'd made, Simon closed one eye, then the other, and went to sleep.

After Kiana registered Percy at the reception, a nurse came out to take the kitten in. She was a small, dour-looking woman with gray hair. "So, we'll just do a quick physical and then we'll take your cat in for the procedure," the nurse said, all business. "Please follow me into the examination room."

Kiana and Jason exchanged a glance and, without saying a word, followed the nurse, with Jason transporting Percy in the pet carrier. Jason hadn't planned on being in the room when Percy was getting treated. He'd assumed his role would stop at the reception, and, after placing the carrier on the examination table, stepped back awkwardly, hands in his pockets. Kiana was standing next to him, twisting a lock of her hair.

"Now, please get the cat ready for me." The nurse looked at Kiana, and Kiana flipped the door of the carrier to the 'open' position, unbolting the latch. Percy didn't move. She was sitting at the very back of the cage, hissing.

"She's beautiful, what a pretty red color. Let's try to get her out; how about that?" The nurse made a move towards the cage.

CHAPTER

Twelve

THE NEXT MOMENT, instead of reaching inside, with a practiced gesture, the nurse unlocked the four sides of the cage and lifted the top off. Before Percy could stick her claws out, she was out of the cage and in the nurse's firm grasp.

The woman gently placed Percy on the examination table, moving the carrier to the side.

"We'll call you when your cat is ready for pick up," the nurse told them curtly.

"So, what do you want to do now?" Kiana asked, as the two of them walked out of the clinic. "Do you want me to take you home?"

All Jason wanted at that moment was to spend more time with Kiana, but he didn't want to appear needy or overbearing.

"They told me Percy will be ready to go back by two or so," Kiana said. "I can just bring her to you."

"Or, if you want, we can go somewhere," Jason said, on the spot trying to think of a location that didn't seem like a date. He had no idea where one would even go, and what their outing would be. Besides, the only places he knew well were H-Mart and a few Korean coffee shops in Annandale.

The pair got in the car, and Kiana turned to look at Jason. "You know what? If you're free, would you like to come to the Mall?"

"You mean, Tyson's?" Jason raised his eyebrows. Cassie was always telling him about meeting her friends at Tyson's Galleria, and he expected Kiana to confirm, but she shook her head.

"No, the National Mall," she said. "The one with the museums. I want to go to the National Gallery of Art."

"I've never been."

"Really? Oh, I guess you've only recently moved to DC. But you're missing out. I love to go, and it's free."

"Oh, nice."

"So, would you like to come?" Kiana turned to face him. Her left hand rested on the steering wheel, and with the right, she shifted the car into drive. "Or I can take you back. It's on the way." She clarified as she pulled out of the parking spot.

Jason's mind raced. He'd never been into art, didn't understand it. The possibility of embarrassing himself in front of her was too much. He wanted to refuse, until Kiana said, as if reading his mind, "You know, I used to be afraid of art. But then I decided to just try to enjoy it. To not overthink."

As they stopped at a red light, she looked over at Jason.

"Yes, sure," Jason said. "I'll come along." He didn't exactly admit to not being able to understand art, but he didn't have to. And now he could spend several hours in Kiana's company while waiting for Percy's surgery to be over.

———

They parked close to the gallery, at a spot, which, according to Kiana, was free, but most tourists didn't know about it. "I always drive here; it's so much better than taking the metro," she noted casually as they exited the vehicle and walked to the building. Jason looked up at it in awe.

He lived just a few miles away, but since moving to DC had not visited the National Mall. At first, Jason was too busy setting himself up, furnishing his apartment, establishing himself at work, and then, as he slowly got more free time, he couldn't motivate himself to do something on his own. And his social acquaintances, few as they were, that he'd so far found in Arlington, went out to bars and wineries, and definitely not to museums.

"So, since you haven't been here before, I'll show you my favorite part of the gallery," Kiana said as they walked into the building. The tall ceilings, the light gently flowing through the windows, the impressive staircase, all struck Jason.

"It's upstairs." Kiana led him to the elevator. They got in, and, for a moment, Jason was transported to their first meeting, the closing doors of the elevator in his building, Kiana rushing in with the swimming bag.

The day everything changed, Jason thought.

They walked into an airy hall, and Kiana pointed to several paintings. They were of large blocks of color. Orange and purple on a yellow background. Two shades of blue with a red stripe in the middle.

"Rothko," Kiana breathed out, her hand lingering on his forearm. They were the only two people in the space, with the gallery still empty in the early morning hours.

"Rothko?" Jason repeated.

"Yes, that's the artist. He's a genius. Look." Kiana pointed at one of the paintings.

"I could draw that," Jason hummed. "It's just some paint–"

"No, look. Just look at the painting. It's almost alive. Rothko made the colors come alive. He lived each block of color, pulled it through himself. It's really incredible how he did it."

Jason stared at the painting, trying hard to understand

what Kiana was talking about. For a few moments, he thought he would never be able to do so. The painting didn't look like anything special. And then, he saw it.

The colors started to separate, each brush stroke revealed a new shade, a new layer, and together they formed a dance of color. A symphony that was beautifully intertwined.

"He lived it, you see, right?" Jason turned and saw Kiana staring at him. "It's incredible. They'll have a Rothko exhibit here soon. I can't wait," Kiana said as the two of them left the exhibition hall. "You know, he was born in Russia," she added after a pause. "Well, the Russian Empire."

"Oh, cool," Jason nodded, and then it hit him. "Wait, remember Anton?"

"The spy? How could I forget?"

"Yes, the spy. Well, the defector," Jason clarified. "You know, I looked into it. And there's that weird death. That was the part the documentary omitted completely. How he died. It was as if they ignored it on purpose. But that was what Audrey mentioned."

"That sounds weird. Why wouldn't they talk about it in the documentary?"

"I know. If you're going to investigate the guy, then why not talk about everything about him? But they only focused on how he lied about what had happened in Russia, but left the whole death mystery alone."

"So, what was the thing with his death?" Kiana stopped walking as she said this, and Jason almost bumped into her. The proximity to her, the attraction was strong.

I wonder if she knows I like her, he thought to himself.

"Audrey mentioned he was the love of her life, or something like that. But then the guy died next to a young woman, apparently his fiancée. And then Audrey also claims she was his fiancée, so it's strange, right?"

"Unless Audrey is deranged?" Kiana sighed. "It's been what, fifty years? And she's still hung up on this man?"

"That's cold." Jason shook his head.

"I'm just being real. I mean, come on, maybe she made the whole thing up, their love story and all that. Did she tell you anything else about Anton?"

Jason shook his head.

"You know what? I think I'm gonna ask my mom about it."

"Your mom? Why?"

"Well, she's Russian, so she might know something about this whole situation. And back in the eighties, when she first moved here, the Russian community wasn't that big. For obvious reasons."

"Oh, yeah. I guess with the Soviet Union and all."

"Exactly." Kiana paused. "She was a ballet dancer and came here with the troupe on tour, then never left. She defected, though not for political reasons."

"That's quite a coincidence."

"Except my mom came here later, that guy defected in 1970, right? And she came here for love."

"How so?"

"She met my dad for the first time in 1981, when her troupe came to DC on tour. And it was love at first sight. But they couldn't date, because he couldn't just visit her in the Soviet Union. I mean, no one really could go there easily. But they had agreed to see each other again, and he told her he would wait for her no matter what."

"Are you serious? That's an incredible story." Jason stared at Kiana in admiration.

"I know. Imagine, with parents like that, it's hard to live up to that standard."

"So, then what happened?" Jason and Kiana had stopped walking and were standing in the middle of the hallway. It was getting more crowded, but they were too enthralled in their conversation to notice.

"Well, then she came back the following year. And that was that."

"So they just saw each other a few times, and that was enough?"

"Yes. So, they tell me."

"But what about their families? Didn't they have to meet as well? I mean, marriage is such a complex thing, there are so many factors to consider." Jason mentioned just a few of the points he had been keeping in mind while setting up his own dating profile, with the AI algorithm aptly measuring his level of suitability against possible matches based on height, income level, education, earning potential, weight, longevity, not to mention the very basics, like, for one, being Korean.

"No, their families met much later. My dad didn't even meet my mom's side of the family until 1992, after the Soviet Union collapsed and we could all go there. I actually remember that trip. I was seven years old, and my brother was about nine, and we all went. My grandmother wept the second she saw us. She cried for probably like a full day, first hugging my mom, then me, then my brother, and then even my dad. It was crazy."

"Wow."

"Yeah. But now I get it. Because when my mom left, you know, no one knew the Soviet Union would collapse like that. And my mom thought she would never see her parents ever again."

"So, do you travel to Russia often?"

"Not really. I've been with my mom a few times. She goes every year to visit her parents. They're in their eighties now, and she worries about them. But they lived through World War II. So my mom always tells me, if I ever complain, how my grandparents had starved as children but they'd made it through the war, and to basically shut up." Kiana chuckled. "And it works."

"My parents do it, too." Jason perked up. "My mom, especially, if I ever complain of pain, would tell me about my grandparents who had lived under the Japanese occupation, and then how she, as a girl, had so little and went hungry. And even now, she's the most resilient person I know. The only time I've seen her cry was when she hurt her foot. I now treat people with the same condition, and they all complain their pain is unbearable at their first appointment. But not my mom."

"Wow, I guess it's good to have immigrant parents, right?" Kiana smiled. "Makes you stronger and tougher as a person."

"It does." Jason nodded. "But the expectations are very high, too."

The two of them started walking again and had made it to the exit. Jason glanced at his watch. It was just after eleven.

"Have they called you about Percy yet?" he asked Kiana.

She checked her phone. "Not yet."

"Maybe we can grab a bite to eat?"

He wanted to keep talking to her. The shared upbringing, the stories they were telling each other, had pulled him in.

"Sure! That would be great. There's the cafe right through here." Kiana pointed at what looked like a gated garden. "There are sculptures there, it's nice. And you can go ice skating there in the winter. It's kind of romantic, actually," she added wistfully.

"Really? That would be a nice date night," Jason said. "I just wish I knew how to ice skate. I never learned."

"I have."

"Of course. You had to, right? As a Russian."

"Yes. There are some non-negotiables. Like ice skating lessons, gymnastics lessons, and piano lessons. And for me, also ballet. Because of my mom."

"I see. Nothing like that for me," Jason said. "Well, other than taekwondo. But even that was on hold for a few years."

"Really?"

"Well, we weren't that well off," Jason clarified and

blushed. That was putting it mildly. Their first few years in America were so financially precarious, it had been a miracle they'd survived at all. His parents worked crazy shifts, but whatever money they made was just never enough. Certainly not enough for things like ice skating or piano lessons. But just enough to put food on the table, though most of it was leftovers from the restaurant where Jason's mother worked.

"Oh, of course," Kiana noted softly.

They'd made it to the garden gate.

"This is beautiful," Jason exclaimed, holding the door open for Kiana.

It was like they'd stepped into an enchanted garden. There were sculptures all around them, and a fountain in the middle.

"It is, right?" Kiana smiled. "DC is full of places like this."

"I had no idea."

"Oh, yes. It's really strange. There's like, the government and all that, so people think DC is very dry and all about politics, but there are some really interesting places. Hidden treasures."

"I'd love to see them," Jason said. "With you," he added after a pause, surprised at his own boldness.

"Well, sure." Kiana blushed. "I guess before you leave."

"Or after I come back." Jason shrugged. "I mean, before your boyfriend moves here, of course," he added and felt the now familiar knot in his stomach.

"Ross is moving here in early September, right around Labor Day, so there'll be a week or two," Kiana said nonchalantly. "The cafe is right through here." She pointed at a green building surrounded by round tables.

Jason followed Kiana, and then she said the words that had given Jason both, hope for the future, while also throwing him into depths of despair.

"And besides, we can be friends even after Ross moves to the area."

CHAPTER
Thirteen

THE SUDDEN REMINDER that it would soon no longer be just the two of them and Percy hit him. There would be Ross. Kiana would be part of a couple and he…

What, a third wheel? Until, if he found a match and she agreed to move here, then what? Would they all be friends? It seemed too ridiculous to even picture.

Friends.

The word reverberated through Jason's mind. His head started pounding, and he pressed his fingers to his temples to stop a headache from coming on. With sudden clarity, he realized that any possibility of a romantic breakthrough with Kiana was impossible.

Up until that moment, there was always a chance, and the prospect, albeit minuscule, drove him on. But now, it vanished.

Did Kiana just friend zone me?

The reason Jason was fully familiar with the friend zone concept and identified it so quickly was because of his cousin, Dave, Uncle Henry's son. Unlike Jason, Dave was successful in love. He dated many girls in high school and college, both Korean and non-Korean, never got into anything serious with any of them, got a great job in investment banking in New York City straight out of college, then did his MBA, got a promotion, and, finally, married the perfect girl: Korean-American, but with traditional values, a great background, with a family of equal social standing to his own.

Dave was the ideal Korean son, and his parents had now become doting grandparents to Dave's two beautiful baby boys. Even in progeny Dave was superior: boys were the preferred grandchildren of most Korean grandparents.

Jason got to know Dave after moving to America. At first, theirs wasn't really a friendship. Dave, despite being younger, adopted Jason, and tried to teach him as much as possible about life in the U.S. Popular culture, how to dress, how to act, how to avoid getting picked on at school. Otherwise, Jason would have completely drowned. He owed Dave his survival and the fact that he'd made it all the way through podiatry school. Through his twenties, Jason used to speak to Dave at least once a week, mostly to catch up, but also to listen to Dave's stories. But now that Dave had become a father to two young children, and Jason moved to Arlington, their conversations became more and more sporadic.

At one point, a year before getting married, when Dave had just finished his MBA, he had developed a crush on a colleague. Her name was Sharon and she worked in HR. Jason remembered the name, though he'd never met Sharon. His cousin gushed about Sharon, everything about her was perfect. Any opportunity Dave got, he would try to pass by Sharon's office. And then, several months later, Dave confided in Jason:

"I'm done, bro. This is the end."

"What are you talking about?"

"Sharon has friend zoned me. I'm sure of it now."

"How do you know?"

"She used the word. Called me a friend. Once a woman

calls you a friend, you've gotta nip it in the bud, or you're done."

"It's that bad?"

"It is. I'll agree to be set up with that chick from church, I guess," Dave said.

That was another reason Jason remembered the story: the woman from church had become Dave's now-wife.

And now Kiana had done the same thing. Jason was certain, he'd reached a point of no return. *Have I been friend zoned from the beginning? Or did it just happen? And what did I expect, Kiana is as good as engaged.*

But Jason hadn't quite bought into the seriousness of Kiana's relationship. How could he? Not with the boyfriend being based abroad and with Kiana only knowing the virtual version of the man. But, regardless, Kiana had used the word.

Friends.

Jason contemplated doing what his cousin had done: cutting off ties immediately. Protecting himself. That would have been the sensible thing to do. But then he remembered Percy.

Percy, who needed a place to stay, who couldn't be returned to an empty apartment, who needed him. *It's only one more week,* Jason told himself, *and then, it's done.*

"Are you ready to order?" Kiana's words reached him as if through a thick fog.

"What?"

"I already placed an order, are you ready?"

Jason found himself standing next to Kiana in front of the cashier, who was staring curiously at him through her gold-rimmed glasses.

"Oh, yes, sure." Jason looked up and saw the menu scribbled in cursive above the cashier's head. He picked the first thing on the menu, which was a chicken salad sandwich, immediately regretted it, but the cashier had already rung it up.

"Together? Or separately?" The cashier asked and narrowed her eyes.

"Together," Kiana responded before Jason had a chance to intervene and handed her credit card to the cashier. "You've been doing so much for Percy," Kiana explained, turning to him.

Friend zoned, of course, flashed through Jason's mind. *If she liked me, she wouldn't have offered to pay.*

"It's not a big deal," he responded and smiled a crooked smile.

"You know, I was thinking," Kiana said after the two of them picked a table in the corner and sat down across from each other. The setting was intimate and would have been romantic and perfect for a leisurely date, had Jason not just had his friend zone revelation.

"What is it?" he asked.

"I'd like to show my mom the documentary. And tell her about Anton. What do you think?"

"Sure, why not?" Jason responded, then paused. "I mean, she wouldn't mind?"

"Oh, no, of course not. My mom's cool. She knows about you."

Jason's mouth hung open. "She does?"

"Yes, I told her. She's been asking about Percy, and of course I told her."

"Told her what?"

"That Percy is staying with Charlie's neighbor." Kiana shrugged. "And I mentioned you were a podiatrist."

"Oh?"

"I just think it's really cool that you've got an actual profession. I mean, you're making a difference in people's lives."

"Thanks." Jason's cheeks turned slightly pink from the compliment.

Fourteen

"SO, I ASKED MY MOM," Kiana said.

Though they hadn't discussed the topic since the previous weekend, the day of Percy's surgery, Jason knew right away Kiana meant Anton Konovalov.

It was Thursday night after work, and they were sitting at the pool, having just swum laps together. Somehow, with Kiana around, pool loungers magically appeared and they were able to get at least one chair.

It had been just two weeks since the two of them first met, but he felt like they had known each other for much longer. Kiana even joked as much.

"What did she say?"

"She told me we should interview Audrey to figure out what exactly is going on."

"Like, question her?"

"Well, I asked my mom about Anton, whether she'd heard anything about that guy. She told me she hadn't, but she came here a full decade after he'd disappeared. So, by the time she got here, likely no one remembered him or his story. But then she watched the documentary, the same one we'd seen."

"And? What did she think?"

"My mom thinks, if we really want to figure out what's going on, we need to first speak to Audrey. I asked her about the other woman, when Anton died and there was the other girl with him, whether that meant Audrey had made up her story. My mom thought the guy probably was dating two women at the same time. That he had two fiancées."

"How could he even do that?"

"My mom told me about this show, *Mrs. Wilson*. It's about this British spy who had four wives, back in the fifties. I just watched it."

"Four wives? At the same time?"

"Yes, the guy in the show didn't divorce any of them. And none of the wives knew about the others. He just kept on marrying new women and lied to the others. And it's based on a true story. So maybe Anton Konovalov was like that British spy, and he was just starting out, you know?"

"That's wild," Jason shook his head. "But it does sound like it could be the case. How would we know for sure, though?"

"I guess we need to start with Audrey. I think my mom is right," Kiana said. "I actually was thinking, if this guy Anton was alive now, it never would have happened."

"What do you mean?"

"The lies, you can't get away with the same stuff now. There's a whole Facebook group for that, actually. It's called 'Is This Your Man?' It's all of these women, and they help each other out. Charlie told me about it a few months ago, and asked me to join, so I could check on her ex. And I've been following it ever since. Because of how many creeps are out there, you can go and put in a name to see if anyone else is dating the same guy as you. Mostly it's the guys from the apps. But the women's group has, like, 80,000 members, and they are all in the DMV," Kiana said.

"What? There's no way."

"Oh, yes. And there are subgroups, for each part of the

U.S. Women post daily the men from the apps. To make sure they aren't being cheated on."

"I had no idea." Jason stared at Kiana. "It's kind of sad, isn't it? That this group even exists."

"I guess so. But it's better than suffering for fifty years, like Audrey." Kiana shrugged. "I think it's great women are helping each other."

"Absolutely, but the men who behave that way! I find that quite awful. Don't you think?"

"Sad but I guess for some terrible people, it's just in their nature." Kiana brushed him off. "Anyway, let's talk to Audrey first. If she agrees, of course. Would she be open to speaking with us?"

"Sure, I'll try to arrange it for when I come back. I'm traveling to Korea next weekend, and I was actually going to ask you when Charlie is coming back. For Percy. I'll be gone for ten days."

"Oh, yeah, Charlie." Kiana averted her eyes. "She's likely not coming back for a while longer. I was going to tell you."

"A while longer?" Jason's heart rate accelerated. He had been seeing Kiana regularly. *Why is she only telling this to me now?*

"Well, she's going to try to sublet the apartment for six months. She said she can work remotely from L.A., and her dad isn't doing well. So she wants to spend as much time as possible with him. And actually, I was going to ask, would you be interested in keeping Percy?"

"For how long?"

"Well, umm." Kiana shrugged. "I mean, you seem to like each other. Right?"

"Yes, but I'm about to go to Korea–"

"I know. I was thinking about that. And I can help, I can come over and take care of Percy while you're away."

"You mean, to my place?"

"Yeah. Or we can move Percy back to Charlie's, but it

seems like Percy is really settled in your place already." Kiana fidgeted. "Listen, I know it's a lot. I thought Charlie would be back by now, but the whole situation, and I feel responsible for Percy. But with you, I know she'll be in good hands. Like, you could even be Percy's forever person."

"Forever person?" Jason's mouth gaped open.

It wasn't that Jason wanted Percy to leave. He loved having the kitten around, enjoyed being a cat owner.

Because all of it was supposed to be temporary.

Yet, the moment Kiana said the word 'forever,' Jason remembered that he was about to engage in another 'forever', a much more important undertaking than adopting a cat. He would soon travel to Korea and meet his future wife. Wasn't that more important than Percy? And whatever else Kiana had in mind.

"Well, or at least, you know, maybe not forever, but for a few months?" Kiana pleaded. She bit her lip and looked away, obviously trying hard to avoid showing disappointment.

"Listen, I don't want to sound harsh or anything, but right now isn't the best time for me," Jason started to say. "I'm going to be getting married soon, and then moving out, likely, I mean, who knows? Things aren't really that stable. I just started this job." As he was listing his reasons not to adopt Percy out loud, Jason realized he sounded cold and callous. Exactly like the type of person he didn't want to be. The person who didn't care.

Hadn't he made a pact with himself to always try to be kind and helpful? Isn't that why he became a podiatrist in the first place? Picked exactly this profession out of all the other possible options because that's where he felt he could make the biggest difference in people's lives?

"Listen, you know what, I have an idea!" Kiana clapped. "Once Ross moves here and he and I move in together, I can take Percy. So, it'll just be a few months. Okay? Please,

Jason, please? And I can take care of Percy when you're in Korea."

Jason's heart sank at the mention of the dark cloud hanging over their relationship: Ross.

The mythical figure emerging from the shadows. According to Kiana, all was on track for Ross to move to DC. He'd just wrapped up his assignment, and was planning on buying the house as soon as he landed in DC. Whenever he heard about the man, Jason felt bile rise in his throat. But each time that happened, just as he did now, Jason reminded himself his suffering had an expiration date: it would all end the minute he got on the plane for Seoul.

"I'll let you know, okay?" He mumbled.

"Alright. And Audrey, you'll arrange the meeting with her after you're back from Korea?"

"Yeah, I guess," Jason added. "Listen, I'll go jump in. I want to do a few more laps," he said and walked over to the pool.

The conversation with Kiana made him feel out of control, like he was powerless to say 'no' to her. Jason suspected, if Kiana pushed a bit more, he would agree to anything she requested, no matter how unreasonable.

Swimming was great for clearing Jason's head. Instead of a few laps, he did his usual forty, then swam a few more, and emerged from the pool refreshed and energized. With a new conviction, his focus and energy had to be on his upcoming trip to Korea. After all, he owed it to himself. This was far too important; he had invested far too much time into the matches not to give them his best. His whole future was on the line. And in order for the trip to Korea to go well, Jason had to do something he'd been putting off: gift shopping.

He needed to bring presents for his parents, his parents' friends that he'd be meeting, distant cousins and their offspring. Also, his childhood friend Hyun-woo, and his wife, and daughter.

Of course, presents for his own parents were a different story. In addition to gifts, Jason also had to buy them specific things they wanted from America. Jason climbed out of the pool, and noticed Kiana giving him an expectant look.

"So, did you decide?" Kiana scanned his face for a reaction, as Jason wrapped a towel around his waist.

"About Percy, you mean?" He rolled his shoulders back. "Percy can stay." In addition to his newfound conviction to focus on the trip to Korea, he had made the decision the cat could stay at his apartment: that way Kiana could keep an eye on the place.

"You mean at your place? That's fantastic! Thank you, thank you!" Kiana jumped up and wrapped her arms around him, then pulled back in embarrassment. Catching a whiff of her perfume, Jason wondered how she managed to smell so sweet instead of chlorine. "So you'll let me know what you want me to do, right? And with the food, I can ask Charlie, or…"

"Sure, we'll work it out. Don't worry. But I've got to get ready to go to Korea," he added solemnly. "I gotta go gift shopping. For all my family, friends, they all need something." Jason expected Kiana to question this tradition: Korea, he'd been told, was somewhat unusual in the extent of its gift-giving culture, but Kiana nodded in understanding.

"I know. My mom always brings a separate suitcase just for the gifts every time she goes to Russia. If you like, I can go shopping with you. Help you pick stuff out."

"Really?"

"Yeah, I like looking for bargains. I love shopping. And I'm good at it, too."

"My mom told me to get some gifts at Trader Joe's. She said people in Korea will go crazy for them," Jason added after a pause. "But I just don't know where to start."

"I love Trader Joe's!" Kiana got up. "Just tell me when. We can go together."

————

It was the second weekend in a row the two of them spent together. This time, they met on Saturday afternoon so that Kiana could do her morning workout and Jason could go for his run at Roosevelt Island. After she checked on Percy and played with the kitten for nearly an hour, while he made them espresso and, at Kiana's insistence, compiled a list of gifts he would need to buy, the pair headed out.

"You need to list the name of the person and what you'll be bringing them," Kiana urged.

"But can't we just see what's available, buy the thing and then I figure out who it's for?"

"That's how you'll end up with things you don't need. If you want to just get generic souvenirs, that's fine. Trust me, I've helped my mom prepare for her trips to Russia plenty of times, so I know."

Kiana's resolve was unwavering, so Jason forced himself to write down the names of everyone he'd be meeting in Seoul and what needed to be bought. The list had over twenty people on it, and, Jason suspected, he'd likely forgotten a few people.

"And by the way, I looked up what gifts to bring to Korea, and for generic gifts, you want to get honey, and also local souvenirs. So we can look for DC souvenirs, like mugs, magnets, t-shirts." Kiana's face lit up as she spoke and Jason's heart melted. She looked incredibly sweet, kind, warm, and beautiful. Even running errands with her was fun.

Could she be my perfect woman? Jason asked himself but immediately stopped that train of thought.

Several hours later, the pair returned to his apartment with five huge bags full of 'junk,' as Jason called it. Toys for the kids, knick-knacks, t-shirts and coffee mugs, gifts from Trader Joe's, and a myriad of other items he found completely unnecessary. Kiana then made him go through his list and check off the items and label them with the name of the intended recipient.

"See, you should be all set now," she noted with satisfaction, watching Jason sort through the stack of gifts. Percy, who had greeted them by the door with a loud meow, moved carefully around the items, sniffing them.

"Thank you!" Jason said. "I really owe you."

"Oh, come on." Kiana shook her head. "This is what friends are for."

"I guess so."

"You guess so? Aren't we friends?"

"Yes, of course we are," Jason squeezed out, remembering the trip to Korea was only a few days away. "We sure are."

PART

Two

CHAPTER

Fifteen

THOUGH HE HAD REFUSED her kind offer, Kiana insisted on driving him to the airport a few days later.

"It's the least I can do, Jason," she repeated until Jason agreed. "Safe travels. And good luck, alright?" Kiana winked at him, as she pulled up in the departure lane.

"Thank you," Jason responded, his stomach in knots.

As the meeting with his matches was getting closer, the reality of what he was about to do was sinking in: he would be making the most important decision of his life next week. Choosing his future wife.

"Come here." Kiana reached to embrace him, and the two hugged. "And don't forget about the hot pockets!" She smiled. Prior to the flight, Kiana had researched the food menu on Korean Air, and mentioned to Jason the 'incredible hot pockets' that were served in economy.

Rolling his carry-on aboard the Korean Air flight from Washington Dulles International Airport to Seoul Incheon, Jason wondered if Percy would notice his absence. And whether Kiana would miss him.

The flight to Korea would take over fifteen hours. Jason had managed to book himself an aisle seat, which would offer some comfort during the flight, but, as he squeezed his six-foot-two frame into the seat and tried to stretch his legs out, he realized the flight would be a challenge. But then, the entertainment system flicked on.

It took a few minutes to figure out the location of the headphone plug, but once he did, he slipped them on and focused on browsing the movies. He settled on *The Godfather.'* Not only had he seen all three movies countless times, he'd also read the novel upon the recommendation of his ESL teacher, Dr. Clark.

"If you want to learn about America, the real United States," the teacher had told him, "read the book. Don't watch the movies, no, first, read the book. It's the greatest story of immigration ever told. A classic. And it'll help your English."

And Jason did. He had been eager to perfect his English, eager to learn all there was about America, and so he read *The Godfather*, first with a dictionary, then, after watching the movies, he'd read it again without one. Jason had kept a list of unfamiliar words that he later memorized for the SATs. When, in just under two years, Jason had learned English well enough to get an A- in an honors English class, he would always credit *The Godfather* for his success.

On the plane, he had planned on watching all three movies back to back, but, after eating and getting through the first movie, his eyes started closing as if on their own accord. The flight attendant had offered him a glass of wine with his meal, and Jason considered drinking, but the possibility of nursing a bad hangover on a long flight was too much of a risk to take. So, to the attendant's surprise, he refused. He covered himself with the blanket, adjusted the pillow and drifted into sleep. He dreamed of Kiana.

The two of them were walking in Seoul, where she was taking him shopping. She was showing him her favorite stores, and telling him where he needed to go, and what he needed to buy.

"But you've never been to Seoul." Jason stared at Kiana in confusion. "How do you know where to go?"

"Of course I have; we went here together last year," Kiana reassured him. She pushed her hair back in her favorite gesture, and then she leaned in and kissed him.

It was the kiss that woke Jason up.

"Kiana," he moaned softly.

The sensation was so real that he reached for her, only to find himself contorted, his feet stuffed uncomfortably under the seat in front of him. The need, the desire to be with Kiana was so strong, that Jason closed his eyes in the hopes of falling back asleep, but to no avail. He checked the time on his phone, then turned on the display to see how much more flight time remained. Another seven hours. Jason groaned.

And then, he realized he was starving. Ravenous. It was a hunger so strong, as if he hadn't eaten in days. Jason had not felt such hunger since his early twenties, when he always kept a pack of ramen by his desk, something he could quickly make and not disrupt his studying.

Jason stretched, adjusted his seat, and went to try to find something to eat. He found the flight attendants engaged in deep conversation. One of them, the same woman who had been surprised by his refusal to drink, offered him some chips and a glass of water, and then Jason remembered the hot pockets.

As soon as he mentioned them, the flight attendant smiled and told him she'd be coming by with one shortly. It was as if Jason had cracked a secret code.

Minutes later, as Jason bit into a steaming hot pocket, while watching the second Godfather movie, he thought, *I gotta tell Kiana she was right. This thing is delicious.*

CHAPTER
Sixteen

HE CALLED his parents as soon as he was at the baggage claim and heard his mother's excited voice.

"Jun! You're finally home, see you soon."

Jason, on the recommendation from Hyun-woo, had booked himself a special transportation van service upon arrival at Incheon airport. This secured him a relatively traffic-free passage into the city. According to Hyun-woo, in Seoul, there was always traffic, and especially in the early evening hours, when Jason's plane landed.

By eight pm, Jason reached his parents' apartment building. Ever since moving back to Seoul, his parents had been living in the Yongsan District of the city, not far from Namsan Park. His parents' move back to Korea had been prompted by the death of Jason's paternal uncle, Kyung-ho, who had died childless and left everything to Jason's father. The inheritance included an apartment in this prestigious part of Seoul, which played a big role in his parents' decision to move back to Korea.

Jason remembered Yongsan well from his childhood, when they had visited Uncle Kyung-ho. Back then, the steep hill leading up to the building appeared insurmountable.

They had always made the journey on foot, and Jason would beg his parents to turn around, to rethink the journey uphill. Now, as the van turned onto his parents' street, Jason felt a yearning so strong, as if all he'd ever wanted was to be back in Seoul. He hadn't felt any nostalgia for his hometown, and the feeling surprised him with its intensity. He missed being back, missed this city, and though he'd grown up in Myeonmok, a completely different part of Seoul, he now felt he'd finally reclaimed a part of him he'd been missing all these years.

His father came downstairs to help him with the luggage. Out of the van window, Jason noticed his father's shoulders had hunched a bit more, and the gray that had become more prominent in his father's hair.

The realization his parents were growing old was like a gut punch. A reminder, Jason had no time to waste. He needed to get married and start a family as soon as possible.

"Jun, my boy," his father said, patting him on the back, as Jason stepped out of the van. A proud smile crossed his father's face, but he didn't embrace Jason. The neighbors could be watching.

They rode up in the elevator together. Jason's mother greeted them outside of the apartment door and immediately dissolved into tears.

"I've waited so long for this, so long, my boy. I'm so proud of you, so happy you came home." She gave him a long look, wiping the tears. "Well, go shower, get yourself changed, and then we'll discuss our plans for the week."

An hour later, the three of them were seated around the kitchen table. Normally, Jason's parents had an early dinner and then went on a long walk together. This was a tradition introduced by Jason's mother, to avoid gaining weight and to ensure longevity. But in honor of his arrival, they had made an exception. His mother had cooked a feast, japchai, bulgogi, and Jason's favorite, homemade Pajeon, served sizzling hot, with huge pieces of seafood and scallion, nicely browned.

"Jun, tomorrow, we have a few visits. Did you remember the presents?" Jason's mother asked, and Jason nearly jumped out of his seat.

"Of course! Let me show you." He made a move to get up, but his mother stopped him. "Finish eating, please."

"No, no, I brought you and Abeoji a few things. I completely forgot." Jason went to his suitcase and returned with a bottle of perfume for his mother and cologne for his father. It was a matching set, by Creed, which, Kiana had assured him, would be well received and was a 'classic.'

"This is beautiful," Jason's mother said as she examined the gift. "And it smells so nice."

"I'm glad you like it."

"How did you know to get this? I've been hearing about this brand. Did someone help you pick it out? I sense a woman's touch."

"Is that so?" Jason's father raised his eyebrows. "Jun?"

"Did you meet someone, Jun?" His mother was now staring at Jason point-blank, with the unblinking stare of a detective on the trail of a criminal she'd been hunting down for years.

"No, well, this was just a friend." Jason averted his eyes.

"A female friend?" His mother pursed her lips. "I see."

His parents exchanged glances.

"Now, Jun," Jason's mother continued, "tomorrow morning, I made you an appointment. Before we do the visits to family and friends, you'll need to take care of yourself."

"But I got a haircut before I came home," Jason protested.

"Jun, I'm not talking about a haircut. You need to take care of your skin." His mother reached across the table and pulled down on Jason's cheek. "See, all these wrinkles you're getting. You look much older than your age."

"I disagree with this," Jason's father grumbled. "But she makes me do it, too."

"Yes, exactly, your father gets fillers every six months," Jason's mother announced proudly. "I'm not talking about plastic surgery. But just the basics. I made an appointment for you at a local clinic, right down the street. This neighborhood is great, I have to say."

"Eomma, is this really necessary?" Jason asked.

"Absolutely! You want to look your best. You'll be meeting your future bride." A knowing smile appeared on his mother's face. "So, we can't take any chances."

———

The next morning, struggling not to yawn and to keep still, jet lagged and out of sorts, Jason found himself seated in the clinic chair as the aesthetician pulled at his skin, took photos, then discussed the procedures with Jason's mother, completely ignoring him.

Two hours later, after Jason, despite trying to push back and agreeing, reluctantly, to a bare minimum, had received fillers and injections, he was swiftly transitioned to a hair salon next door for an emergency intervention to correct his haircut. According to the salon owner, who came to greet her favorite client and to honor her son, the way 'they cut hair in America was atrocious.'

"They just don't know what to do with Asian hair over in the US," the salon owner ruminated, shaking her head. "You'd think with all the different nationalities living there, that wouldn't be the case. But I can always tell if someone got a haircut over in the U.S."

"Thank you for this." Jason's mother smiled proudly at the salon owner, then turned back to look at Jason in the mirror. "This is an important visit for us."

Jason also examined his reflection in the mirror. His face

looked somehow cleaner and fresher, the lines on his forehead smoothed out and the hair neatly brushed to the side.

Catching his mother's careful stare in the mirror, Jason flinched. It was as if he was seeing himself through his mother's eyes, and it unsettled him. He felt the weight of her expectations, the importance of his mission. His trip was a make-or-break one for the whole Lee family.

———

The rest of the day was a blur of visits. Jason was paraded to the aunties, cousins, friends of the family. The distribution of gifts from America, inquiries about Jason's podiatry practice, his plans to come back to Korea and whether he would ever join his parents in Seoul. Each time, he dispelled the questions, described his profession and told the curious family members he had no plans to return to Korea.

"Is that because you haven't done military service? I suppose it is too late now, right?" Someone would note, and Jason would nod.

He'd decided this was as good an excuse as any. Indeed, not having done military service in Korea meant he would have almost no future in the country. As a man, he was expected to have completed it, to have paid his dues to the Korean society. Each Korean man, with some rare exceptions, did military service and in return received promotions, acknowledgement, and more important, social capital to last a lifetime. Without it, even if Jason wanted to, he could not thrive in his home country.

After graduating from college, Jason had considered going back to Korea for his military service. But by then he had started preparing for podiatry school and did not want to lose the momentum. The stories he'd heard from Hyun-woo about military service in Korea made Jason wonder if he'd made the right choice. Sure, it was tough, painful, long, but it was a rite of passage. It bonded and united people. Jason wondered if he'd somehow escaped a fate that would have made him more of a man.

Checking himself in the bathroom mirror before bed that day, Jason wondered what version of himself he preferred. This one, with fillers and injections, about to go on several first dates or the one he'd seemingly left behind in America.

He thought back to the changes in his life since the arrival of Percy and Kiana. Images of the three of them sitting on his sofa filled his mind.

CHAPTER
Seventeen

HIS MOTHER'S eyes ran over his outfit, as Jason stood stock still. She brushed the invisible lint from his shirt, then made him readjust his collar.

"Good luck, Jun," she said, as Jason headed out the door to his first date.

It was with So-young, a lawyer. So-young spoke great English and was ready to move to the United States, despite having passed the rigorous bar exam to practice law in Korea and never having lived anywhere outside of Seoul.

Jason was meeting her for dinner at a restaurant in Itaewon, where So-young could get easily after work. The restaurant was on a side street, away from the thoroughfare, and Jason wandered through the crowd of tourists who were moving up and down the narrow street, some shouting drunken songs, though it was still early in the evening. It took him a few minutes to find the place.

The restaurant was completely empty. A sleepy waitress stood at the counter, flipping through a magazine. She waved at Jason and he took a seat in a booth in the corner. There was an electronic menu stuck to the wall, and he browsed through it. The impersonal setting struck him. Clicking through the flashing screen, which was written in English and Korean, accompanied by photos of the dishes, targeting, no doubt, the tourist crowd, Jason frowned. *Am I about to meet my future wife here? Is this where I'll stumble upon my great love? The woman of my dreams?*

It seemed unlikely.

He was just unfolding the napkin when he saw her.

So-young walked in wearing a gray skirt suit and a crisp white long-sleeve shirt, despite it being hot out. She had on sensible black flats and a matching purse. Small pearl earrings and a pearl necklace completed the outfit. White, gray and black, as if no other colors existed in the world. Jason rose to greet her. He shook her hand and smiled. So-young nodded in acknowledgement, then took out her mobile, which was in a black case, pressed several keys, and explained:

"I just put it on silent, so the office doesn't bother me. They sometimes call around this time." she sighed. "Clients."

"Oh yes, clients can be quite challenging," Jason said.

They sat across from each other.

"Do you also have demanding clients in America? You're a doctor, right? A foot doctor?" She furrowed her brow.

"Well, the clients are all different," Jason explained. "Some of them aren't demanding at all, but their problems are demanding, and then they don't follow through with the right treatment. So, it becomes an issue." As he was speaking, Jason noticed So-young took out a notepad and jotted something down.

"I'm just noting key points," she said. "It'll help me remember our conversation."

"Okay, sure." Jason immediately stopped speaking. The scribbling had thrown him off, and he lost his train of thought.

"Please continue. You were saying something about your clients." So-young held her pen up.

"I was just saying, they are different, that's all," Jason said. "Would you like to order something?"

"Yes, I always get the same thing. I would like the Naengmyeon." So-young pointed at the screen, expecting Jason to place the order. "It's very good here. I'd recommend it."

He obliged and decided to also order the cold buckwheat noodles for himself. As he was punching the selection in, he heard So-young's voice:

"So, have you found you've fit into American society?"

"How do you mean?" Jason looked up at his date, who was tugging on her pearls.

"I mean, the American mentality, the lifestyle, it's so different from how we live in Korea. Isn't it? Do you think you've made a full adjustment?"

"I don't know," Jason responded. "I haven't really thought about it."

"How can you not have thought about it? Do you see yourself as more Korean or more American?" So-young drummed her fingers on the table.

"I suppose, both at this point."

"Both?" So-young insisted. "And what if you had to choose? What if you had to pick one country? Where do your loyalties lie?"

"I think I would say I'm Korean-American." Jason shrugged. "I've now spent most of my life in America, but I still speak Korean, and I'm proud of my heritage. It's a part of me. So, I would say, both."

"You're a people pleaser, aren't you?" She twisted her mouth into a smile.

"What makes you say that?" Jason's face flushed red.

"You don't like offending people. I can tell. I forget, what's your Myers-Briggs?"

When setting up his dating profile, Jason had been briefed by his mother about the importance of the MBTI, or the Myers-Briggs Type Indicator, which broke down all people into 16 personalities based on degrees of introversion, types of thinking, their relationship with intuition and logic, thinking and feeling. Jason had taken a free version of the test and had added his MBTI to his dating profile but hadn't given it much thought since.

"I think it's INTJ," Jason noted. Then, immediately corrected himself. "No, INFJ."

"That's so weird for a guy. It's a very rare type, isn't it?"

"I guess so. Listen, I'm not really that into the whole Myers-Briggs thing," Jason started to say. "And besides…"

"Why not? Are you afraid someone might crack the code?" So-young interrupted.

"What code?"

"You? Do you think yourself so unique no one can understand you?"

Jason opened his mouth to respond, but a waitress appeared with the tray of food, and Jason stopped himself, grateful for the interruption. The server expertly set two large bowls on the table and left, without saying a word. So-young pulled one of the bowls towards herself, as she started speaking again.

"But tell me, are you afraid of being understood? I think most men are emotionally stunted. They really are. You know, working in courts, I see all kinds of criminals."

So-young cut her noodles in precise, quick movements with the scissors she took out of a drawer on her side of the table. "Most of them are, you guessed it, men. No one talks about it, really, but most violent crime is committed by men. I don't understand why no one tries to address it. Men are the reason for the way of the world today. And now in Korea, we have a strong feminist movement, but guess what? The men, they can't take it. They're all weeping and complaining now, because the Korean women are tired of being pushed down."

So-young cut the remaining noodles, set down the scissors and picked up her pen.

While she was scribbling in her notepad, Jason had cut his own noodles. He took the chopsticks and was about to grab a mouthful when So-young opened her mouth to speak again. Jason immediately put down his chopsticks, so as not to offend his date by eating while she was speaking.

"It's social justice, that's the reason I became a lawyer. And it wasn't easy. But I believe in making the world a better place. And it starts with you." She pointed her finger at Jason, and he noticed her nails had been trimmed very short.

"With me? But I'm just here for ten days," Jason said, pushing the bowl of food closer.

"I'm not talking about only Korea. I mean the whole world," So-young said with satisfaction and took a bite of her food. It was a dainty bite, clean, deliberate. As if every movement of the chopsticks cost So-young a fortune and she had to ration it carefully and purposefully. So-young was now focused on inserting bites of food into her mouth. Jason, grateful for a break in the conversation, which was more of an interrogation, also started eating. They both finished their noodles in silence.

After So-young asked him a few more questions, noted his answers in her notebook, and Jason paid their bill, So-young rose from her seat, indicating the date was over.

"It was great meeting you," So-young said. "I hope I didn't come on too strong. But I'm passionate about changing the world." She shrugged in mock self-deprecation.

"Nice meeting you, too," Jason said, following So-young out of the restaurant.

As soon as she disappeared into the Itaewon crowd, he pulled out his mobile and called Hyun-woo.

"Hey, buddy." Hyun-woo picked up the phone immediately. "It's Jun," Jason heard Hyun-woo say and guessed his friend was talking to his wife, "I'm just gonna step to the other room, so we can talk. How did it go?"

"Disaster!" Jason exhaled.

"That good? Come on!"

"It was a complete and total disaster. That algorithm sucks, man," Jason announced so loudly, a passerby turned to look at him.

"What happened?"

"I thought I was focused on my career but that was a whole other level. I almost choked on the food."

"She was one of those?"

"One of what?"

"Those weird feminists. They're crazy," Hyun-woo said. "You should have screened for that."

"How do you screen for that?"

"Just ask her the questions on the app ahead of time."

"But I'm not against the feminist movement. I think women have a right to be upset," Jason countered. "It wasn't what she was saying, it was just *how* she was saying it. I just felt like she was interrogating me as if I was testifying in court."

"For real?" Hyun-woo chuckled. "But be careful with those feminists. They're all crazy, I'm telling you, man. The way they keep going, they'll get rid of all the men out there. Turn us into lapdogs."

"Come on. That's not going to happen."

"I'm telling you, man." Jason could hear the crackle of the lighter going off. "You should have had sex with her, buddy, that's what you should have done. That would have gotten those crazy ideas right out of her mind."

"You're still smoking?"

"Can't kick the habit, man. It's the damned military. Got hooked and here I am almost twenty years later."

"You need to quit."

He and Hyun-woo had been having the same conversation for over a decade, ever since Jason had realized how serious his friend's smoking habit had gotten. Hyun-woo would agree to quit, but then move the target date further and further out. First, it was because he was courting his now-wife. Then, he was too stressed out because of the wedding. Then, it was a situation at work. But Jason never gave up. He had long ago decided that, regardless of Hyun-woo's reaction, he would give his friend a hard time about smoking. As a doctor, Jason thought he had the moral leverage to do so and owed it to Hyun-woo.

"I know, I know." Hyun-woo chuckled. "So, you got a few other dates lined up, right? Just avoid the crazies, man. See you on Friday. Listen, I gotta go, it's bedtime, I gotta go give the kid her bath." And Hyun-woo hung up the phone.

Eighteen

"IT'S NOT A BIG DEAL. Don't worry, Jun," his mother consoled him after he'd shared the disappointing outcome of his first date. "You have two more. That's why you don't put all your eggs in one basket. I am certain with these two other ladies things are bound to go well."

"Yes, I hope so," Jason said, changing into slippers. Sure it would upset his mother, Jason was careful not to mention So-young's stance on feminism and her criticism of men in Korea. Jason's mother still believed in traditional patriarchal values and disapproved of the feminist movement. If a woman didn't make as much money as a man, it was because she had to stay at home and take care of the children. She believed a man needed to earn more so that he could provide for his family. And if you introduced equal pay, women would not stay at home and raise their children, and society would fall apart.

But Jason disagreed. He wanted women to earn an equal wage because it was a question of fairness. If you did the same amount of work, you should be paid the same, regardless of gender.

"So, who is your next date?" His mother followed him down the corridor into the kitchen.

"It's that kindergarten teacher, Min-jung." Jason smiled.

From the start, Min-jung had been his favorite. They had been exchanging messages through the app for over a month now, with Min-jung asking him how his day was, sending him cute messages and lots of emojis that Jason appreciated, despite finding them a bit silly.

"How nice, and what a lovely profession she's got." Jason's mother nodded in approval. "Now, did you eat? You must be hungry, Jun. Come, sit, have something to eat." She pointed to table. "I've got some manduguk ready for you. Your favorite."

Though he wasn't hungry, Jason could not resist his mother's cooking. He moved to help her, but his mother stopped him.

"Just sit, Jun, it's not often that you come to visit." She gave him a careful stare.

Sliding into the chair, he watched as his mother served his meal, freshly made dumpling soup with kimchi. Jason was transported to when he was little and they had dinner together, just him and his mom, night after night, when his father worked late. It was the same in Korea and then in America. It was in the kitchen they had the best chats, just the two of them.

Mostly, though, his mother spoke and Jason listened. She loved telling him about her family. His mother had so many stories. They were always stories of survival, of overcoming loss and suffering, of persevering. Now, sitting across from his mother, Jason remembered what Kiana had shared with him, how she, too, had a similar upbringing and had heard stories of suffering from her own mother. Jason smiled at the thought of how similar the two of them were.

"Now, Jun, tell me, who's this friend who helped you pick

out perfume?" his mother asked, and Jason's heartbeat accelerated. *I swear she can read my mind.*

"Just someone I met in the building," Jason said, staring at his food so as to avoid eye contact. "She's taking care of my neighbor's cat."

"A cat? I never liked cats. Those animals can't be trusted."

"I was thinking of getting a cat," Jason looked up only to see his mother shaking her head. He hadn't yet told his mother about Percy.

"Jun, please get married and have some children. And forget these silly ideas."

"Alright, Eomma," Jason agreed. There was no sense in antagonizing his mother now by mentioning that he had been keeping a cat in his apartment.

———

Wiping the mirror after a shower to see his reflection, Jason examined his face. He had to admit, the fillers and injections, coupled with the new haircut, had made him look several years younger.

As he made his way to a casual coffee shop, where his next date, Min-jung, had agreed to meet, Jason wondered whether most of the men on the street had also had fillers.

He recalled how the aesthetician had told him half of her clients were male, and it was perfectly normal for men to take care of themselves. That was what had convinced him to go along with the treatment in the first place and not to question his mother's wisdom.

"The expectations are very high. Korean women are very demanding," the woman told him as she injected his face with chemicals.

Jason and Min-jung were to meet during her lunch break, near the exclusive school where she worked, which was not far from Lotte Young Plaza. Min-jung told Jason she preferred to meet at a coffee shop rather than a restaurant, because she loved to have a latte for lunch and it was 'like a meal.'

Jason walked into the café, which was all light. Large floor-to-ceiling windows, light beige panels, white tables and chairs. The white, gleaming counter stood in the center, with two baristas, frozen in expectation.

As soon as Jason took a seat by the door, a message from Min-jung arrived:

On my way

She accompanied her text with an emoji of a cat drinking out of a cup, and Jason's heart melted, as he immediately thought of Percy.

He opened WhatsApp and texted Kiana, realizing he had sent the text at midnight in DC only after hitting 'send'.

Hey, how are you? How's Percy doing? Send pics.

The second he placed his phone down, he looked up to see his date.

"Hi, you must be Jason." She was standing next to him, and Jason rose from his seat. Dressed in a beige dress, tied with a belt that made her waist look tiny, Min-jung was short and had a very small frame. Her hair, jet black, lay thick on her shoulders in a perfectly straight line, expertly cut. Huge sunglasses perched on her nose.

"Hi, Min-jung," Jason said, and his heart leaped. *She could be the one,* he thought with excitement. He'd been trying to contain it, thinking something could go wrong during their first date, but now, with Min-jung standing right next to him, Jason thought his luck was finally about to turn.

"It's so nice to finally meet you," Min-jung said, her voice melodious.

"Same here. What would you like to drink?"

"A latte, please," Min-jung said and took a seat. Jason walked over to the bar and placed their order. He decided he'd have another espresso. His third day in Korea, and he was still jet lagged. With his dependence on caffeine, Jason was grateful Seoul had plenty of excellent coffee places.

When Jason walked back to their table, he saw Min-jung scrolling through her phone. Only then did he notice a Louis Vuitton bag casually sitting on the table in front of her. At the sight of the bag, Jason clenched his jaw. He didn't know all the expensive brands, but he knew this one, and had been told by his cousin Dave that those bags cost an absurd amount of money. A Louis bag had been part of the gift exchange for Dave's wedding.

His date pulled her sunglasses off. Jason noticed the Gentle Monster brand, but that didn't ring a bell.

Now Jason wondered whether everything else Min-jung owned cost a fortune. If that were the case, and the two of them were to get married, the expectation would be to get her and her family very expensive gifts. Korea still functioned as a traditional society, with an elaborate set of rules followed for weddings. The groom provided a house for the couple. The price of the house was assessed, and the bride's dowry had to be ten percent of the price of the home. Additionally, there was the gift exchange between the two families.

"So, I love this place. They have the best quality espresso. The company actually grows its own coffee beans. It's so impressive," Min-jung noted. "I'm so glad we finally met. I have a really good feeling about you."

Pausing for just a moment, Jason, eager for this match to work out, said: "Same here."

The barista called the order, and he walked to the bar to pick up the two cups.

"I work just down the street," Min-jung said, when he returned. "It's the most exclusive daycare in Seoul." There was pride in her voice. "They hired me because of my English. I lived with my parents in the US for ten years."

"Really? Where?"

"Manhattan." Min-jung smiled casually. "Upper West Side."

"I also lived in New York City. In Queens," Jason said. "Did my fellowship there during Covid."

"I've never been to Queens." Min-jung stretched. "But you live in DC now?"

"In Arlington," Jason clarified.

"Is that a suburb?" Her noise twitched.

"Well, it's right across the river from DC. But it's a different state. Virginia."

"Sounds like New Jersey," she said. "But anyway, you're a doctor? That's so cool," Min-jung gushed. "Such a noble profession."

"Thank you." Not expecting a compliment, Jason blushed.

"I mean," Min-jung yawned and put her hand to her mouth to cover it up, "that's so impressive. I could never be a doctor." She rubbed her eyes. "I can't stand the sight of blood. So, what kind of doctor are you?"

"I'm a podiatrist," Jason said.

"What's that? Never heard of that."

"It's a doctor who treats feet."

"For real? That's crazy. Actually? A doctor for feet alone? How did you choose to do that?" Min-jung curled her lips in what was almost a smile.

"I decided to become a podiatrist so I could help people. It's hands on. And I love my job." Jason straightened up in his seat.

"You should have become a plastic surgeon. They make the big bucks." Min-jung sniggered. "From what I hear."

Something in the way Min-jung was speaking was off, but he couldn't tell what it was. She took another sip of her latte and then moved her eyes, blinking fast. And then Jason noticed the dark circles under her eyes, covered by a thick layer of makeup.

"So, what do you like to do outside of work?" Jason asked. He vaguely remembered Min-jung's questionnaire mentioned reading and 'watching Korean dramas' as hobbies, but now wondered if he hadn't confused her with So-young. Min-jung did not seem like a reader.

"I love clubbing," Min-jung said casually and yawned again. "I go out dancing four nights a week with the girls."

"Really?"

"Yes, it's my passion. And the great thing about my job is that I don't have to be awake for it." Min-jung giggled. "Not really, at least. I mean, the kids won't know the difference; they just play." She shrugged. "All I've gotta do is make sure I speak English to them, and that's enough. That's all their parents want."

"So, did you go out last night?" Jason asked, but he already knew the answer. The dark circles under her eyes, the yawning, her drooping eyelids.

"Yeah." Min-jung giggled. "That's why I can't eat right now. We usually have a huge breakfast at six in the morning, after the clubs close. And then I go home and shower, and I go straight to work. It's the craziest thing, being at work all day after clubbing. So trippy." Min-jung moved her hands in the air.

He stared at the latte in front of her which suddenly seemed completely full, like she'd barely taken a sip.

———

Just as Jason was leaving the coffee shop, he opened the dating app and, without a moment's hesitation, clicked 'no' when the app asked him whether he would like to see Min-jung again. This was the one thing he appreciated about the way the app had been set up: no awkwardness in agreeing on a second date during the first one.

On the way to his parents' apartment, his phone buzzed. He saw a WhatsApp message pop up. No text, just a photo of Percy on the screen. The kitten was curled into a ball on Jason's couch. One of Percy's ears stuck out, like she was listening, undoubtedly paying attention to the photo being taken, while maintaining the appearance of slumbering. Percy looked so cuddly and adorable that Jason immediately got homesick.

What am I doing here, on the other side of the world? This was the dumbest idea ever. Just one left, he thought with a bit of relief, *and then I'll be done with this whole stupid thing.*

CHAPTER
Nineteen

"JUN, PLEASE LOOK FOR MORE MATCHES," his mother urged, turning the TV down, after Jason had told her about the disastrous date with the kindergarten teacher. He spared his mother the clubbing details but told her the woman was vapid and had encouraged him to become a plastic surgeon.

"I don't think that's a good idea. There isn't enough time," Jason countered.

"Of course, there is time. You have one full week left. You can meet three more matches."

"But it's been a waste of time. If this is what the algorithm produces, what's the point?"

Jason went to bed, thinking he had one last chance. On Thursday night, he would meet his third and final match, Yuna. He'd already decided he would not look for any more matches, were this one not to work out.

Jason would have scheduled the date sooner, but Yuna worked at the largest Korean bank and could not go to dinner earlier in the week. They were meeting in the Yeongdeungpo District at a Chinese restaurant, not far from Yuna's office building.

Jason walked in and tried to get a table, but the hostess refused to seat him alone, and so he stood by the door, waiting. Everybody was always early in Korea, at least by five minutes, but not when it came to dating.

Yuna came in ten minutes late, when Jason had nearly decided to leave. She was out of breath, and the second she saw him, she ran up to him and apologized profusely.

"I'm so sorry! I was almost out of the door, but my boss caught me in the elevator and gave me another assignment." She pointed at her briefcase that was bursting with papers. It was a navy-blue case, which exactly matched the navy-blue suit she was wearing. To Jason's relief, the brand of the case wasn't Louis Vuitton.

"Is this not a good time? We can reschedule," Jason suggested, but Yuna shook her head.

"No, no, I was really looking forward to meeting you." She stared directly at him. Jason thought her eyes looked kind.

"Same here. They should still be holding our table." Jason held the door open for Yuna, and, following her inside, noticed she was very tall. Her hair had been pulled back in a ponytail, revealing her slender neck.

"So, how's the jet lag?" Yuna asked, after they took their seats. She was the first of his dates to ask him this question, and he took it as a good sign.

"I guess I'll be fully adjusted to Seoul time by the time I go back to DC." Jason opened up his menu. It was his fifth day, but he was still waking up in the middle of the night ravenously hungry.

"I travel a lot for work, so I feel your pain," Yuna said.

"Where do you travel?"

"Normally, London or New York," she said. "Probably two or three times a year. My bosses love taking me along, because of my English, in part. I'm the only one of the analysts who is fluent."

"Oh, that's impressive. How did you learn to speak English so well?"

"I lived in the US when I was in elementary school. My parents almost immigrated to the United States. After the Asian Financial Crisis, our family really struggled. My dad lost his job at Daewoo then."

"No way, that's where my dad worked, too. And he was also laid off."

"For real? Maybe they know each other." Yuna added eagerly.

"I'm sure they do. Though it was a large company, but my dad was there for fifteen years."

"Mine also. Something like that. So that's why we went to the US. But my parents couldn't take it, and then my dad got a big break, so we came back to Korea four years later."

"My parents also came back after retirement, but I stayed," Jason noted, pushing the menu to Yuna. "Do you know what you want?"

"I think so." A sly smile crossed her face, and Jason reddened at the double-entendre. But before he could feel any embarrassment, Yuna added, "I love the dumplings. They are so juicy."

"Thank you, I'll try those too."

"So, you stayed in the US after your parents left? How come?" Yuna asked, once their order was placed and the waiter brought over their drinks. She'd let her hair down, and was playing with its strand, flipping it with her fingers.

"Well, it was mostly because of what I decided to do. Because of my degree. I decided to practice medicine in America."

"Why not here? Why not in Korea?"

"That's interesting. No one ever asks me that." Jason gave Yuna a careful look. She wasn't just pretty, she was insightful and showed genuine interest in him. "I like how podiatry is practiced in the US. And I really found my calling with podiatry."

"Really? So, why feet?"

"Because without feet, we can't move. And without movement, we can't live. That's why."

"Wow. That's deep. I'd never expected that." Yuna looked directly at him.

"Thank you. And why did you want to work at a bank?"

"I got into finance because I'm not good at anything else," Yuna shrugged. "I can't stand the sight of blood, so medicine was out, and then I hate arguing. So, I could never be a lawyer."

"I hate arguing too."

"Really? That's funny. Did your parents argue a lot when you were young?"

"My parents? Is that related?" Jason swallowed hard.

"Yeah. Usually, if your parents argued a lot, or if you faced adversity as a child, you hate arguing. And also, you are drawn to trauma. Like, do you like watching crime thrillers, for example? Or things like true crime?"

"For real? Is that what it is?"

"Yep. People who grow up around arguments usually end up having those two characteristics." Yuna's lips curled in a sad smile.

"That's wild. I had no idea. I love watching *Law & Order*."

"Well, then, probably borderline. If you were obsessed with true crime, then it would be serious." She sighed.

"That's pretty intense for a first date." Jason pulled apart his chopsticks, watching as the waiter had brought their food, and two steaming bowls of dumplings were sitting in the middle of the table. He felt grateful for the diversion.

"I know, right? I usually wait until the third to share my insights, but you're going back to America soon." Yuna bit her lower lip. "So, I figured, why hold back?"

"Very good point," Jason said. And then, completely

forgetting about the app and how he should have left the delicate task of letting the date know whether he wanted to see her again, he said, "I hope this isn't the only time we see each other."

"Same here." Yuna straightened up. "I have a good feeling about this."

———

Dinner turned into a long walk along the river at the Yeouido Hangang Park. Their conversation flowed back and forth naturally. Covering everything, from their likes and dislikes to the pros and cons of living in America. The more they spoke, the more Jason liked Yuna.

After their walk, he saw Yuna home, taking the train with her and walking his date to her apartment building. By the time Jason got back, it was after midnight. He completely forgot all about jet lag and walked into his parents' apartment whistling a tune. *Dynamite* by BTS. The song was everywhere in Seoul, playing in every mall, coffee shop, and Jason's mood aligned with its upbeat tune. He snapped his fingers just as he heard his mother's voice:

"I guess the third time's the charm?" His mother's hair was in curlers and Jason was transported to their first few months in America. He could picture his mother, her hair also in curlers, late at night, trying to stay fashionable, while working non-stop at a tiny, hole-in-the-wall restaurant and being paid cash under the table, just so that their family could survive.

"Eomma, I love you." Jason gave his mother a hug, and she hugged him back. The hugging, the expression of affection between the two of them, was relatively new. When Jason was little, his mother never told him she loved him. She never hugged him, either. But after several years in America, Jason said it first to his mom. He'd seen it on TV and decided to try it. She was shocked to hear it at first, and then she cried. Now, even Jason's father said it from time to time, though not as often as his mother.

"I love you, too," Jason's mother responded. "Come on, let's have some tea. Your father is already asleep," she pressed her finger to her lips. She puttered to the kitchen and Jason followed.

"So, when will you see her again?" His mother put the teakettle on.

"We're going to the BTS museum on Saturday," Jason said, sitting down at the kitchen table. "Yuna will be getting us tickets. It's a convoluted process, but she told me I must check it out, since I'm in Seoul."

"So, a second date!" His mother clapped excitedly, forgetting all about being quiet. "Are you going to meet other dates?"

"I don't think so, Eomma." Jason said, reaching for a teacup. "I'd like to focus on Yuna."

"Very good, very good. I have a good feeling about this," Jason's mother said, and he paused at the realization it was the second time he had heard this expression that night.

CHAPTER

Twenty

TO MEET HYUN-WOO, Jason traveled to their old neighborhood, Myeonmok, where his childhood friend still lived. The short walk from the subway to the bar, where the two of them agreed to meet, filled Jason with unease. This was a completely different Seoul, the part of the city no one saw in K-drama or K-pop music clips.

Jason remembered it well.

He'd grown up walking up and down these streets, had missed them when he first came to America. Had romanticized his childhood neighborhood. When he thought of Seoul, this was the first image that popped up in his memory.

Now, all he saw were the gray high-rises entirely devoid of charm, the storefronts catering to the tired commuters. There were no gawking tourists, just the worn-out residents of this drab neighborhood, rushing to get home to the safety of their apartments. Jason could have been one of them: a fate he'd narrowly escaped by chance, by a sequence of events that had propelled him out of Korea and to America, and he felt relief mixed with guilt.

He didn't want to be there.

With some trepidation, Jason opened the door of the bar

and walked in. It was loud and very busy. Right away, he noticed Hyun-woo sprawled out at a table in the back, and Jason carefully maneuvered to join his friend.

"Hey there, buddy, ready for some fun?" Hyun-woo winked and pointed at a bottle of what Jason guessed was soju that stood in the middle of the table. Without waiting for an answer, his oldest friend poured them drinks. "Let's toast to our friendship. Proud to still be your friend, after all these years, buddy." Hyun-woo lifted up his glass, exclaiming: "Now, let's toast!"

Jason lifted his to clink, but then immediately set it down. "Remember, I don't really drink. So, I'll just get a tonic water."

"Oh, yeah, I keep hoping you'll start drinking anyway." Hyun-woo shrugged.

Each time he saw Hyun-woo, Jason had to remind his friend of his predicament. It was as if Hyun-woo thought Jason's body would somehow go through a transformation and allow him to consume copious amounts of alcohol, just as his father and grandfather, and most Korean men, could do.

But something had gone wrong with Jason's genetic code, and, whenever he drank, he turned red very quickly, his cheeks flushing a deep shade of crimson. A pounding headache was not too far off. It didn't take much alcohol for him to reach that stage. And if he had strong liquor, the effect was immediate.

"Brought you these, for you and the family." Jason smiled at his friend, handing Hyun-woo a bag filled with gifts.

"Thanks, buddy!" Hyun-woo nodded at him and stuffed the bag under the table without looking at its contents. "The little lady will be happy. This was the only reason she'd let me out of the house tonight." His friend wiped an invisible drop of sweat off his forehead and added, "Married life is rough. You'll see."

"I can't wait," Jason said, only half-joking.

"So, how is the dating going?" Hyun-woo asked. "I gotta warn you, buddy, once you find a decent chick, and the standards are low these days, trust me, you just hold on to her. She doesn't have to be perfect, you hear me?"

"Alright, man." Jason chortled. "I love your optimism."

"Well, I'm just sharing my experience. Trying to help. That's how I met the wife. You can't aim for the moon. You and I, buddy, we aren't the K-pop stars. Gotta be realistic about our looks."

"But what about our amazing personalities?" Jason shook his head in mock astonishment.

"Women are shallow, buddy. All they care about is your wallet. Well, and you know what. They like jerks. It's been proven long ago. You gotta treat'em bad, real bad. That's when they start realizing they are in love. And once that happens, then you know you've got them. No woman wants a nice guy. Nope." Hyun-woo shook his head. "If you're nice to them, they think something's wrong."

"I can't be a jerk. And you already know I disagree with your stance on women." Jason sighed.

"See, that's your problem. That's why you're still single. At thirty-seven!" Hyun-woo leaned back and opened his arms. "You need to become tougher. At least in the beginning. Don't call. Don't show interest. Be mysterious. And then the girls will be all over you. Trust me. I used to be all nice. After the military, I was desperate."

"Really?"

"I swear, the military, it's like they starve us in there on purpose so we settle for any stupid woman once we get out. Did you know that?"

"You think?" Now that the conversation turned to the military, Jason hung on to his friend's every word, but was immediately disappointed.

"Yeah, that's my theory. But anyway, so when I got out, I got with this one chick, the one from our building, remember?

Lived on the third floor. And she cheated on me right away. Like, within a month. So, then I got smarter. I realized what I had to do was to be the top dog. So, I was the one calling the shots. That's what you gotta be doing, buddy."

"Well anyway, I think I met someone," Jason said carefully.

"You did? Great! So now, follow my advice, and you'll marry her. Treat her like dirt, remember, buddy."

"She's a good girl, Hyun-woo. I think I like her."

"Good girl? Please!" Hyun-woo scoffed. "They're no good girls out there. They're all bad, but some hide it better than the others."

"Hyun-woo, I'll prove you wrong. You'll see. Nice guys can win." Jason pushed back.

————

After seeing Hyon-woo, Jason could barely sleep. Jason kept waking up, picturing Hyon-woo's eager face, and his friend's words, 'they're all bad, but some hide it better than the others,' swirled over and over in his mind. Jason kept coming up with counterarguments and regretted not standing up to Hyun-woo more.

I should have told him off, I should have said something. He didn't want to fight with his oldest friend and the only connection he had to his childhood. *But does a last bit of nostalgia matter more than my principles?*

After tossing and turning, Jason finally gave up trying to go to sleep. He flicked on his phone. The first thing to arrive was a message from Kiana.

So? How's Seoul?

Jason, to his shock, realized he hadn't responded to the photo of Percy Kiana had sent three days prior.

> Hi! I can't believe I didn't respond. Totally forgot. My bad.

> No worries. You alright?

> Yes, doing really well. Met someone.

He hit 'send' too fast, then paused in hesitation, staring at the screen and wondering at Kiana's reaction. She responded in mere seconds.

> Nice. Congratulations. Can't wait to hear all about it.

> Thanks.

Jason felt compelled to add an emoji of fingers crossed.

Three dots appeared, then were deleted, as Jason stared at the screen in anticipation. Her response didn't arrive until a few minutes later.

> Btw, I got an idea about Anton Konovalov. My mom and I watched the documentary together, and she pointed out a few things to me.

> Like what?

> Can you talk?

Jason checked the time. It was almost two in the morning, but he couldn't sleep. He dialed Kiana's number.

"Hey, that was fast!" She chuckled. "How's Seoul?"

Hearing her voice made him smile. Jason sat up in bed and propped himself up with the pillows.

"It's been great so far, for the most part. I went on two

dates, crazy ones, a woman who was grilling me about my stance on global feminism and then another one with a party girl."

"So, the Korean AI dating algorithm isn't all that?" Kiana's laugh was throaty.

"I'm about to find out. I met my third date, Yuna," Jason breathed into the phone. "I think she's the one."

"Wow, really?"

"Yep, we're gonna see each other again tomorrow. Well, today, actually."

"What time is it?"

"Like, two am," Jason cleared his throat.

"OMG, go to bed! What are you doing up?"

"I can't sleep. Percy's okay, right?"

"Yes, don't worry, Percy and I hang out at your place all the time. I've been coming every day. I go to the pool, and the woman with the ankle monitor is still there. Everything is still the same," Kiana said and Jason felt a strong yearning to be next to her. He closed his eyes to dispel the emotion.

"But tell me about Anton," he said, his voice cracking.

"So, my mom figured out something really important. You know how the documentary mentions all these claims Anton had made in his book, right? And then, most of these claims are preposterous, and the people interviewed in Russia are appalled. My mom pointed out that the book had been published posthumously. After Anton died!"

"Why is that important? Oh, wait... wow!"

"Exactly! Because how do we know who actually wrote this book? And the book made millions, apparently. At least back in the seventies, it sold like hotcakes. Just imagine a young, sexy Russian, a defector suddenly dead but with an amazing story of an escape and conversion to Christianity. But my mom says the book was likely redacted after his death, and maybe was even written by someone else. Not

Anton. And it may have been the reason he died. Well, was killed."

"He was killed?"

"That's what my mom said. She said there was no way a guy like that would have committed suicide. No way it could have been an accident. She said, the guy was a trained soldier, a naval officer. He would have *known* how to use a gun."

"So, is this what we should tell Audrey?" Jason fidgeted.

"I think we should meet with her and try to get more of the story. Because there's that weird other woman in California. It's not clear which one of them was the real fiancée. Or maybe he had two women, or maybe Audrey was making it all up. My mom thinks that's possible. I mean, some women do get obsessed and make up stories, you know?"

"Alright, sure. Though I doubt Audrey is lying. She's a serious person."

"Anyway, so let's try and see Audrey as soon as you're back, like we discussed."

"Deal," Jason responded. "I'll call her and we can have that meeting. I promise."

"Well, good night then. See you soon. I'm excited to figure out the story of Anton."

"Good night." He put the phone to the side and fell asleep immediately.

———

Jason jumped out of a cab and right into a puddle. He shook the water off and almost slipped on the sleek concrete that led to the entrance. A line of people had formed outside, cuddling together under umbrellas. Jason didn't heed his mother's warnings and had left an umbrella at home. Now, he cursed himself for his lack of foresight.

Purchasing tickets to the museum of the most popular K-pop group was an ordeal, and even with the tickets, they had to arrive at least thirty minutes before the designated time, but, Yuna assured him, it was worth it. The museum was a 'must see' in Seoul. It didn't matter whether you actually liked K-pop and BTS. It was a sign of the times, and he could share the experience in America and remember it for years to come.

"Hey," he heard and saw Yuna standing in the middle of the queue, in a dry spot.

"Hi!" Jason made his way to her. They hugged, and right away, Jason felt better. Gone were his doubts, his nerves, even his wet foot didn't feel so uncomfortable.

"This is so exciting," Yuna said. "This is basically the most unique thing Korea has done. Historical. You know, K-pop?"

"Yeah." Jason didn't quite understand the phenomenon of K-pop, or K-drama, for that matter, but if it gave Korea a good name globally, then that was enough for him.

Submerged in semi-darkness, the museum felt more like a nightclub. Music videos played on full blast in the rooms, with photos and costumes of the BTS stars, none of whom Jason knew by name, on display. Taking photos was strictly forbidden. Guards appeared out of nowhere and warned rule-breakers.

There were several stages, where eager fans could dance and practice K-pop dance moves. One room was larger and was nearly completely dark, except for strobe lights. Loud techno was pumping, and Jason thought of Min-jung and the dark circles under her eyes and felt sorry for the tiny kinder-gartners who had to put up with the party-girl teacher.

Most of the time, it was impossible to hear what Yuna was saying because of the music. In the last room, when they were about to exit, Yuna started moving gracefully to the music, twirling in the middle of the dance floor. She looked beautiful with her long, flowing hair, vulnerable, and sweet.

Jason remembered his museum visit with Kiana, the walk

through the National Gallery of Art, and shook his head. How wistful he was with Kiana, how insecure. Now, with Yuna, he felt in control.

This is it, Jason thought. He wanted to embrace Yuna right there and then, but then he remembered Hyun-woo's warning. Although he disagreed with Hyun-woo a lot, maybe it was worth trying something different. To be less eager, more confident. But before he could decide either way, Yuna walked up to him.

"Ready?"

She stood close to him, and he could feel her breath.

"Yes, this was a great idea," Jason said, leaning closely. He meant it.

They made their way through the exorbitantly priced gift shop, full of eager shoppers, ready to fork over hundreds of dollars for BTS merchandise and were now back outside. The rain had ended, so Jason and Yuna walked down the street together. He took her by the hand to make sure they weren't separated on the crowded sidewalk. His gesture felt so practiced, as if he'd done it all of his life. Her hand, so small, so narrow in his, felt fragile and Jason felt like a large and protective man next to her. He liked that feeling.

"Is there anywhere we can go and sit?"

"I know a great place where we can go." Yuna flashed him a smile. They were standing so close to each other. Jason wanted to kiss her. He was smitten.

"Do tell," he said, his eyes sparkling. The time with Yuna was precious. This date was likely his last chance to really get to know her before he left.

"The Grand Hyatt," she said. "It's not far. We can go there for brunch."

"Sure," Jason nodded, hiding his surprise. The Grand Hyatt was not far from his parents' apartment in Yongsan. It dominated the skyline and was a fixture of the neighborhood, but Jason was sure the establishment was long past its prime. When he was little, each time the family visited his now deceased uncle Kyung-ho, his mother gushed about how posh and beautiful the Grand Hyatt was and how she wished to spend just one night in the beautiful, luxurious property. Back then, his parents constantly argued about money, and the Grand Hyatt, with all its glory, represented the impossible: wealth.

But that was thirty years ago.

———

Jason and Yuna arrived at the hotel within minutes, thanks to a quick taxi ride that was almost entirely uphill. The hotel was like a fortress, overlooking the city from a hill, and as the two of them walked up to the dining room, Jason understood why Yuna had suggested the place. Even if outdated, the hotel boasted an incredible view of Seoul. With the dark storm clouds hanging low above the city, it felt incredibly romantic.

"This is amazing," Jason said, taking in the view. Inside of the dining room, almost every table was occupied. Children were running around, the clanking of dishes, hotel staff clearing the plates. Jason and Yuna had caught the tail end of brunch, and most of the crowd had finished their meals. There were a few couples, mostly middle-aged, sitting side by side, and Jason caught himself thinking he wanted to be part of such a couple, and to have Yuna by his side.

"This is post-Covid revenge spending," Yuna whispered into his ear, as they stood, waiting for the hostess to seat them. Her warm breath excited him. "We used to come here with my parents when I was little."

"Oh yeah? You know, we live nearby, but I've never been here till now," Jason noted casually, omitting the part of his childhood he'd spent in a completely different, less luxurious part of Seoul.

"Well, then, I guess it was meant to be." Yuna gave him a meaningful look.

CHAPTER
Twenty~One

Just made it to DC!

JASON TEXTED Yuna as soon as he landed at Dulles International Airport. He stuffed his phone into the pocket of his backpack, preparing to deplane, and noticed the envelope.

After their brunch at the Hyatt, they saw each other once more, the night before his departure. Yuna had to work late that evening, but she'd stepped out from the office to meet Jason outside of her building and handed him a thick envelope.

"Don't open it until you get back home," she said and kissed him on the cheek. Now, that envelope was sitting in his backpack, a promise of something wonderful to come.

As soon as Jason opened the door to his apartment, he heard a loud meow and Percy waddled over slowly to him, arching her back and stretching. The first thing that struck Jason was Percy's size. In the ten days he was away, Percy had gotten bigger, and now he couldn't exactly call her a kitten. She was a young cat.

"There you are!!" He picked her up. "I missed you." He nuzzled his face into her neck and kissed the cat on the nose. "How have you been, little girl? My little Persimmon."

Carrying the cat into the kitchen, Jason cradled her in his arms. Percy's bowl looked freshly emptied, while there was a large heap of dry food in her other bowl. "Was Kiana just here?" Jason guessed. "Did she come this morning, Percy?"

After refilling both bowls, so that the dry food was now almost spilling over, he turned the espresso machine on. While his drink was brewing, he poured himself a glass of water and sat on the couch. Percy climbed up next to him and started kneading, while Jason reached into his bag and got out the envelope.

His stomach flipped in anticipation of discovering what keepsake Yuna had prepared.

I'm about to open the envelope

He texted Yuna, and tore open the seal.

To his surprise, instead of pages of writing, the envelope contained a greeting card. It was printed on very thick, dark-blue card stock. Several pop-up orange koi fish appeared when he opened it, with three lotus flowers surrounding them. The fish were outlined in gold, and the lotus flowers done in various shades of pink. It was beautiful.

The card wasn't signed, but he noticed a small white insert that had slipped out. In neat handwriting, the note read:

I am incredibly glad we've met.
Hope to see you soon.
Yuna

Next to the name was a neatly drawn heart symbol.

"Look, Percy, isn't this pretty?"

At the sound of the machine, he got up to get his espresso.

Returning to the couch, Jason saw Percy pawing at the lotus flowers.

"Percy, no," Jason yelped, but it was too late. He rushed to pick up the card, but one of the lotus flowers was torn near the crease. "Come on, girl, why did you do that?" He sighed in quiet resignation and tried, in vain, to secure the flower back into its spot. Downing his espresso in one gulp, he went to take a shower. He'd have to go to work the following day, and there was no time to waste. Groceries, laundry, the list of tasks was daunting.

When Jason was planning his trip to Korea, it all made sense: in his mind, right upon landing, he would take care of all the errands and show up at seven in the morning at work the following day fresh and ready to go.

Now, faced with reality, Jason wanted one thing: to sleep. Having read his fair share of jet lag advice that warned a weary traveler against sleeping until it was dark out, advised to go outside to maximize exposure to the sun, to eat healthy foods and to avoid unnecessary caffeine consumption, Jason tried his best to resist the urge to crash. But Percy gently purred right next to him, so he picked up the cat, set her on the pillow in his bedroom and promptly fell asleep.

He woke up to Kiana's voice.

"Jason? Are you home?"

Jason swallowed hard. He checked the time. Six pm.

"Hey." He stretched, threw his sweatpants on and walked out of the bedroom.

Kiana was standing in the middle of the living room. Next to her was the cat, both of them bearing almost identical, expectant, expressions on their faces.

"Hi." She greeted him with a smile.

"I was just napping." Jason rubbed his eyes. "Thanks for waking me up. I forgot to set the alarm."

"When did you get back?" She threw a look at his suitcases, that stood abandoned by the door.

"Around noon, not sure." Jason shrugged. "I just got in and crashed. Didn't realize it was gonna hit me like that." He yawned and covered his mouth.

"Oh, that's crazy. How was it?" Kiana smiled and pointed to the card. "And I guess that's from her?" She bit her lip. Without waiting for an answer, Kiana continued. "Those cards are crazy expensive, by the way. I guess she really likes you, Jason." She made the heart symbol with her fingers.

"Oh, really? I had no idea."

"Yeah, they're like twenty dollars."

"For a card? That's wild." Jason darted his eyes to the cat. "Percy almost tore it up."

"Maybe Percy is jealous?" Kiana giggled. "So, guess what? Ross is coming this weekend! He advanced the dates of his move." Her eyes sparkled.

Jason's stomach flipped at the mention of Ross, and he wondered whether his dislike of Ross was due to a general distaste for what the man represented: a tough go-getter who was his complete opposite.

"Already? But that's great." Now that Jason had met a promising match, surely it didn't matter that Kiana was about to settle down, and he did his best to sound supportive.

"Yes, I'll go to the airport to meet him on Friday night. His flight will land at eight, so I can go there after work to pick him up."

"Nice," Jason mumbled.

"I know! I get to meet Ross in person. Can you imagine?"

Jason rubbed his eyes again.

"Wait a second." Kiana came up to Jason and stood right in front of him. Jason thought she was about to give him a hug, but she squinted and scanned his face.

"What's up with your face? It looks different."

"My face?" Jason went to the mirror. "Oh, that's the Korean me."

"What? You ARE Korean, man. What's going on? You look weird."

"Umm, I had a few things done when I was over there."

"What do you mean? What things?"

"Just had some fillers. I don't really know. But everyone does it in Korea."

"What do you mean? But don't you have to do it in, like, six months again? Isn't it dangerous?"

"Of course not. It's fine. Everyone does it in Korea."

"Even the men?"

"Yeah, absolutely. Even the men. It's almost expected these days." Jason shrugged. He wasn't sure, but that's what his mother had told him about the procedures. "Does it look okay?" Jason asked hesitantly, walking to examine himself in the bathroom mirror. Kiana followed and stood next to him, both of them staring at Jason's reflection.

"You know you look fine, Jason," Kiana said after a pause. "But kind of strange. Like a different person. That's all."

"It was just a few things. I'm still the same guy." Jason examined his face carefully, as if seeing himself for the first time.

"But that girl you met, when will you see her again, tell me all about it," Kiana said, heading out of the bathroom.

"Yes, she said she will be coming to New York City for work in September. I'll go up to see her there."

"That's really soon, September is next month!" Kiana furrowed her brow.

"Yes, it is."

"I'm really happy for you, Jason. By the way, let me know if you'd like to hear more about the whole Audrey thing. I mean, with Anton. My mom got really into it."

"Oh, yeah, maybe not tonight. I'm so beat, and I have to work tomorrow. I have to do the early shift and then another one the day after. I think they may have put me on the early schedule for the next two weeks straight, too."

He wasn't exaggerating. He hadn't paid much attention to what Betsy was telling him about scheduling after his vacation, so engrossed he had been in planning his trip to Korea. But now, Jason realized, August would shape up to be a tough month.

"That sucks," Kiana said. "But at least your trip was worth it, right?"

"Yep. By the way, I got you something." Jason dug into his carryon and handed Kiana a huge package of face masks, one of several he'd picked up at the airport. He'd gotten her another gift, a traditional, very elaborate tea set, but now decided it was too much.

"Thank you!" Kiana exclaimed, accepting the masks. "I love these."

CHAPTER

Twenty-Two

"WHAT DID you do to your face?" Were Betsy's first words to him as soon as Jason walked into the office the following day. Six forty-five in the morning, but Betsy was already seated at the reception desk, a huge steaming cup of coffee in front of her.

"What do you mean?" Jason asked.

"You know what I mean. Look at your forehead. It looks all smooth. Like a baby's bottom!" Betsy shrieked. "Cassie, come over here, check out Dr. Lee's face."

Cassie rushed to them from the PT space.

"Can I feel it?" Betsy asked. "Let me touch your forehead." She tapped her finger along Jason's hairline. "That's impressive, Dr. Lee."

"Did you actually get some fillers done?" Cassie's mouth gaped open, as she leaned in to examine Jason's face.

"You know he did, you know he did," Betsy said. "Well, well, while we're over here, working hard, Dr. Lee was in Korea on a little cosmetic adventure."

"They forced me to do it." He sighed, and the three of them burst out laughing.

"I'm surprised they let you leave Korea, a good-looking guy like that, Jason." Cassie giggled.

"I know, right?" Betsy shook her head. "But Dr. Lee, aren't you concerned you'll end up looking too young? What if your patients don't believe you're actually the doc?"

Jason chuckled. After Kiana's reaction, he'd expected as much from his colleagues.

"I got you these." He produced a set of face masks for Cassie and another one for Betsy. "And some treats for the office." Jason took out a bag of individually wrapped matcha cookies he'd also found at the duty free.

"Thank you, Jason," Betsy exclaimed. "By the way, your first patient is here." She pointed at the door.

———

Eager to update Audrey on Kiana's ideas about Anton Konovalov and the suggestion to meet, Jason called his former patient as soon as he got home from work.

"I was looking forward to your return," Audrey said as soon as she answered the phone.

"How have you been?" Jason asked.

"Dr. Lee, I have to tell you. I've had an incredible week. My son had been staying with us for a while, with me and my husband. It was a huge strain on our finances, he'd moved in during Covid, lost his job. I hate to say it, the whole situation was beginning to drive us nuts. But the day I had my appointment with you, he announced he'd found a job and three weeks ago, he finally moved out. Even started paying us back. He got a well-paying job. It's amazing. It's like you've got the magic touch, Dr. Lee."

"Me?"

"Like I've told you, Dr. Lee, something good happens every time I see you. It's like magic."

"I don't believe in magic, but I'll take it. As long as I can help you, I'm happy." Jason chuckled.

"So, did you watch the documentary? About Anton?" Audrey asked without missing a beat.

"I did," Jason said. "I also showed it to a friend, who speaks Russian."

"What did you think?"

"I thought a few things were strange about the documentary. But mostly, it didn't make sense why they didn't look into Anton's death at all."

"I agree."

"They made a whole documentary discrediting his book." With clarity, Jason remembered Kiana's text from when he was in Korea and reproduced what she said exactly to Audrey. "The person I showed it to, her mother is Russian, so she watched the documentary as well and she thought likely Anton's memoir, wasn't actually written by him."

"Really?"

"Yes, that's what she thought. She'd like to meet you." Jason cleared his throat.

"I'd like to meet her as well. Will you be able to arrange it?"

"Of course."

———

Right after hanging up, Jason texted Kiana.

> Hi! I just spoke to Audrey and she's on board to meet your mother. Can you ask your mom when works for her?

Just as he put down his phone, it pinged. Expecting a response from Kiana, he picked up the phone, but it was from Yuna.

Jason spent the rest of the evening exchanging texts with his third match. A whole day passed before he noticed Kiana hadn't responded to his message.

Friday! Jason remembered she was supposed to pick up Ross from the airport.

> Good luck tonight!

He texted her.

No response came that evening or overnight.

It wasn't like Kiana to disappear. There was no reason for his friend to ghost him. Panicked thoughts crept into Jason's head.

> How's it going?

He texted Kiana on Saturday morning, as he was getting ready to go to for his run at Roosevelt Island, stretching just as he used to do before taekwondo practice.

No response.

What is she up to? Jason wondered when he got home after the run. He wasn't one to exaggerate danger, but, since meeting, he and Kiana had been in touch almost every day. The only exception was his trip to Korea. *Maybe she is just caught up with Ross?* But something felt off. *What if Ross has done something?*

He jumped up. Percy, who'd been sitting next to him, meowed and got off the couch. Jason dialed Kiana's number. It went straight to voicemail.

That's it.

Remembering Kiana's place from having walked her home, he clearly recalled the number on her door, 2023C. He headed straight for her apartment, turning on Wilson Boulevard, made a left onto an alley that led into the sprawling block of garden-style apartments, where Kiana lived. The shaded streets looked ominous, danger lurking behind every corner.

What if I'm too late? The thought pierced his imagination, and he burst into a sprint.

He made it to Kiana's door in minutes, panting, as he stopped outside. Jason took a deep breath and knocked softly. At first, there was no response. He knocked again, harder now, and heard the shuffling of footsteps.

"Who is it?" she asked.

"It's me. Jason."

The door opened and Kiana appeared on the doorstep. Her face was red and puffy.

"It's not a good time." Tears streamed down her face. "I've been crying non-stop since, like, Thursday night."

"What's going on? Come on, what happened? Is it okay if I come in?"

She nodded. "Just don't look at me." Kiana went inside and sat down on the couch, burying her face in her hands. The drawn curtains made her living room look sinister.

"Listen, let me get some light in here, sitting in this dark room with no fresh air can't be helping."

"No, no, it's because of him. Ross," Kiana said, her voice nearly a whisper. "I found him on the site."

"What site? You told me you met him on a dating website, right?" Jason stared at her in confusion. Kiana's face was turned away from him and he couldn't see her expression.

"The 'Is this Your Man?' Site. Remember, I told you about it."

"The one with the cheaters?" Jason let out a deep breath and sat down next to her.

"Yes." Kiana swallowed hard.

"Alright, so you found Ross there?" The second Jason said those words, the corners of Kiana's mouth drooped.

Her voice cracking, she said, "His name isn't even Ross."

She shook her head and wiped a tear that rolled down her cheek. "He lied about *everything*."

Jason didn't answer, but silently continued listening.

"He's the worst." Kiana took a deep breath. "He's actually married. And he's got three kids."

"What? So, what was he doing on a dating website?"

"Well, it's actually crazy. He's estranged from his wife, but he's definitely still married. He's moving back to the area to try to make up with her and the kids."

"But didn't you go check out houses for him? I don't understand. Are you sure there isn't some sort of mistake?"

"I'm sure. There are two other women just like me. He was using us for different things. Like, I was the one to get him from the airport and to see the houses. So, I guess I was the 'logistics' woman. Then, there was another one picking out furniture for him."

"This is terrible."

"I know!"

"How did you find out?"

"I checked the Facebook group right before going to the airport. It was like my sixth sense telling me to go on there. I saw a post from his actual wife, with his photo, age, and just a red flag next to it. That's the thing with the group, you can only do the minimal stuff, like nothing in the main text, so the algorithm doesn't block you. That's why it's so hard, and sometimes you don't even see the person."

"So, you just saw it by chance? The photo?"

"Yeah, I don't even know. It was like divine intervention. On Thursday night, after I got home from work, I was just sitting there, and a text from Ross arrived. I was about to respond, because he was getting ready to board his flight, you know. He would have a long layover in Germany, or whatever." Kiana sniffled. "I just logged onto Facebook. I don't even go on there anymore. That's for old people, I mean, other than this group and another one for Arlington people, that's all I really read on there. But I got on and opened the group. The first thing I saw was Ross hugging this other woman. And there are three kids next to them, their faces blotted out. My hands went numb, you know, from the stress."

"Wow!" Jason exhaled.

"I know, it was like I was this investigator, except it's my life. My heart was beating so fast as I clicked and there were lots of comments. So with that group, if there are lots of comments, that's a bad sign. Because it means the other women also know this guy and they've got something to say. And there are these reactions to the post, mostly angry and sad."

Kiana held up her phone as if to show Jason, but instead tossed it on the couch in disgust. "Also, not a good sign. So I read the wife's comments, because you're supposed to put everything in the comments. There are so many things in there, like Ross has been lying, his real name is Ryan. They're actually married. She's just now finding out everything. And all that. It was sick."

"But how do you know the wife wasn't lying?"

"I contacted her. That's what I did on Thursday night." She sighed. "We talked, and I told her everything, and she was crying."

"So why was this guy sending you to look at houses?"

"I don't know. Maybe the houses were options for him to show the wife, as a kind of getting back together plan. Like he was looking for a nicer family home to move into." Kiana shrugged. "I guess that's why he was asking me to go over there and check it out. All this time, he was just using me." Kiana started crying again, and Jason leaned over to hug her.

"Thank you, I'm sorry." Kiana sniffled into his shoulder. "I'm such a mess."

"You're not a mess. But it's good that you found out now, at least, isn't it?" Jason said after a pause. Kiana sat back and looked at him.

"Yeah, I think you're right. It is good. I was thinking about it, and I almost went out there to meet him. I nearly got myself tangled up in this thing. And I don't even get it. What was his plan? Was he going to just lie to me forever? And the other women? Why did he do that?"

"I don't think it matters," Jason said, biting his lip. Seeing her tears, her distress, caused him an almost physical pain. "People are just strange. That's what I've learned in my thirty-seven years."

"You're thirty-seven?" Kiana perked up.

"Yep, born in 1985."

"For real? You look younger. I thought you were, like, thirty. And now, even more so, with the skincare stuff…"

"I'm definitely not thirty," Jason huffed. "If I were thirty, my mom wouldn't have been freaking out so much about marriage."

As soon as he said those words, Kiana turned pale and fresh tears rolled down her cheeks.

"Oh my God, oh my God, I can't do this," Kiana cried out. "I'm gonna be single forever."

"Kiana, stop. Please, what can I do?" Jason got up and threw a frantic look around her kitchen. "Let me get you some water." A pile of dirty dishes was sitting in the sink. He found a clean glass in the cupboard, filled it up with water and brought it to her.

"I'm thirty-seven, too," she breathed out, taking a sip from the cup.

"You don't look it, either."

"But I am, and now I'm just gonna die alone, and I won't even have any kids."

Jason didn't respond but watched as Kiana finished her glass of water. Then, he gave her a hard look and said, "Come on, you're coming with me to stay at my place."

"What?"

"Yep, I don't want to leave you by yourself."

In response, Kiana started crying again.

"Please don't cry," he begged.

Wiping tears with her hand, Kiana managed to say, "It's because you're being so nice. I'm just so grateful we're friends."

Jason sighed. He could never understand women. How was one to tell the happy tears from the sad ones?

CHAPTER
Twenty-Three

THE PROCESS of leaving Kiana's apartment took an inordinate amount of time: first, she washed her face, then packed and repacked clothes to take with her. She also included toiletries and make-up. Finally, the two of them went for a snack. By the time they made it to Jason's apartment, it was almost midnight.

Percy settled on the couch, observing the pair.

"You can sleep in the guest bedroom," Jason said.

"Thank you again, Jason. I'll be comfy enough here on the couch."

"Oh no, I have a guest bed. I can make it up for you."

"You don't need to go to any more trouble."

"Why? I've got an actual spare bed, it'll be much nicer."

Since moving into this apartment, he hadn't made up the guest bed once, and it stood in the second bedroom as a reminder of his loneliness. He'd rented a two-bedroom apartment so that there would be extra space if his parents ever came to visit. Now, as he got the sheets out of the closet, he felt proud of himself for his foresight, for having purchased these bed linens and a second set of blankets and pillows, for actually owning these items.

"I'm so impressed," Kiana said, watching as Jason piled the sheets and blankets on top of each other and carried them to the bed. She was much calmer now, though from time to time still sniffled.

"Are you?" Jason chuckled.

"You're amazing, you really are. How many single guys out there keep a guest bedroom so tidy and not just used as a storage space? Let me help you," she offered.

Jason could tell another bout of tears was coming, so he nodded and quickly changed the subject.

"Listen, I'm just glad you're here. Percy misses you. And in the morning, we can do something together, how about that?"

"Really?"

"Yes, really. Don't sit here feeling sorry for yourself."

"I'm not. I mean, I just got my heart broken."

"Well, if I were your parent, I would tell you some inspirational story about the challenging lives your family members had," Jason said. "But instead, let me tell you about, hmm, let's call him Mikhail…Cohen, that'll do."

"Who?"

"This client of mine. This guy got huge blisters on his feet. Do you want to know how?"

"No. Where's this story going?" Kiana threw him a confused look.

Once he adjusted the corners of the fitted sheet around one side of the bed, Jason moved to the second side. Satisfied, he sat down on the bed and invited Kiana to sit next to him.

"So, Mikhail lived in one of those subsidized apartments near Rockaway Beach. But he really wanted to have an ocean-view apartment. He'd moved to the US in the early nineties, and he waited for twenty years to get his subsidized apartment with an ocean view. When he finally got it, he was already eighty-five years old. So then, the guy moved to the apartment and every morning he walked on the beach. Every day."

Jason patted the bed. "Everything was going well, except he was so old, but he didn't feel old. He felt great, and for the next nine years, he was perfectly fine. But then Covid happened. This guy was now in his mid-nineties, and it was scary for even much younger people. Mikhail Cohen was afraid of leaving his apartment, because if he got infected, he stood a much higher risk of it getting serious. But Mikhail wanted to stay in shape. So, you know what he started doing?" Jason paused for effect. "You'll never guess!"

"What?" Kiana had stopped crying and fidgeted in anticipation.

"He started walking in his apartment. Up and down the apartment, ten miles a day."

"No way!" Kiana straightened up.

"Yes! Ten miles going back and forth in his living room. He would walk barefoot, and that's how he ended up with blisters on his feet. I treated him, and that's the story he told me."

"That's crazy."

"It is, right? All that time, he was trying to stay healthy and fit. Walking in his apartment, back and forth, back and forth. Can you imagine? And he was in his nineties by then."

"It's a good story," Kiana said.

"It is. So you should never lose hope, and you're never too old to take care of yourself. I have another idea for you, by the way," Jason continued. "The gratitude practice. A colleague does it. You write things you're grateful for every day. And that helps."

"That sounds like a better idea. I like it more than walking ten miles a day barefoot." She forced a smile.

"I saw that! Was that a smile?"

"Maybe." Kiana blinked fast. "Thank you. I'm grateful to you, Jason."

"Good night," Jason said and closed the door to the guest bedroom behind him.

———

He sat down on the couch, absorbed in thought. Percy was curled up next to him, and Jason ran his hand through Percy's fur. When he had offered his place to Kiana, he hadn't thought of the consequences. Their strange friendship, his attraction to Kiana, which was still there. Her face, even when tear-streaked, looked beautiful.

But then, immediately, the image of Yuna popped into his mind. His perfect girl, who was almost certainly his future wife. Jason knew he would propose to Yuna, as soon as he got the chance. It was just a matter of time. First, they needed to see each other once more, and if everything went well, he would do it.

His life would finally be on the right track. He would make his parents happy and settle down. With Yuna, there were no butterflies in his stomach. But there was a calm understanding of everything moving in the right direction. It was fate. Jason knew it.

He considered watching TV, but thought the sound might wake Kiana up. So he texted Yuna, and went to bed without waiting for a reply.

———

Opening his bedroom door, Jason peered into the living room, looking for Percy. He'd gotten so used to waking up to the little cat next to him, it felt odd not to hear her eager purrs wanting breakfast. The guest bedroom door stood slightly ajar, and Jason peeked inside. Percy was curled next to his guest. Kiana's red hair lay in a massive heap on the pillow, entangling with Percy's red fur. The two of them made a fiery glow, creating a scene so beautiful it made Jason's heart ache.

This was almost his perfect life, but he was quick to remind himself the cat wasn't actually his, and Kiana was just a friend.

Kiana stirred, and Jason was about to step away, but he heard her voice:

"Hey. Good morning." She sat up on the bed.

"Hi, how was your night? I was looking for Percy," Jason said, slightly embarrassed.

"Oh, Percy wanted to keep me company. You know, cats can tell when you're distressed. So, I guess Percy knew she needed to help me out." Kiana stretched. She was wearing a cropped shirt, and Jason noticed her pale stomach. He averted his eyes.

"I guess so. I hope you're feeling better."

"Yes, I am. First night I've slept since I found out about Ross," Kiana said and got out of bed.

"Well, I'm glad. Listen, I'll go make coffee. You want one?"

"Yes, definitely!"

Ten minutes later, Kiana emerged from the bedroom, looking refreshed. Jason handed her a cup of espresso, and she sipped it slowly, savoring the taste.

"This is fantastic, thank you," she said. "I feel human again. I don't know what happened, I'm sorry I broke down like that."

"We're friends, right?" Jason said. "I'm here for you. And it sucks to find out things like that about someone. I can't even imagine."

"I guess so."

"Do you want to go get some food?"

"Or I can make us some breakfast?" Kiana suggested.

"Umm, sure," Jason agreed. "I went grocery shopping yesterday, so there should be eggs, butter, whatever you need," He pointed to the refrigerator.

"Great. I make the best scrambled eggs, you'll see." Kiana opened the refrigerator door.

"I can help," Jason offered.

"No worries, I like making eggs," Kiana said. Jason was about to protest, but, as soon as he stood up, his phone beeped, and he saw a text from his cousin, Dave.

It'd been over two weeks since they last spoke, and, without hesitation, Jason dialed Dave's number to update his cousin on the trip to Korea.

"Hey, man!" He heard Dave's familiar voice. "I guess congratulations are in order."

"What do you mean?"

"I heard about Yuna."

"What? You even know her name?"

"Yep. *Your* mom told *my* mom last night. I know everything."

"Wow." Jason's mouth gaped open. He knew, of course, how thrilled his mother had been when he told her his third match was successful. He even let his mother pick out a farewell gift for Yuna, a silver charm bracelet, that he presented on their third date. Still, he was shocked his mother went so far as to share this information with her sister-in-law, Dave's mother.

"Yeah, so, when's the wedding?" Dave was chewing. The man was always eating. He boasted a very high metabolism and always had snacks available. As a teenager, Dave could eat two extra-large pizzas in one sitting, and Jason, whose parents had so little money back then, was grateful his own body could do with a much smaller amount of food. Most of what Jason ate back then, in their first years in America, were the leftovers from the restaurant where his mother worked. Which was almost exclusively fried rice. Containers of it, for breakfast, lunch and dinner. To this day, Jason equated it with poverty.

"The wedding?" Jason yelped and caught a strange look

from Kiana. She had finished whisking eggs in a bowl and poured them on a skillet. "Come on, man, we just met."

"Well, you know, things can move fast. I'm rooting for you. I really am. And don't be mad at your mom, she's just excited."

"Alright, alright."

"Besides, I wanna come to your wedding. Party like it's 1999! Listen, June's a good month."

"I'll keep that in mind. Listen, I've gotta go," Jason said curtly.

Kiana dropped a spoon, and he rushed to pick it up, while still holding the phone.

"Sorry, I'm so clumsy," Kiana said loudly enough for Dave to hear.

"Who's that? You got a woman, too? Wow, Jason, look at you."

"It's not like that," Jason started to say, and caught another look from Kiana.

"I had no idea, Jason, I had no idea. Listen, I won't tell anyone, alright?"

"There's nothing to tell."

"Is she hot? Tell me, how does she look?" Dave clicked his tongue. "I know you got good taste."

"I'll talk to you later," Jason said and hung up the phone. "That was my cousin," he explained.

"I see." Kiana shook her head and Jason wondered what Kiana had overheard.

"I guess my mom is telling everyone I met a girl." Jason opened his arms wide.

"Well, I suppose this is it for you." Kiana curled her lips in a half-smile. "I guess one of us has to be in a relationship, right?"

"I guess so." Jason reached for the plates. "Let me help you."

"I'm almost done with the eggs." Kiana pointed at the

pan, and immediately yelped, "Oh, wait, do you have a stirring spoon?" She grabbed one, locating it immediately on the counter, then started stirring the eggs around. "Just in time, they almost burned! But I think they'll be alright. Do you have any bread?"

"I got some bagels." From the refrigerator, he produced a bag he'd stored before his trip. "They're a bit stale, but I don't think they went bad." Jason examined them.

"That's because of all the additives," Kiana said, frowning. "I've been reading a lot about food safety. But we can still make egg sandwiches." Kiana expertly sliced two bagels open, toasted them, while Jason watched. He wanted to help her but got so carried away with observing her swift motions, with how quickly her hands moved, as if they almost flew, that he didn't dare disturb her.

"You're almost a professional chef," Jason noted, once she was done.

"Far from it. But I like cooking. I watch cooking shows a lot." Kiana brushed a strand of hair off her forehead. "And I sometimes practice, too."

"Nice. I guess it makes sense, so you don't just watch people make food, you try to make it, too. I've never been a fan of cooking shows myself, though," Jason said. "Just *Law & Order*."

"I remember." Kiana smirked. She'd assembled their food on two plates and pushed one across.

"Yeah. And I learned the other day it might be because of childhood trauma."

"Really? How's that connected?"

"I guess if you had a traumatic childhood, you like to watch crime shows. Find it comforting." Jason turned the fork in his hand. "I'm not sure if it's true."

"Did you have a traumatic childhood?" Kiana asked. Laying her fork down, she looked straight at him, her forehead creased.

"Kind of." Jason cleared his throat. "Things were stressful when we first came here. But I wasn't that young. I was fourteen."

"Fourteen is barely a teenager," Kiana said. "It's okay if you don't wanna talk about it."

"What about you?"

"My childhood was great. But I'm still messed up." Kiana rolled her eyes. "I mean, look at me. Almost got into a relationship with a cheater."

"But you didn't."

"Yeah. I guess I've got some guardian angels protecting me."

"I believe in them. I definitely do," Jason said. "Though I'm not religious, but some things, you gotta wonder."

"Well, I think you're my guardian angel. You came and saved me. And even told me a story about an old man, who walked up and down his apartment to stay fit. I actually think I dreamed of him last night." Kiana rose from her seat and rushed to hug Jason. "Thank you!"

"That's what friends are for," Jason said and hugged her back.

Twenty~Four

"BY THE WAY," Jason said, "Audrey is on board. She really wants to know what had happened. Will you ask your mom?"

Mid-morning sun shone on the Custis Trail ahead of them, as they walked in the direction of Roosevelt Island. The outing had been Jason's idea. Though he didn't say it, he thought Kiana needed to spend as much time as possible outside to lift her spirits.

"On your left!"

Jason jerked and pulled Kiana aside, as five bikers zoomed past them. The cyclists, all men, were dressed in special bike gear, tight shorts and reflective jerseys. One of them yelled, "Watch out!" and spat, as he passed, another shouted something incoherent that sounded vaguely threatening.

"These guys seriously think it's the Tour de France or something." Kiana gaped after the group.

As the bikers disappeared from view behind the curve in the trail, Jason frowned. "If even one of them crashes into you, forget it."

"And here you are, saving my life again." Kiana turned to Jason.

"Well, hey, I'm a doctor, after all." He winked at her. "But back to getting Audrey and your mom together."

"Let me see what I can do." In a practiced motion, she pulled her hair back and secured it with a scrunchie. "My mom will definitely agree to it. It's just a matter of figuring out when it would work, with my job and your job and all that. And my mom teaches ballet on weekends."

"Oh, wow."

"Yeah. She's always busy. Even during Covid, she taught online classes. My mom's amazing. Which is kind of strange, 'cause I'm so messed up."

"You're not. You're so accomplished. Come on, give yourself some credit."

"But in terms of personal life. My mom and my dad, they have a perfect relationship. It wasn't like things were easy for them, but they just always knew they'd found the right person in each other. I wish I had that." Kiana's voice cracked.

"Listen, don't worry," Jason said. "You'll find your man. Just give it time."

"I just always thought it would be easy for me, too." Kiana opened her arms wide. "Even my older brother, he's been married since he was twenty-five. So, I'm the black sheep of the family. Divorced. Late thirties! No prospects. When my mom was my age, she'd married the love of her life and had two kids. So I'm way behind."

"You're being too hard on yourself. You really are." Jason gave Kiana a rueful look. "I know how it is, but it's not worth it."

"You sound like a self-help book now." Kiana averted her eyes.

"I want to help. And look at me. If I managed to find someone, I'm sure you will too. Just give it time."

"I guess I got used to being alone during Covid." She shrugged. "I actually loved it. Loved being by myself, going on walks. It was totally fine, but now I feel like time is running out. And it sucks."

"Really? That's so weird," Jason stopped. "I actually hated Covid. It was a crazy time. So much pain and suffering. I barely slept."

"Sorry you went through that."

"Yeah. But you know what? I learned I was doing what I was meant to do. I really love my job. Even now, in outpatient, it's the best."

"I love my job, too. But I just wish I also had more of a personal life," Kiana noted gravely.

———

On Sunday morning, Kiana and Jason walked through the door of the Silver Line Diner in Tyson's Corner. A week had passed since Kiana's breakdown, and the two of them had reestablished their daily contact now that she'd returned back to her place.

At Jason's insistence, they got there fifteen minutes early. He always operated based on the Korean concept of time, where an early arrival was a sign of respect.

The location had been Audrey's idea. She told Jason she avoided Arlington because that was where she'd met Anton all those years ago, and the place still gave her 'chills.' Tyson's Corner was an area of Northern Virginia easily accessible from Arlington, and was also convenient for Kiana's mom, who drove from Leesburg for the meeting.

Jason and Kiana picked a booth in the back of the diner and sat down next to each other, with a view of the entrance. Squeezing in to sit next to Kiana, Jason wondered whether she also felt the intimacy of the moment.

The second Kiana's mother walked in, Jason knew who she was. Her face was like a time projection of her daughter's, the same features, the same shape of the nose. The same round eyes, only gray, where Kiana's were dark-brown. Well-defined eyebrows, high cheekbones and even her hair looked remarkably similar. Shorter than her daughter, the woman held her head up high and had impeccable posture. Jason rose to greet her.

"Mrs. Nasiri." She turned to Jason, extending her hand. "You can call me Zeena. Short for Zinaida."

"Mama, this is my friend Jason," Kiana said. "I've told you about him. Jason is taking care of Charlie's cat, Percy."

"Of course, of course," Zeena smiled. "That's very kind of you. And very responsible. And I heard you also helped Kiana the other day."

"Mama, please." Kiana opened her eyes wide, as if trying to telepathically tell her mother to stop speaking.

"Alright, alright." Zeena reached across the table and patted Kiana's hand. "So, this friend of yours, I did watch the documentary, and I even ordered the book that gentleman wrote, *I'm Sorry, Dasha*." Zeena carefully pronounced the title. "But I'll save my analysis for later."

The waitress came over to check on their table, followed by Audrey.

"Hello, I'm Audrey Simmons." She turned first to Kiana's mother, then to Kiana, nodding to Jason.

"I'll be right back to take your drink orders." The waitress spun on her heels and disappeared.

Audrey sat down and placed her purse on her lap. Jason noticed it had flowers painted on it. Following his gaze, Audrey said, "You know, I've got a friend, she paints purses. And all the proceeds she sends to this little village over in Kenya." Audrey fumbled with the flaps of the purse, then opened it and put on her reading glasses. "Now, this is better," she announced with a disarming smile.

"I'm Zeena," Kiana's mother said, turning to Audrey, who was sitting next to her.

"I don't know how to thank you. I am so grateful you

agreed to meet with me. I really appreciate your time and how you'll give me your perspective on Anton." Audrey spoke quickly, as if the floodgates had burst open. "It's hard, and after all these years, I just don't understand. I remember the guy I knew, and he was a hero. Brave, smart, handsome. So strong. Anton was hilarious, too. He took me grocery shopping, you know. And he was over six feet tall, and he'd lift me up and sit me on his shoulders, like I was a little girl, right in the dairy aisle. People were staring, but Anton couldn't care less. And now, with this documentary that came out, they paint him as a terrible liar. And I refuse to believe it. They've discredited his whole book, you see."

"Audrey, I'd like to tell you my opinion of Anton." Zeena put her hands flat on the table. "As someone who defected from the Soviet Union ten years later than Anton, but who lived in the USSR during the same time, I can tell you quite a few things in his book *were* false."

"Ah!" Audrey gasped. "So, are you saying the documentary is correct?"

"Yes, a lot of what Anton had mentioned in his book," Zeena emphasized the last word, "is false. In particular, the claims that he tortured people because they were reading the Bible. You definitely couldn't read the Bible openly, that much I can confirm, but you could buy it on the black market without too much trouble. I had plenty of friends who were active and traded banned books and made quite a bit of money that way. And no one was tortured."

"Is that so? But why would Anton lie?"

"Possibly because he was told to lie," Zeena said. "I have some suspicions about his involvement with the church. And his authorship of the book."

"But he was a man of God. He'd found Jesus." Audrey paused. "Though, now that I think about it, I never saw him writing. And he never mentioned the book to me."

"I have a few theories about the book. Perhaps someone else wrote it." Zeena turned more towards Audrey.

"Really? But why?"

"Because of sensationalism," Zeena said. "Back then, there was the Iron Curtain, no one could go back to fact check information. So either Anton was very clever, and quickly figured out the more lies he spun, the better off he would be in the US. Or someone groomed him to say things that would help sales. Simply finding Jesus wasn't enough, they wanted a story of redemption."

"So, you're saying Anton invented everything for profit?"

"Or he'd been made to do it."

"But then what about his death?" Audrey yelped.

"This is what I wanted to ask you. Can you tell us what you know about his death?"

"We said goodbye right before Christmas. Anton wanted to join me, but my father worked at a secret base, where Anton wasn't allowed. The next thing I knew, I got a phone call informing me of his death. That was it. You know, I didn't speak of his death with anyone for thirty years? I had the FBI come to my apartment. They questioned me, and then, that was it. After that, I didn't tell anyone about my connection with Anton."

"That must have been so traumatic. Not being able to share with anyone."

"Yes." Audrey drew a sharp breath. "I still get chills when I think about him. I miss him. To this day, I miss him."

Kiana, who'd been sitting quietly, winced at those words.

"I'm so sorry you had to go through this," Zeena said. Jason wasn't sure, but he thought he saw her wipe a tear. "What about the young woman who was with him when he died? Have you ever met her?"

"No." Audrey pursed her lips. "Mary Ward. That was her name. I think it's fake. It's just too plain. What kind of name is that? There must be thousands of women with that name."

The waitress reappeared with four waters, surveyed their group and asked, "Now, folks, are you ready to place your orders?"

"We should probably go ahead," Kiana said softly, and Jason nodded.

"I'll just have some dessert," Audrey glanced at the menu, "apple pie, please."

Jason ordered a hamburger. Kiana and her mother split a large salad and a sandwich. The waitress scribbled down their orders in her notepad and left, and Zeena spoke again.

"You don't think she's real? Did you ever try to look into the story?"

"I was terrified. Just imagine. We were in love. We were supposed to see each other right after the new year. We made plans to get married, and then I found out he had died of a gunshot wound to the head. The next time I saw him was in a casket." Audrey's fingers trembled, as she pulled the glass of water towards her, the ice cubes making a clinking sound.

"I think you should try to find her. Mary Ward. This is the missing piece of the puzzle, in my opinion." Zeena unfolded her napkin, pushing her own glass of water away.

"You think it's that important?"

"Yes, absolutely. That's the only way to find out the truth about Anton's death," Zeena said eagerly. "Maybe Kiana can help you."

"Mama? How?" Kiana stared at her mother in bewilderment.

"Well, don't you dig on the internet all the time? Might not be so difficult to find this woman."

"Mama? Mary Ward might not even be her real name!" Kiana exclaimed.

"That's what I was thinking, too," Audrey said, taking a sip of her water. "I was thinking maybe they gave her a fake name, just to hide her identity. It said she was his fiancée, but she didn't even come to his funeral. And she was seventeen! None of it adds up. I was Anton's fiancée, not that woman."

"And what if Anton was a conman?" Zeena gave Audrey a pointed stare. "Is that possible?"

"Anton? A conman? Of course not." Audrey raised her hands up in protest. "He was a genuine, kind person. Look. I brought these." She reached into her purse and took out a stack of yellowed photos, some frayed at the edges, placing them in the middle of the table.

"May I?" Zeena's hand hovered over the photos.

"Of course."

In the photos was a much younger, but very much recognizable, version of Audrey Simmons. Wearing flared jeans and a white sweater, hair hanging to her shoulders in thick curls, her face lit up with a happy, carefree smile. Her eyes sparkled how only the eyes of someone in love do. Audrey was sitting next to Anton, the two of them holding hands. The defector's face bore the same happy, pure expression of love.

"You see." Audrey smiled wistfully. "This is how we were. This was taken in November, just six weeks before his death. Does this look like a man who had another fiancée?"

"No," Zeena said. "Absolutely not. But I still believe the only way to get closure is to find the woman who was with him when he died. Audrey, would it be okay if we tried to find Mary Ward for you? Are you open to the idea?"

"Yes, sure. I don't see why not," Audrey, who'd been holding one of the photos, dropped it on the table. "I'm very grateful for all the time you took, for everything."

"When I heard your story, you know, it really resonated with me. Back then, defecting from the Soviet Union was like going to the moon. I'm not exaggerating. We left everything behind. I had no idea if I would ever see my parents again. I was lucky, of course, in that I married such a wonderful man, and that, after 1991, once the Soviet Union collapsed, I could go back and see my parents. But for ten years, it was nothing." Zeena unclenched her hand. "And for Anton, well, I feel so sorry for him. It must have been terrifying to leave everything behind. He was so young, barely twenty years old when he left."

Audrey listened attentively, nodding at every word Zeena shared.

"I'm so glad Jason connected us," she said once Zeena finished speaking, and both women turned their attention to him.

"It's really thanks to Kiana," Jason said, and Kiana blushed.

CHAPTER

Twenty~Five

"CHARLIE IS about to sign a sublease, for a whole year. So with Percy, I just wanted to confirm you're okay to keep her. I mean, you guys seem to like each other," Kiana petted the purring cat, sprawled across her lap, "a lot."

Jason and Kiana were spending most Saturdays together, and that weekend was no different.

"Sure, I don't mind. The only thing is Yuna." Jason handed a cup of espresso to Kiana, then sat down on the couch next to her. "The plan is to eventually have her move here, if everything goes well. So, I'll have to make sure she's okay with the cat." The hesitation in Jason's voice didn't escape Kiana, who looked at him carefully.

"Well, hopefully there won't be an issue," Kiana said vaguely. "Thank you, by the way." She took a sip of her espresso.

"But I really love having a cat," Jason added. "And I get to see Yuna at the end of the month."

"That's right, of course. In New York, right? Where will you stay?" Kiana raised her eyebrows.

"I was thinking I'd just stay with my cousin Dave."

"Are you sure that's a good idea?"

"Why not? Dave knows about Yuna."

"But what if you want some privacy?" Kiana asked, her cheeks turning bright red.

"Oh, yes." Jason cleared his throat, suddenly keenly aware of the touchy topic of being physically intimate with another woman. "I guess I should get a hotel."

"Yep," Kiana mumbled, setting her cup down and focusing her attention on the cat.

———

Following Kiana's suggestion, Jason booked a hotel in Brooklyn Heights. He'd initially considered staying in Manhattan, but he'd always felt more comfortable in one of the Boroughs. And so, he settled on a place right by the Brooklyn Bridge, several blocks away from the AC subway line. Jason pictured how he and Yuna would walk across the bridge, staring at the Manhattan skyline, holding hands. The image was so perfect, so romantic, symbolizing the vision of an idyllic life that awaited him with Yuna.

After considering different options, Jason decided to get to New York by train. The idea of a peaceful train journey aligned perfectly with the romantic mood of walking across the Brooklyn bridge together with Yuna. So, Jason booked his ticket on Amtrak without hesitation.

He settled in his seat, staring out of the window. The train gathered speed, quickly leaving DC behind and passing a forested area. The leaves were still green, but with tiny hints of yellow, the signs of fall already in the air. Jason opened the Notes app on his phone, and was about to jot down his gratitude list, which he'd been doing sporadically. And then, the train pulled into the BWI airport station.

A large group of loud tourists got on, occupying every available seat around Jason. Their loud chatter was insufferable no matter how hard he tried to block them out. He'd learned everything about their disrupted vacation plans, the delayed flights, and the miraculous appearance of the train that had saved them from spending the night in Baltimore and was now transporting them from BWI to Newark airport, where they would continue their trip to a tropical paradise.

When he finally emerged at Penn Station, Jason felt exhausted. He navigated to the AC subway line, anxious to get to his hotel. On a busy Friday night, the train was full of commuters. Jason squeezed into a corner of the subway car and observed.

When they first moved to America, his family lived in Palisades Park, New Jersey, right across the Hudson River from Manhattan. New York City was close, but somehow unattainable. Uncle Henry had taken the Lee family to New York City on several occasions, and Jason remembered the feeling of awe mixed with a slight revulsion. This wasn't a place where one lived. It was a place to see and immediately leave.

The podiatry fellowship in Queens had given Jason another perspective on the city, along with more feelings of unease associated with treating patients at a busy hospital during the pandemic.

Quickly making his way out of the subway, Jason located his hotel, which was just two blocks from the stop. The hotel's sleek interior contrasted sharply with the facade of the building, which had been done in the Victorian style, with intricate wrought-iron railings and bas-relief flowers. Once in his room, Jason decided to order room service and watch TV rather than face the bustle of the city.

———

Can't wait to see you!

As the morning sun spilled through the curtains, Jason rubbed his face with a smile and responded to Yuna's text:

Same! Getting ready now.

Ever since meeting, they had been exchanging daily texts and speaking on the weekends. Yuna worked a lot, and most of their conversations were about mundane, routine things. She didn't have any hobbies, which, according to her, was because she was extremely busy at work, but she was close to her family, especially her mother. Jason liked that about her, how mindful Yuna was of her mother's needs.

"It's just me and my sister," Yuna had told him. "My mom, she did everything for us when we were little, so now it's our turn to help her and to take care of her."

To that, Jason could relate. He, too, felt indebted to his mother for her sacrifices while raising him.

Yuna knew about his cat because Percy had popped into view once when the two of them were speaking on FaceTime, brushing her tail against his cheek.

"You have a cat?" Yuna exclaimed. "That's so cute! I love it. What's its name?"

Jason told Yuna the story of Percy, and also mentioned Kiana and her role in the cat's appearance.

"So, you guys are good friends? You and this woman?" There were jealous notes in Yuna's voice and Jason tensed.

"Yes, we've gotten to be good friends."

"Does she have a boyfriend?"

"She's seeing someone, yes," Jason responded, and that information had been enough to stop Yuna from prodding any further.

Kiana had, indeed, started seeing someone almost immediately after the Ross debacle. Although he'd gently suggested taking some time, she insisted finding another love interest was the best idea, and cited a Russian saying, which meant "like cures like." After sifting through what she referred to as 'hundreds of matches' online, Kiana found Sid.

"He's former military, but now he's in government contracting," she told Jason proudly. "Totally my type."

"That sounds a bit like Ross, doesn't it?" Jason tried to keep his voice steady, but his concern was palpable. Worried that Kiana would be stepping into another heartbreak, Jason wanted to warn her of the risks without sounding overbearing. But his approach was failing.

"I guess I'm just attracted to the strong, masculine types." Kiana's eyes sparkled. "He's really cute, and he's got a great job. Sid's looking to settle down."

"Show me his photo, please," Jason asked, and Kiana shared Sid's dating profile. In the main photo, Sid was smirking. His arms were crossed, the protruding biceps peeking through his t-shirt stretched tightly against his chest. The second photo pictured Sid on a motorcycle, with the same, low-key bicep flex and the smirk.

"See, he is manly." Kiana breathed out.

"Did you check the group?" Thanks to Kiana, Jason was now fully versed in the utility of the 'Is This Your Man?' Facebook community.

"Yes, and there's nothing. So that's a good thing, but don't worry, I'm taking it slow." Kiana blushed. "He's a really nice guy. We're going on our second date this weekend. And he's so thoughtful. He asked me out on the second date right at the end of our first one. We're going to a cute winery near Leesburg. So it'll be great, because I'll just pop in to see my parents right after, so it's not a big deal that it's a bit out of the way."

Twenty-Six

RIGHT AFTER ANSWERING Yuna's text, Jason got ready and made his way to the second floor of the hotel, where, he'd been assured the night prior by the receptionist, he would get his complimentary breakfast.

The space was crowded, with hungry hotel residents circling the counter like vultures, waiting for the next tray of breakfast sandwiches to appear. When it did, brought out by a hesitant and apologetic server, the crowd dove right for it and picked it clean in seconds. After observing for several minutes, but failing to get any closer to the food, Jason realized he would not be able to get breakfast in time to meet Yuna. Instead, he poured himself a cup of coffee from the dispenser, and left the hotel on an empty stomach.

He went straight into the first bodega he saw, grabbed a bagel sandwich, and headed for the Brooklyn Bridge. The idea of getting to Manhattan by crossing the bridge on foot occurred to him the night prior, after he saw it out of his hotel window. Though it was only eight in the morning, the bridge was already busy with runners and bikers.

As a few tourists had emerged, Jason joined their ranks, making his way across while snapping photos. He paused in the very center of the bridge to read the dedication plaque. With the fresh breeze blowing, the sun reflecting in the water, and the anticipation of seeing Yuna, he felt on top of the world.

Forty-five minutes after leaving his hotel, Jason found his way to their meeting point, which was several blocks from Yuna's hotel, near Wall Street. He saw her right away, standing at the corner, and his heart leaped. His date was wearing a jean miniskirt and a black leather jacket, with matching black, high-heeled boots. Her hair, which in Seoul he'd seen her wear in a ponytail, lay in thick locks on her shoulders. Yuna looked striking.

"Hi!" Jason said.

"Hi." Yuna smiled coyly.

"You look beautiful." He reached to embrace her and kissed her on the cheek. It felt natural to do so.

"I got some shopping done." Yuna gave him a proud smile. "I always go to the same boutiques when I'm in New York." She did a twirl to show off her outfit.

"Amazing. You look great. It's so good to see you."

"It's good to see you, too." Yuna looked him straight in the eye, and Jason took her by the hand, which felt so small in his.

Yuna was beautiful. His perfect woman. They had a whole day together, and the possibilities were endless.

"I was thinking maybe we can go to the High Line?" Jason said. "Have you been yet?"

"I have," Yuna said, "but I love it. Let's go. There are so many cute places on the way. We can post on Instagram."

"Sounds good," Jason agreed.

"I have five thousand followers," Yuna said casually. "I always post when I travel for work, and that's when I get the most likes."

"Oh, really? That's cool."

"So I kind of also want to check out this one place. It's the cutest," Yuna continued. "It's this adorable bakery, Korean, but French inspired, actually, and they have these croissants to die for. And their pastries are amazing, like a work of art. Do you want to go there as well?" Yuna blinked fast, the expression on her face flirtatious and adorable.

Dazzled, Jason immediately said, "Yes."

"Where is it?" he asked, still holding Yuna's hand.

"It's in Gramercy."

"Oh, great."

He had a vague understanding of the various parts of Manhattan, having spent most of his time in Queens. "So, I guess we can take the train there?" He scanned the area for the closest subway station.

"The train, oh, no." Yuna giggled. "You're funny. I never take the subway in New York. It's not like in Seoul, it's just disgusting." She crinkled her nose. "There are all these rats and homeless people, and whatever. Yuck."

"Oh, alright, well, let's take an Uber then," Jason said and pulled out his phone. "What's the name of the place?"

"It's called Musée, that's French for a museum, and also a play on words, like Muse. You see?" Yuna said, while Jason typed the name of the cafe into the app.

"Three minutes," Jason noted, as the Uber app populated their ride.

"Great, oh, wait, stand right here!" Yuna ordered. She got out her own phone and flipped the camera on. "Smile!" she said as she stood next to him, snapping a selfie. "I'll post this on Insta. Is it okay if I tag you?"

"I don't have Instagram."

"Oh, that explains it," Yuna tittered. "I was trying to find you, in Korean and English, and there were so many Jason Lees, but not you. You really need an account. I can set it up for you."

"But why would I need social media?"

"Why wouldn't you?" Yuna shook her head in disbelief. "I

mean, you could also probably advertise your business. Don't you want more clients? You could be the cool doc, this sexy Korean man."

"Well, I'm not sure that is the look I'd be going for." Jason chuckled. Despite himself, he was flattered to be called sexy by Yuna, who was so openly into him.

"Listen, leave the image thing to me," she said expertly, flipping her phone off and stuffing it into her purse. Jason noticed her fingernails had been studded with tiny sparkles.

Their Uber arrived, and they rode through Manhattan to the café. Jason expected a quaint place, something small and adorable, but instead, as the Uber pulled up to the yellow storefront with the name 'Musée,' written in cursive, they found a line snaking down the street and turning the corner.

"I guess it's a popular place," Jason noted, as they got out of the car.

"It's no biggie." Yuna grabbed Jason by the hand. "The line moves really fast. There's one for pickup and the other one to eat-in."

"Alright," Jason said. He didn't particularly mind waiting in line, as long as he was with Yuna.

She confidently led him to the end of the line and, while still holding his hand, asked, "Listen, what's your Korean name?"

"Jun," Jason responded.

"How cute." Yuna giggled. "I love that name. But I guess in the States you had to change it. I'm lucky with my name."

"Yes, Yuna is a beautiful name."

"And it sounds awesome in English. Unique, but also easy to pronounce."

"Absolutely," Jason said, kissing her on the cheek. "Just like you, beautiful and unique."

Yuna blushed. "Let's do a selfie, but with Korean hearts," she suggested, holding up her phone.

"A Korean heart? What's that?"

"You just make a little sign with your fingers. I thought you knew. Like this." She crossed her thumb and her second finger, making a tiny cross with her right hand. "See? That's the Korean heart."

Jason tried to copy her movement.

"No, like this." Yuna placed her manicured fingers over his and adjusted his thumb by moving it slightly to the left. "You have beautiful hands," she said, running the tip of her finger along his middle finger. "So strong."

"Thanks." He felt his breath catch. The café, the streets of New York, all of it was secondary. In that instant, he knew Yuna was the one. She flipped her hair and took a step back, seemingly oblivious to her effect on him. For a few minutes the two of them didn't speak, with Jason processing what had just happened and Yuna scrolling through Instagram. Then she spoke.

"I was thinking. Your name, Jason. Have you ever considered changing it?"

"What? Why?"

"Well, what about Jamie? I think it's really sexy, and you can be like Jamie from *Outlander.*"

"Who's that?"

"Oh my God, you don't know? It's an amazing show, and Jamie is a Scottish guy from the past. He's just the sexiest man there is."

"But I'm used to Jason. It's the name I picked when I moved here."

"Jamie Lee flows so nicely," Yuna said, giving him a careful look. "We're next in line," she yelped.

Jason expected to be seated within minutes, but it turned out being 'next in line' only meant they were about to enter the cafe, and, once inside, there was another long line moving around the perimeter of the crowded storefront. Several servers, dressed all in white with matching yellow aprons, stood behind the counter. Equipped with tongs, as customers pointed, they picked up and placed various pastries on trays. This reminded Jason of the scene at his hotel that he had so eagerly escaped.

Maybe everyone in New York loves to wait in line and compete for food, Jason thought, as he and Yuna chose their pastries and made their way to the next counter, where they could place coffee orders and pay.

The process took close to an hour and, by the time they sat down in a crowded area upstairs, Jason felt exhausted. Yuna, on the other hand, looked fresh and energized as she bit into her croissant, which had lavender stuffing.

"This is so insanely delicious." She placed the croissant on a plate and snapped a photo, which focused on the croissant's bright purple stuffing. "So cute! I'm sure I'll get a ton of likes!"

"It is." Jason glanced at his watch. It was already after eleven. His plan of going to the High Line and then walking across the Brooklyn Bridge was still possible, but barely so.

And then Jason reminded himself of his gratitude practice. Each moment was to be treasured. There was no reason to rush things, to fulfill some list of activities. What mattered was spending time together with Yuna.

His future wife.

CHAPTER
Twenty-Seven

"SO, HOW WAS IT?" Kiana asked, stepping into Jason's apartment. Immediately, Percy jumped off the couch and ran up to the door, her tail raised up high, to greet the visitor, then let Kiana pick her up. This was something the cat wouldn't let him do consistently. *I bet she prefers Kiana,* Jason thought, observing the reunion.

"It was great!" Jason gushed. "Well, not the Amtrak, but everything else was great."

"I can see that." Kiana winked at him. "You're perfectly glowing."

"It was just amazing. It really was."

"So, what's next? When will you guys see each other again?" Kiana said, sitting down on the couch after placing Percy gently on the floor.

"I think I'll go home for Christmas. To propose," Jason said, pacing between the kitchen and the couch. This was the first time he'd voiced the decision, and it felt monumental. Pausing for a moment, Jason trotted to the kitchen and poured himself a glass of water.

Kiana's words reached him:

"As long as you're sure, I say, go for it. You only live once."

"Well, hey, I think I'm sure." Jason took a sip.

"You know what I just realized? You said, home. About Korea. That's definitely a sign." Kiana gave him a pointed stare, as she rose from the couch and walked over to join him in the kitchen.

"Did I?" Jason scratched his head. "I gotta call my parents, too." He glanced at the time. "I guess in a couple of hours."

"Your mom will be so excited." Kiana clapped. "She must be so proud her plan worked. Did you tell her you'd be meeting Yuna in New York?"

"No, not yet. She would have told my uncle Henry, and then Dave would have found out, remember."

"Oh, yeah, that makes sense. My mom says hi, by the way." Kiana smiled at him.

"Please tell her I said hello as well. By the way, we've gotta figure out the rest of this Anton thing. Did you look into finding Mary Ward? Is there anything I can do to help?"

"Not yet." Kiana said. "I will get on it, though. But I've been busy. Sid and I went on a date this weekend. Our third. It was so sweet. He took me to this cute place in Ashburn."

"That's nice. What was the place?"

"Just this coffee shop." Kiana bit her lip. "But there's something weird about him, I'm starting to suspect."

"What do you mean?" Jason sat down on a stool and prepared to listen, relieved the topic of conversation had switched from his love life to Kiana's.

"Well, so, he keeps telling me he's going to invest in land near Harper's Ferry. Now, it's like the second weekend in a row, he keeps going to check out that area." She crossed her arms.

"So, what's weird about that?"

"Well, you know I work in commercial real estate?"

"Of course."

"So, I offered to look into it, but he was all cagey about it. Like he wasn't being truthful."

"Kiana, maybe you shouldn't help guys with real estate purchases?" Jason rubbed his chin. "I mean, what's up with this? With Ross, and now this guy?"

"I know, it's maybe just a coincidence, I guess." Kiana sighed. "But now I'm all paranoid. After the Ross thing. So, I'm just wondering what to do. I mean, it doesn't make sense. Unless he's lying about the real estate thing, but then that's such a random lie, isn't it?"

"I told you I didn't like how that guy looked."

"But he's not been posted in the group." Kiana pulled out a stool and sat down across from Jason. She wasn't wearing any make-up, and her under-eyes were dark, like she hadn't been sleeping well. "At least there's that. Though I don't actually know his full name. I don't think his first name is just Sid, either."

"Wait, what? You've gone on three dates with him, and all you know is that his name is Sid? This dude could be a serial killer." Jason set his glass down on the counter with a clink.

"No, come on, Jason."

"How can you be so lighthearted about this? This is serious. Kiana, please, this could be something dangerous. How well do you actually know this guy?"

"Maybe I should post him in the group."

"Yes, please. Post him in the group. Do it right now." He urged.

Kiana had long ago told Jason he could never see the 'Is This Your Man?' group, because it operated on a strict code of secrecy and was open only to women. But Jason had formed in his mind the idea the group was a powerful, ever-present resource, able to solve any issue related to dating in the Washington, DC area.

"Well, it's like, 80,000 people, posts take forever to get approved. But I'll post about Sid, I promise. Now, let's talk about Yuna, so at least there is something positive and I start believing in love again." Kiana titled her head. Despite himself, Jason smiled.

"See! How happy you look. I love it! So happy for you, Jason!" She reached over to squeeze his hand.

———

Jason had considered delaying proposing to Yuna, but it was impossible. Not with the distance. And not with the urgency. A part of him wanted to spend a few more months getting to know Yuna, and, of course, he'd been telling Kiana the very same thing: to get to know the person, to not assume, that things like love took time. But Jason decided his own advice didn't apply in his case because the Korean dating algorithm had done the heavy lifting for him, and it was far superior to the shabby American dating apps.

Kayeon had done the background check, had reviewed the candidates' health information, their current financial health, their future earning potential and even screened people for debt and gambling issues. And both he and Yuna had passed those checks with flying colors. Not only were they perfectly matched, but their fathers had similar professional back-grounds and had even worked for the same company. This was further proof of their unique compatibility.

Hesitating for only a brief moment, Jason picked up his phone, turning on video chat mode.

"Eomma," he said, as soon as his mother picked up. "I am going to propose."

"Jun," his mother's whole face lit up, "my son. I'm so happy," Before Jason had a chance to answer, she said, "I'm so proud of you. I love you. I knew you'd turn your life around, Jun."

As far as Jason could remember, this was the first time his mother had told him she loved him unprompted.

Like clockwork, the call from his cousin, Dave, came shortly after.

"So this is it?" Dave asked as soon as Jason picked up the phone.

"I guess so."

"Congrats, cousin. I'm proud of you. And there I was, worried you'd end up single forever."

"Come on!" Jason furrowed his brow.

"Oh, never mind, just teasing." Dave cleared his throat. "Have you gotten the ring yet?"

"The ring? Oh, not yet. I thought we were supposed to go ring shopping after she accepts, in Korea. That's what my mom told me."

"You've gotta get the ring. I mean, to her, you're an American, so she'll expect it from you. Like in the movies. Gotta live up to the expectations. So that way she'll definitely say yes."

Hearing those words, Jason a pang of anxiety. The possibility of rejection was very real and gnawed at him.

"I still have a few months, no rush," Jason said, trying to keep his cool. With Dave, it was the only way. If Jason showed any sign of weakness, Dave would pounce.

"Listen, go over to Costco, get her a nice-looking ring and make sure to save all the papers in case it doesn't work out, 'cause they got a great return policy. It's nothing."

"Alright, thanks for the advice," Jason said, choosing to ignore the point about the implication of Costco's generous return policy.

———

"Tiffany's. You've got to go to Tiffany's," Kiana said as soon as Jason told her he was planning on buying a ring for the proposal.

"Really?"

"Of course, they are the best."

"But Dave was telling me I could get a nice diamond ring from Costco," Jason started to say, but Kiana raised her eyebrows.

"No, no. You want Yuna to say yes, right?"

"Of course I do."

"So then, get her a ring from Tiffany's. No one wants to think their future husband went to a wholesaler to get the engagement ring."

"Alright, I guess I'll go over there next week. They have a store in Tyson's, don't they? I think I've seen it."

"Yep." Kiana nodded. "Listen, if you want, I can come with you, to help you pick it out."

"Thank you, sure. That would be great."

"And by the way," Kiana sighed, "you may have been right about Sid. All I've gotta say, there won't be a date number four with him."

"What happened?"

"So, after you told me the guy might be a serial killer, or whatever," Kiana rolled her eyes, "I actually posted in the group. And one woman, I swear, they're like, actual detectives, she offered to look him up. Well, to look up his number. The comments were actually, like, also concerned when I told them he didn't tell me his last name or anything else."

"See," Jason opened his arms wide, "I told you so."

"Don't gloat." Kiana smirked. Despite the bad news, she looked better than she had over the weekend. "I can actually laugh about it now. Kind of. So then, this woman searched his number through a database, and she gave me his actual name, which was Siddhartha. And I can't remember the last name. But then, and this is the part that makes no sense, she told me he actually already owned real estate near Harper's Ferry. He had a whole land parcel in that area."

"What? But he was telling you he was looking into it?"

"Yes, exactly." Kiana nodded with conviction. "That is the

part that makes no sense at all. So after I learned that, I decided I will just stop talking to this guy."

"So that was it?"

"Yeah, this is it. I mean, if he's lying about that, what else is he lying about?"

"You really should have the same screening that we have in Korea," Jason said, pointing to his phone. "It's so rigorous."

"I wish!" Kiana sighed. "But I have a few other dates lined up. Not wasting my time."

Jason opened his mouth to react but decided against it. It was unlikely Kiana would listen to his advice. At least, not right away.

Twenty~Eight

THE TRIP to Tiffany's didn't happen for a few weeks.

At first, because of Jason: he wasn't ready to spend the money, having just booked a round-trip ticket to Korea. The price at Christmas was exorbitant, so Jason settled for a flight in the middle of December instead. But even that was over his budget and complicated his student loan repayments, not to mention saving for a house.

The excitement over the upcoming proposal, the promise of a joint future with Yuna, the marital bliss that was, at last, awaiting him, however, pushed him to ignore the financial hit.

But then Kiana was busy. She got very serious about dating and told Jason that she had two weekends in a row booked solid with dates. Apparently, meeting several men each weekend, rotating between them to avoid 'getting stuck.' This was a new method she'd learned about 'in the group.'

Kiana had come over to drop off a cat treat, and all three of them were sitting in Jason's kitchen, as Percy devoured the snack.

"Jason, the deal is that we, women, get so excited about just one guy. Like, it totally happened to me with Ross. And then even with Sid at first. So we all get stuck on one guy, and he's likely not worth it at all. But it's much better to date several guys, to have fun, to go out as much as possible, and that way, one guy will eventually become more serious. It's the proverbial 'don't put all your eggs in one basket.' You know what I mean? It's a numbers game. Men do it all the time." Kiana gesticulated excitedly, and almost knocked over her glass of water.

"I guess so," Jason responded vaguely as he steadied the glass. He had come to find, Kiana reacted better if he challenged her ideas softly, without outright dismissing them.

"But isn't that what men do? You all date around, you don't actually focus on one girl. Right?" Kiana pressed him for an answer.

"Well, umm, that's not exactly what I do," Jason said. "But maybe I'm not your typical American guy, and maybe," he scratched his head, and, unable to resist, continued, "that theory is just not a good one?"

"Not a good one? But you've got all these success stories in the group. Like, these women, they met their actual husbands after they stopped being serious. It gives you a lighter feeling towards dating, you match the energy."

"What energy?"

"The men's energy. You've gotta match it. That's what it's all about."

"But why would you want to match the men's energy? You're a woman," Jason said, forgetting about his intention to be more diplomatic.

"Jason, that's not what I'm saying."

"I don't think your theory makes any sense at all. If you like someone, just like them. Why would you want to go out and waste your time on some other random people just so that you are matching some energy of some person who isn't even real? Just let the guy know you like him. If it's mutual, then there you go."

"Jason, please, why are you being so annoying? Don't you get what I'm saying?" Kiana pouted.

"I do, but I don't agree," Jason said. "I'm trying to help, that's all."

"But I don't need any help. Anyway, for Tiffany's, I can go in two weekends. I've got a few guys already in rotation, and I'm about to meet a new guy in person, Greg. He's a real estate agent, so we'll have a lot in common. And he wants to hang out, but then he might be going to Colombia for a month or so."

"To Colombia? The country?" Jason gave Kiana a curious stare.

"Yeah. Why?"

"Well, I know my cousin Dave went there on a solo trip. This was before he was married, and, I mean, the stories he told me. I don't think it's a good sign."

"Like, what do you mean?" Kiana opened her eyes wide. "Greg says he goes there all the time. Like, he's there several times a year."

"I mean, single guys only go there for one thing. It's not exactly a cultural exchange." Jason said, remembering Dave's account of the trip, which his cousin had shared in excruciating detail.

"Oh? Are you just saying this so I cancel Greg?"

"You decide for yourself. But he doesn't sound like a serious prospect to me. I mean, not if he's going to Colombia all the time."

"Jason!" Kiana pleaded. "Must you ruin everything?"

"Well, I'm not the most worldly guy, but even I know what goes on there."

"Alright, fine, and then I've been chatting with this other guy, Ricardo. He lives in Rockville, and he seems very smart. I'll show you." Kiana opened the app, and the yellow background popped into view.

"See, there he is." She pointed at a photo. It showed a guy smiling at the camera. His face was open, clean-shaven.

"This guy's bio is interesting… but no, wait is that a neck tattoo? Kiana!" The man was wearing a white shirt with its collar slightly opened, revealing a neck tattoo going up all the way covering his throat. Jason drew in a deep breath. "Okay, on to the next one." Jason swiped to the next profile. "Look, this guy looks decent. And he is standing in front of the National Gallery of Art. That's a good sign, isn't it?"

'Yeah, it is." Jason looked up and Kiana was giving him an odd look before turning away. "Anyway, I'm just trying to have lots of options, that's all."

———

"Wow, I can't believe we're here," Kiana said, as they parked in front of Tiffany's in Tyson's corner. It was early November, and she adjusted her colorful scarf, as she zipped up her jacket. "You know, I got my wedding ring here with my ex."

"You never told me that." Jason raised his eyebrows. "It's not going to be weird, is it?"

"No, I'm over the whole thing. I mean, that was, like, ten years ago, and we didn't stay married long."

"But still, you were married, right? It must have meant something."

"Well, it did, of course, but the whole thing was kind of crazy. My ex was really ambitious, and I think he was really trying to get my father to like him. My dad, you know, he's a professor at Georgetown. My ex-husband," she sighed, "he'd just finished his Ph.D. and was trying to get my dad to help him. So I think he kind of used me to try to break into the academic circles."

"What? Are you for real?"

"Yeah, I mean, we figured it out later. Well, he was really smart, of course, but I think he only wanted to marry me because I'm my dad's daughter. Like, he didn't love me for myself."

"Kiana, that's awful."

"I guess so," Kiana said. They were still sitting in the car, and she turned to face Jason. He noticed tears had welled up in her eyes. "I'm sorry, I never speak about it. This is the first time in a while I've thought about Vlad."

"So, did he actually manage to get ahead?"

"Getting ahead was just part of the problem. There was also the issue with Vlad's mom. She was a total monster-in-law. I actually now think that, if it weren't for the mom, he and I probably would have stayed married for much longer. But she was really terrible, and, honestly, when I got divorced, I felt nothing but relief."

"If you don't want to go in, it's okay."

"Come on, of course I do." Kiana flipped open the passenger-side mirror and checked her make-up. "It's okay. Let's go."

She got out of the car first, the expression on her face purposeful. Jason followed. They walked through the glass door, with Jason holding the door open for Kiana.

Once inside, an associate, a man in his forties, dressed in all black, gave them a practiced smile, as he enunciated, "Welcome. My name is Eric. How may I be of assistance?"

"I'd like to buy an engagement ring," Jason croaked.

"Wonderful. Congratulations!" The man's face lit up. "Let me help you." He led them to a display on the side. "Here, we have our engagement rings. Of course, you may have looked on our website?" He glanced at Kiana. "Is there a particular ring that caught your attention?"

'Oh, it's not for me." Kiana darted her eyes to Jason. "We're just friends. I'm helping with the selection."

"Of course, of course. You're the bride's friend?" The associate nodded in understanding. Kiana looked about to correct him but just smiled. Jason sighed. The process of buying an engagement ring had barely begun and was already proving to be tedious.

"Now, have you thought about the setting? We've got yellow gold, rose gold, and, of course, platinum, for that clean look." The associate focused all his attention on Jason, completely ignoring Kiana.

"What do you think?" Jason, oblivious to the associate's snub, asked his friend.

"Get the yellow gold for sure," Kiana said. "Don't even think twice about it. Platinum is out."

"Okay, great, I'd like to see your yellow gold bands, please." Jason turned to the associate.

"If I may," the man cleared his throat. "Platinum is a premium metal and offers clean, effortless lines. It's a classic, which has been popular for years now."

"That's alright, thank you. I think yellow gold is a better choice. Could you show us a few options, please?" Beads of sweat started to form on Jason's forehead. He wanted to be out of the store as quickly as possible.

"Absolutely." The associate walked behind the counter and, throwing a disgruntled look at Kiana, unlocked the display and placed a single ring on a velvet case, handing it to Jason.

Jason lifted the ring and showed it to his friend. A large diamond sparkled in the light.

"It's nice," Kiana said. "Pretty."

"How much is this one?" Jason asked, carefully placing the ring back.

"This one," the man paused, turning the ring over, "is $17,000."

"Alright, I see." Jason swallowed hard. If he spent that much on a ring, he would barely have enough for the gift exchange that followed the engagement.

"$17,000? Are there any cheaper rings?" Kiana asked, and Jason was grateful for her intervention.

"Of course," with some reluctance, the associate said to Kiana. "We've got rings in different price ranges." Then, turning back to Jason, Eric continued, his voice buttery-soft, "Now, are you familiar with our upgrade program? If you purchase a ring at Tiffany's, we'll credit you the purchase price, and you can get a bigger diamond later on."

"Thank you," Jason said, doing his best to avoid eye contact with Eric.

"The price is determined by the four c's," the associate noted, curling his lips in a condescending smile. "These are what determines the diamond's quality, which is the deciding factor. And that's color, clarity, cut and carat." He opened and closed his fingers. "So, we can look for a more affordable diamond, which could be smaller in size, or not as clear."

"That would be great." Jason smoothed down his jacket.

"Absolutely. Please tell me, how much are you looking to spend?" Eric asked, raising his eyebrows, while the corners of his mouth turned downward.

Jason's cheeks flushed red. He wanted to spend as little as possible, but admitting it now seemed nearly offensive.

Seeing his confusion, Kiana said to the associate, "Could you please give us a minute?"

"Of course." The man quickly placed the ring behind the display and locked it, walking away.

"Let's just look online," Kiana whispered to Jason as soon as the man was out of hearing range. "You can order online. And not deal with this."

"Is it that obvious he is stressing me out?" Jason chuckled.

"Yep." Kiana put her hands on her hips. "He's stressing me out, too. It's like you're supposed to be made out of money or something. I can't stand the attitude. No, I don't want to drop $17,000 on a ring out of the blue."

"Are you sure we can order online?"

"Of course! I don't know why I didn't suggest it sooner, but I just kept thinking you had to go to the store, you know, 'cause that's what I did with my ex, and it's like a tradition. But who cares? The world is changing." Kiana opened her eyes wide. "Listen, let me just check something." She opened the Tiffany's website on her phone. A few seconds later, she announced. "Yep, you can even play with the setting and size, everything. And then, boom, you'll get the ring delivered to you. No pressure."

"Alright, I'll tell him," Jason said, then walked up to Eric. "Thank you for your help so far, but I'm not ready to make the purchase today."

"No problem," Eric said. "Here's my information just in case." He handed Jason a business card and shook his hand. "Come back when you're ready."

Eric didn't say goodbye to Kiana.

———

As soon as they walked out of the store, Jason and Kiana exchanged glances.

"Wow, that guy hates me." Kiana giggled.

"Well, maybe just a little bit," Jason admitted.

"I think he does. He probably thinks I'm the reason you didn't just drop 17K on a ring."

"Yeah, as if I can't make up my own mind," Jason said after a pause. "Want to go get something to eat? We can go to the Silver Line Diner."

"Sure! Like that time with Audrey and my mom," Kiana said. "By the way, I haven't even started looking for that other woman. For Mary Ward."

"Oh, yeah. I also completely forgot about the investigation. Just so much going on with the proposal, and the trip to Korea."

"You know what I just realized, Jason?" Kiana said, opening the car door. "If that group had existed in the seventies, Audrey would have known if the guy was two-timing her. So, she could have avoided this whole story."

"You mean that Facebook group?"

"Yeah, 'Is This Your Man?' group.'"

"Maybe you can ask there. About Mary Ward." Jason turned to face his friend, as he pressed the ignition button. "I mean, didn't you say those women are all amazing detectives?"

"Wow, you're a genius!" Kiana's mouth gaped open. "Totally! What a great idea!"

They pulled out of the parking lot and were waiting at a light to cross Leesburg Pike.

"These lights take forever." Kiana sighed. "I don't know why they designed this place like this. It's like they don't want people to ever make it on time."

"Yeah. One of the reasons I take the metro to work." Jason cleared his throat. The light changed, and he lifted his foot off the brake. Jason liked having Kiana next to him, liked their chatter, and though the visit to Tiffany's did not yield the results he'd expected, he felt happy. Kiana had that effect on him: she brightened up his day.

"You know, I think right after I post about Mary Ward, I'll just stop reading the group." Her words pulled him out of his thoughts.

"But what about dating? Don't you want to check the guys out in the group?"

"I do, but then, it's always bad news. Like at least once a day, there's some cheater, or abuser. Or even, remember the guy with the neck tattoo?"

"I sure do." Jason tapped the steering wheel.

"So, I looked him up in the group. And guess what!" Kiana fidgeted in her seat. "He'd been secretly filming stuff, then selling the videos."

"What?" Jason's mouth gaped open. "That's wild. And he's on the apps? Dating? How's that allowed?"

"I have no idea. But I guess he's free to date, whatever. So, I actually had a date scheduled with him. We were about to meet, and I ran him through the site. At first, his name didn't pop up, but then I tried a nickname. And it came up." Kiana bit her lower lip. "So after that, I haven't gone out with anyone. It was a close call, you know."

"This sounds really dangerous, Kiana. Maybe you should look somewhere else?"

"Like, where?" Kiana said. "I don't really have time, and on the apps, at least there are lots of options."

"Aren't there in-person events where you can go?"

"I don't know. I'm just taking a break for now." Kiana said. "And besides, it's about to be cuffing season, so all the crazies are coming out."

Jason pulled up into the Silver Line Diner parking lot. "Shall we?" He looked over at his friend, choosing not to respond to the cuffing season comment, but Kiana gave him a sad smile.

"The weather's turning colder, and, of course, the holidays are coming, so all the singles, you know, like me," Kiana rolled her eyes, "feel super lonely and everyone tries to get themselves into a relationship. So they're not too discerning, to say the least."

"Oh, I see."

"Yeah, and basically, right now, the risk is I'll end up in this short-term thing, but it's not real, and then, when cuffing season ends, it's all over."

"That's wild," Jason said, opening the Silver Line Diner door for Kiana. For a moment, he felt like they had gone back in time, and were about to have a meeting with Kiana's mom and Audrey, and to hear about Anton Konovalov. He looked over at Kiana, and said, "Audrey."

"I know. I was just thinking about that time we saw her here. I've got to look into it."

Twenty-Nine

WITH THE TRIP to Korea approaching, Jason became more and more immersed in his relationship with Yuna. They texted twice a day. Once in the morning, when Jason first got up, when it was nighttime in Korea, and at night, right before Jason went to bed, when it was the morning of the following day in Seoul. Every Sunday morning in DC, Jason and Yuna had their weekly call, which lasted for over an hour.

They talked about everything, covering their favorite foods, their likes and dislikes, their dreams and ambitions. There was never any doubt in Jason's mind about the seriousness of their mutual intentions. Even though he hadn't yet proposed, they had talked about a future together. Yuna wanted to have two kids, and often mentioned how good it was to have one sibling, citing her relationship with her sister. Jason agreed. He was an only child and felt like it was too lonely. Yuna was excited about moving to the States, and was sure she would be able to find a job in the DC area.

"I can probably get something in private client services. I've got good experience, and I can get strong references. And maybe you can open your private practice," Yuna insisted. "After you change your name to Jamie." She laughed.

Ever since their meeting in New York City, Yuna repeated she saw great potential in him as a 'superstar doctor.' Jason, though he didn't take her ideas too seriously, listened to them patiently.

"I can just tell, Jason, you're young and handsome, you can become a poster boy for podiatry. Just think about it," she urged him.

"I'd rather just do good work," Jason countered. "And I like my practice now. My colleagues are very sweet. Regardless, I can't really leave yet, I've signed a three-year contract."

"Sure, but then you can prepare. Just think how happy your clients are now and just imagine if you build your own practice."

That was true.

Jason, though he'd only been at the practice for a little over a year, had gotten several new clients. His schedule had been filling up, and he was consistently booked. After covering several appointments, Jason found that Dr. McGrath's clients had switched over to him. At first, Jason thought this was an accident, but then one morning, when it was just him and Betsy in the office, she told him, keeping her voice low:

"Dr. Lee, Jason, I gotta tell you, you're getting really popular."

"Oh?" Jason straightened his scrub top.

"Everyone's asking for you. All my recent bookings, they all wanna have you as their doc. I'm not allowed to switch people over, but some of them won't take 'no' for an answer," Betsy shared.

Several days later, Cassie mentioned their Google reviews had gotten several high ratings.

"Jason, have you read the recent ones? There are quite a few people gushing about you."

"For real? I don't ever read those." Jason glanced at his phone.

"Reviews are so important, are you joking?" Cassie said. "People really care about them. Let me find one." She opened her laptop and started scrolling. "There it is!" Cassie smiled, pointing at the screen.

"I love this practice. Feet care," Cassie turned her laptop so Jason could see it, while continuing reading, 'is definitely the best podiatry practice in the DMV. If you go, make sure your appointment is with Dr. Lee. He's got the magic touch."

"Wow, they say that about me?" Jason looked at Cassie in amazement.

"Yeah! Here's another one." Cassie scrolled down. "Jason Lee is a gem. He'll never recommend any treatment that isn't reasonable. Dr. Lee takes time to listen to his patients, understands the problem and finds the most practical solution. So lucky I found him."

"I should really take a look at these," Jason said.

"Yeah, you should. If you're ever having a bad day, just read the Google reviews. People love you, Jason," Cassie added and closed her laptop. "And I said to Betsy the other day, one of your patients told me after she started seeing you, her life changed for the better. She really struggled during Covid, then it just continued, but after she saw you, things improved for her."

"I know who it was," Jason said, remembering Audrey. Immediately, he felt a knot form in the pit of his stomach at the realization he hadn't yet provided an update on her case. "It was Audrey, right? Mrs. Simmons? An older lady? She'd mentioned something about her daughter."

"No, this woman was in her forties."

"Are you sure?"

"Yes, the one who had the sprained ankle, remember? You diagnosed her, and then she came to me for physical therapy. She and I really clicked. She said she got a promotion at her job the day after her appointment with you. And this was completely unexpected, because she was stuck in this one department with a horrible boss, some woman who hated her guts, but then she had the appointment, you treated her, and boom, the next day, she hears she got a promotion."

"And she thought it was because of me?"

"Yes, she said, you had this way of grounding her. She's a little woo-woo, this woman, but she said she could feel how you'd connected her to Mother Earth."

"Alright, Cassie, you lost me with the Mother Earth reference. But hey, if she's happy, and she's better, let her think whatever she wants. I just want my patients to get better and to be healthy," Jason said emphatically.

This was the motivation for becoming a doctor: healing his patients. "All I want is to never see them again," Jason added, quoting Dr. Herman, his mentor. At times, it was as if Dr. Herman lived in his head.

"See, and that's the difference between you and so many other doctors. Most of them want patients for life. But not you. That's what makes you a great doctor, Jason."

"Thanks, Cassie." Jason smiled.

———

Thanksgiving came and went. Jason picked up extra shifts in preparation for his trip to Korea, and the ring he and Kiana had picked out online after their failed visit to Tiffany's had arrived in a signature robin's egg color box.

"See, this is so much better," Kiana told him after he showed her the ring. She'd come over after her Saturday morning workout to say 'bye' to Jason before he left for Korea. "Easy, and it took us, what, less than an hour to pick it out? And no shaming into spending more money than you wanted to, right?" Kiana flashed a victorious smile. "I love how it looks, by the way!"

"It's nice," Jason agreed, closing the box, as he set it on the table. "I think Yuna will be happy."

"Absolutely," Kiana reassured him and picked up Percy. "Are you ready to hang, little girl? It's going to be you and me alone, when Daddy leaves."

"Wait, did you just call me her daddy?" Jason gaped at Kiana.

"I did. You're her cat dad."

"If my mother heard that, she would flip out." Jason chuckled. "But thanks for taking care of Percy. I really appreciate it."

"It's nothing. Come on, Jason. Percy's like my own. I would take her in a heartbeat if my landlord allowed it."

"Would you like an espresso?" Jason pointed at the machine.

"No, thanks, I'm wired as it is after my workout. So, these gifts, are they for Christmas?" Kiana pointed at a stack of boxes Jason had arranged near his two suitcases. "Didn't you just bring a ton of stuff over in August?"

"I did." Jason turned the espresso maker on. "But now I'm going back, so I gotta bring more gifts. And thanks to your shopping method, I made a list and ordered everything online, so I'm all ready."

"Good job," Kiana surveyed the set-up with approval. "What if you didn't bring the gifts? What would happen?"

"Well, it's just not done," Jason shrugged. "You have to show people you care. It doesn't have to be expensive, something small even, just a sign that you remembered them. And besides, it's *almost* Christmas."

"That's true."

"Don't forget the ring." Kiana looked over at the Tiffany's box. "I'm excited for you, Jason. This is a big deal. Once you get married, you'll be my proof there's hope for the rest of us. That there are some good guys out there."

"Thanks," Jason said. "I'm so lucky to have a friend like you."

"Same here.

Percy wriggled out of her grasp. Letting the cat jump off, Kiana said, "Oh, and by the way, I've got some major news. I didn't want to tell you, because I wanted to make sure she was the one, but basically, I think I've found Mary Ward."

"What? Are you for real? And you're just telling me now? How?"

"It was through Ancestry.com, actually. Because, of course, there are so many Mary Wards, and at least twenty of them in California. But this one woman from the group, she was so nice. She told me she was an historian and really wanted to help."

"And?" Jason, having poured his drink, was now absent-mindedly stirring it with a spoon.

"So, in one of the newspaper clippings they mentioned the full name of Mary Ward's father. When Anton Konovalov died, she was seventeen, so we calculated she must have been born in 1955, but we put the range from 1954 to 1956 just in case. What helped was that her father's name was Gerald, which is pretty unique."

Kiana pulled her hair back, and quickly affixed a scrunchie. "Anyway, so then the woman from the group found their whole family tree on Ancestry.com and from there, she found the right link. Mary got married and had changed her name, and her new name is now Invernizzi, which is pretty unusual, so after that it was easy. I've got her address and everything." Kiana glanced at her phone, "She lives actually not far from where Charlie is, in Pasadena."

"That's something. But we must tell Audrey right away."

"I know, right? Will you do it? Audrey might want to reach out to Mary Ward, don't you think?"

"You know what, I'd love to be there when Audrey makes that call," Jason said. "So, let's wait until after I get back from Korea."

"Sounds like a plan."

CHAPTER
Thirty

"YES," Yuna said, wiping a tear.

She looked gorgeous, in an off-white cashmere, turtleneck and matching wool pants. Soft snow was falling outside. The first snow that season. Jason stared at his now-fiancée in awe. It felt as if the two of them were on a movie set. Seated in a private corner of the dining room at the Grand Hyatt, with a view of the Namsan Tower.

A tea service had been arranged, booked by Jason in advance. He picked the Grand Hyatt as the setting for the proposal because it was the location of their incredibly romantic second date. The day he first knew Yuna was the one.

As soon as Yuna said 'yes,' the attendant, prepped in advance by Jason, snapped several photos of the happy couple.

And then Yuna asked, "Maybe we can film the proposal?"

"What do you mean?" Jason looked at his new bride in confusion.

"Well, let's pretend like you're proposing for the first time. That way, I can upload it to Insta. That will look so good! I want this to be documented." Yuna blinked fast and curled her lips in a smile. "And you look so handsome. I want everyone to be jealous!"

"Alright," Jason agreed. "So what do you want me to do?"

"Excuse me." Yuna waved at the hotel attendant, who had just moved away from them. "Could you please film us?"

"Alright," the attendant said, throwing a brief glance at his watch. "Just let me know when you're ready."

Yuna directed Jason to stand next to her chair, then sat down, looking out of the window.

"Now," she told the attendant. "The weather is just so romantic today, don't you think?" She pointed at the soft snow, as she turned to Jason. "I love this time of year."

"Yuna, will you be my wife?" Jason asked and handed her the box.

"Jason, stop, you've got to bend one knee," Yuna yelped and, turning to the attendant, directed him to stop recording. "Let's start from the top."

They all retook their positions.

"The weather is just so romantic today, don't you think?" Yuna pointed at the windows. "I love this time of year."

"Yuna," Jason said, and his beautiful bride turned to him. Obediently, he got on one knee.

"Oh my God!" Yuna exclaimed, her face was full of awe and surprise. If Jason hadn't just proposed to her, he would have been sure she was genuinely surprised.

"Yuna," Jason repeated, opening and holding up the box, "will you marry me?"

"Yes," Yuna responded, wiping a single tear. She stared at the ring. "Wow, it's beautiful." Jason slipped the ring on her finger. The fit was just a little too loose, and she curled her finger to stop the ring from sliding off.

The attendant stopped recording and quickly handed Yuna her phone.

"Thank you so much. I'll edit the video later and I'll add a few close-ups of the ring. And the box, I love it. How did you know I love Tiffany's?" she asked Jason, while twisting the ring on her finger to examine the diamond. It sparkled beautifully in the light.

"I just guessed," Jason said, deciding against mentioning Kiana's role in purchasing the ring. Yuna's questions about Kiana had gotten more and more pointed. Ever since his friend had embraced being single and had stopped dating altogether, he decided it was best not to mention her to Yuna, who might misinterpret their friendship and feel as if Kiana was a threat. There was a part of him that still remembered how attractive he'd found Kiana in the beginning, when they first met. The memory caused Jason some discomfort. It was a reminder of how pathetic and out of control he'd felt as a single guy with few romantic options in Arlington. Now, coupled with Yuna, he wanted only to focus on his future as a happily married man.

"I can get the ring readjusted later on," Yuna said. "But I love it! Just love it." She stuck out her left hand and stared at it in admiration. "Jason, this is like a dream."

"Come here," Jason said and kissed Yuna on the lips. "I love you." He exhaled. It was the first time he said it, and it felt strange saying the words after proposing. But this sequence felt right. After all, he'd decided to make Yuna his wife on their second date, and what did it matter if he'd told her he loved her *after* proposing.

Isn't it more important that I've found her at last, and will soon be a happily married man, with the perfect woman next to me on my life's journey?

"I love you, Jason." Yuna looked directly at him. "We're going to be so happy together."

"Yuna, yes, we are," Jason croaked and squeezed her hand.

She was twisting the blue box in her hands. "I love the box, too!" Yuna batted her eyelashes at him. "So, you know what happens next?"

"What?" Jason threw a look full of love and admiration her way.

"The *sang-gyeon-rye*."

"Oh, yes. Of course, the sit-down." Jason tensed.

The sit-down, a Korean tradition of introducing the bride's and groom's families to each other, and the process of discussing the life of the newlyweds, including all the financial details, was gruesome.

Jason had heard of many a couple who had failed right at this very step, at least according to his friend Hyun-woo. The complications of having the two families meet, connect and bless a union were many and the subject of endless jokes and K-drama plots.

"But remember, we figured out our dads worked together at Daewoo in the nineties," Jason said after a pause. He took Yuna's hand in his and gently ran his finger along her palm. She squeezed his hand, and that connection, the soft touch, the bond between them, said it all. Jason's heart melted.

"Yes," Yuna murmured. "And that's the most important thing. Also, my mom can't wait for me to get married. I'm the older daughter, you see, and they say I'm holding up my little sister." She winked at him.

"You look so cute when you do that." Jason leaned to kiss her again. "Love you," he whispered into Yuna's ear.

"Love you, too," she said and then froze in place. "Wait, wait, Jason!" She took out her phone. "Here, let's do this." Yuna switched the camera into selfie-mode, positioned her face next to Jason's, then stuck out her left hand with the ring finger adorned by the new Tiffany's diamond. She paused to shift the too-big ring until it sat straight. "Smile," she ordered and snapped a photo. "Another one!" she said after examining the first selfie. "And let's do one with the Korean hearts. I'm gonna try to do it with my ring finger sticking out," she noted, trying to maneuver her fingers in a way that would make the new ring visible.

———

After Jason told his parents he'd proposed and Yuna had said 'yes,' his mother immediately sat him down and started making a list of gifts and gift requests, and quizzed Jason on his most recent finances.

"Jun, how much have you put away for a house?" His mother gave him a concerned look, rearranging a stack of papers on the coffee table.

"Eomma, not much. But it doesn't matter, the prices are so high in Arlington now. It's almost impossible to get a place. I would need at least $300K down payment to get a decent single-family home," Jason said. As soon as he said the amount, he remembered Kiana's mythical fiancé and his lies and sighed at having been jealous of the guy who'd turned out to be a liar.

"How much have you saved so far?"

"Eomma, I've got student loans, you know that. I want to pay those off first."

"Yes, but we need to let them know. This is how everything is calculated, Jun. We have to set the expectations." His mother gave him a pointed stare. "I know this isn't pleasant, I mean, speaking about money to people you've never met, but this will be the foundation of your relationship. Of your marriage. And it's tradition, after all. And once you get money matters out of the way, things will fall into place, trust me. We're lucky we can afford to do this, Jun," his mother said, referring to their relatively recent inheritance.

"Alright, alright." Jason made the okay sign with his fingers. "Listen, with the house, since I'm renting, can we just tell them we'll get a $1,000,000 home within two years? Maybe the interest rates will come down, or, I don't know, there'll be a miracle. Otherwise, it makes no sense to me how to make it work."

"Your father and I can probably help with the down payment," Jason's mother said.

"Eomma, no, please, you need money to live here." Jason shook his head. He'd prided himself on supporting himself financially since starting college, and he wasn't about to change that.

"It's fine, Jun, we need to help you. We can't take it with us to the grave."

"Eomma, don't talk like that, you're still young!"

"But look at your uncle? Just like that, a heart attack, and there you have it."

"You guys aren't like my uncle. He was a heavy drinker," Jason countered.

Two hours later, after some tedious calculations, estimates, subtractions, and after perusing several Arlington real estate listings, Jason's mother was pacified.

"You are right. Even though you don't own a home right now, you do have great earning potential and have a stable job," she noted proudly. "Now, I will show this to your father, and I think we should be set."

Jason's father was a quiet man, who left most of the decision making to his wife. She ran their day-to-day lives, and he never got involved in the mundane matters, like what to have for dinner, how to spend the weekend, or whether it was time to replace the upholstery on their chairs. But there was never any doubt in Jason's mind, his father was the head of the family. Min Suk Lee only got involved on rare occasions, but it was on the occasions that truly mattered. Jason's father had avoided all the matchmaking, the conversations about Yuna, the back-and-forth so far. Now that Jason had proposed and the sit-down was about to happen, Jason's father was all in.

———

The meeting between the Lees and the Parks was arranged three days after the proposal, just one day before Jason was to fly back to the States. Jason didn't like waiting until the last moment, but Yuna's mother had been abroad. According to Yuna, her mother went to Vietnam three times a year to golf resorts. She stayed there for several weeks at a time, and the last trip of the year traditionally happened right before Christmas.

"My mom loves playing golf," Yuna told him, a dreamy smile crossing her face. "She's been into sports all of her life, but golf has become a real passion. I think it's so cute she has a hobby."

Jason and his parents drove to the Park family apartment, an immaculate three-bedroom flat in Gangham, where the meeting would take place.

As soon as the Lees had walked through the Parks' front door and introductions were made, Yuna's father recognized Jason's father. Yuna's mother took Jason's mother away for a quick chat. Meanwhile, the two men immediately hit it off and started reminiscing about the lost glory of Daewoo, as well as its untimely demise. They transitioned straight to soju and toasted to their company, their connection, and to their friendship, which now would, without a doubt, blossom thanks to the union of their two children. After shaking Jason's hand, Yuna's father didn't ask Jason any questions, seemingly did not notice Jason's refusal to drink, and focused all of his attention on the older Mr. Lee.

Yuna's father was an imposing man who had to be at least in his early sixties, judging by his daughter's age and his stint at Daewoo before the company failed in the late 1990s. But the man's face looked sleek, his cheeks were plump, and his forehead was smooth, the telltale signs of recent plastic surgery.

Jason remembered his own procedure in August and breathed a sigh of relief at the realization his mother had likely forgotten to have him do a repeater injection before he went back to America. Mr. Park had thick hair, a rich shade of black. Jason was sure the man's natural hair color had at least some gray in it, but the hair dye had been done so skillfully, if one didn't know Mr. Park's age, there was no way to guess the hair had been dyed at all.

After the women emerged from the kitchen, Mr. Park invited them to a low-set square table, which had red fabric on top. A white couch was positioned by the window, and two bright red armchairs stood opposite. Yuna brought over tea and refilled soju for the men, and then the six of them sat on the low cushions, three to each side of the table.

Jason, having spent most of his adult life in America, had never experienced anything like this gathering.

Only now did he understand Hyun-woo's warning about the sit-down. Right away, the conversation immediately moved to Jason's earning potential, to his current financial obligations and to what type of home he could get within two years.

After some discussion, they agreed the wedding would be in Seoul, in June of the following year. The exact date would be determined once the families had reviewed the availability at the five-star hotels in Seoul, where it would be taking place. Yuna's family suggested that their first choice should be the Grand Hyatt, where the couple had shared two special moments, including the proposal.

"It would be so special if the wedding were there," Mr. Park said, giving his daughter an encouraging smile. "With the couple leaving Seoul after the wedding, it would be important to make it as memorable as possible."

"Of course," Jason's father said, "but we do want to make sure our children are off on the right foot in America. Life in Washington, DC, is expensive. We should do a cost comparison with several other hotels."

"Yes," Yuna's father scratched his chin, "I agree, getting a good deal is important." He turned to his wife, who feigned a smile. Jason wasn't sure if he'd imagined it, but he could almost see his future mother-in-law's nostrils flaring ever so slightly.

The two families agreed Jason would purchase a home for the family within two years of the sit-down, at the cost of no less than one million dollars. Once the agreement was reached, his mother gave him the 'I told you so' look and he smirked. She loved being right.

Then, the families discussed the gift exchange. Yuna would get a new handbag, and so would her mother. All three of the Park women, including Yuna's little sister, would get brand new mink coats. Mr. Park would get five hand-sewn Italian wool suits with matching shoes and belts. Jason and his father would also get hand-sewn suits, and his mother would get a pair of diamond earrings. Though the brands weren't mentioned, the expectation was that these would be the likes of Chanel and Hermes. The sit-down lasted nearly four hours, but the Lees left the residence of their future in-laws elated.

"Why is it that the house purchase needs to be within two years, exactly?" Jason asked his mother, when they were driving back. She turned back to him from the passenger seat.

"It's because of the kids. You're expected to have a child within two years. That's why."

"Oh, I didn't realize it would be so fast."

"Fast? I've been waiting for my grandchild for almost forty years!" His mother scoffed.

"Eomma, do you mean to say you wanted a grandchild as soon as you had me?"

"Never mind, you know what I mean."

His father's neck tensed, but Min Suk said nothing, gripping the steering wheel.

———

"Congratulations, Jun," his father told him after they got home. "Let's mark this new chapter in your life. Maybe you'll have some soju?"

"Thanks, Abeoji," Jason said. He rarely spent time alone with his father and would have welcomed this special occasion. But drinking the night before his flight back was a recipe for disaster. "How about we just sit together? I still can't drink, but I'll have some tea."

"I'll leave you two alone," Jason's mother said and retreated to the bedroom, clutching the phone in her hand. There was no doubt in Jason's mind: his mother was about to call everyone she knew to share the good news: her son was getting married.

PART

Three

Thirty-One

BLINKING in the bright daylight as he stumbled out of the plane, Jason landed in DC hungover and with a headache. Thankfully, not jet lagged, having slept almost the entire flight back to Washington. His father had managed to convince him to have soju together, a decision Jason didn't regret. This was a special occasion, and spending time with his father was worth the inconvenience.

Two days later, Jason was almost back to normal. That's when he invited Kiana to come over, eager to share the details of his trip in person.

"Congratulations!" His friend said as soon as she walked through the door. "Tell me, how did it go? How did you do it?"

"Here it is on video." Jason handed his phone to Kiana, as he flipped to Yuna's Instagram page.

"Oh wow, so Instagram official then! You don't look nervous at all," Kiana pointed out after watching the clip. "And I love the snow in the background. It looks like a fairy tale setting."

"That's the second time I asked her." Jason chuckled. "Yuna wanted to do it for her Instagram."

"Oh, no way! So, she made you do another proposal? I think she just wanted you ask her to marry her twice."

"Ha, you might be right." A fond smile crossed Jason's lips. Everything Yuna did was lovely and Jason couldn't wait to marry her.

"By the way, we had a great time here. I really think Percy's an exceptional cat. She's so sweet, Jason."

"Oh, yeah?"

"Yes, like this one day I had a really bad migraine, and Percy came over and lay next to me, and then she actually moved on top of the couch next to my head. I think she actually cured me."

"Really? You believe in that stuff?"

"That cats have healing abilities? Of course I do." Kiana kneeled on the floor, and Percy approached her, purring loudly. "Percy is a sweet girl."

"By the way, the wedding is in June. I don't have the exact date yet. Yuna's family is checking out a few hotels, and we'll decide on the date after that."

"That's so exciting, Jason. I wish I could be there." Kiana looked up at him. She looked paler than usual, but Jason wrote it off as just the lighting.

"Why don't you come?" Jason said. In his head, he'd been going over the list of people he'd invite to the wedding: his cousin Dave of course, perhaps Hyun-woo, and friends from university, podiatry school, taekwondo. He wasn't sure about Kiana, mostly because of how Yuna had reacted to the mention of his friend, but now that he'd said it out loud, the idea of having Kiana at his wedding seemed natural and logical.

"Me? Are you serious? You're inviting me to your wedding?" Kiana got up to walk over to him.

"Yes, of course. We're good friends now. I'd love for you to come."

"But it won't be weird?" She tucked her hair behind

her ear.

"Of course not. As long as you and I don't think it's weird. And that way Yuna can meet you in person, and she'll know someone other than me when she moves here," Jason said with conviction.

"Very true! Sounds good to me. I'd love to come to your wedding." Kiana smiled. "Who knew when I'd agreed to take care of Percy last summer that I'd meet you and get invited to a wedding in Korea! Life is so strange, isn't it?"

"Definitely. And here I am, a cat owner." Jason gave Percy a fond look. "I mean, Charlie is never coming back, is she?"

"I don't think she is, not before next summer," Kiana sighed. "Her dad is actually doing better, but she's extended this sublet and she really likes it out in L.A."

"I've never been there," Jason said.

"Me neither. Though Charlie invited me to come, like, a hundred times. But there's always something, and L.A. seems so stressful."

"Talk about stressful. I gotta figure out the presents for the family."

"More presents?" Kiana raised her eyebrows. "You've got to be joking, Jason. You just took two suitcases of presents over to Korea."

"Yes, well, so, in Korea, we have this tradition. We exchange gifts before the wedding. The families of the bride and the groom."

"Gifts for the family? For the in-laws?"

"Yes, it's very important. We just had the 'sit-down', after I proposed, and we agreed on the gifts."

"So the gifts aren't a surprise?"

"No, no, the value is related to the value of the house." Jason started to explain what his mother had told him, but immediately got confused. "Or, what I bring to the table. The groom, that is, the value of what the groom provides, and then there's a percentage that's applied to the value of the gifts. Or something like that. But regardless, it's a ton of money. The gifts are expensive."

"That's crazy, so that's on top of what you'll be spending on the wedding? Plus, what you've already spent on the ring?" Kiana's forehead creased with worry.

"Yep. But it's worth it."

"That's insane. If I'd known that, I wouldn't have suggested Tiffany's. I would have taken you to, like, Kay Jewelers."

"I'm glad I got the ring at Tiffany's, by the way. Thank you for the suggestion. It was a hit. And she loved the box. Posted it on her Instagram right away."

"I see. Well, I've also got news. Though not as awesome as your wedding."

"Really? What is it? Did you meet someone?"

"Nope! But I've got a new dating method I've started applying. And it's supposed to be the cure for all the losers out there, and to even get rid of those who're out there during cuffing season."

"Oh yeah? What is it?"

"It's called the 'Drain the Bucket Dating Method.'"

"What?" Jason laughed. "This can't be for real, can it?"

"It's definitely for real. The idea is that most of the pool of men out there is pretty much trash. Which, of course, I've experienced firsthand. So, you need to drain the bucket to find your drop. Like 'drop in the bucket'. Get it?" Kiana stared at Jason expectantly.

"Who comes up with this stuff? So how do you drain the bucket?"

"Basically, you block all the men on the apps without giving them a second chance. And to determine the losers, you read and review their profiles carefully. And if they're not respectful, if they use weird language, if they're overly sexual, boom, they're blocked. And there are these success stories, Jason. Women, even older than me, are applying this method, and they're meeting really nice guys. They'll post stuff like 'I've met my drop in the bucket,' 'I think I've found my dropman.'" Kiana's eyes lit up. "It's so cute!"

"I think the filtering thing sounds good, get rid of anyone who doesn't meet your standards straight away. You deserve someone special."

"Thanks!" Kiana crossed her arms.

"If there's anything you need me to do, let me know. I'll help you drain the bucket, or whatever, fill it up if need be. And by the way, I got in touch with Audrey Simmons, like we agreed." Jason rushed to change the subject. Kiana's irritability when it came to discussing dating lately was palpable, and contrasted sharply with his own happy love life.

"Great." Kiana straightened up. "I've got all the materials ready. I even printed things about Mary Ward for her. Mary Invernizzi, rather, so that Audrey could look at it." Kiana brushed her hair back. "I mean, older people like printed things, so Audrey would probably prefer that."

"Thank you. I am sure Audrey will be very happy."

"Isn't it weird that Audrey still refuses to come to Arlington?" Jason said as Kiana got into his car, the pair heading for the Silver Line Diner. His friend was holding a thick manila folder, which she placed carefully on her lap, with the printed documents ready for Audrey's examination.

"I know, it's because of trauma. But it's been fifty years. Just think." Kiana snapped the seatbelt on. "But at least the roads will be empty, no traffic this time of year."

Audrey was already waiting for them when they entered the diner. She'd picked the same booth where they'd sat the first time, only now Audrey was the one facing the entrance. As Jason and Kiana approached, they saw Audrey holding up the menu, moving her finger, as if trying to memorize the items.

"Oh, hello," Audrey said to the two of them. "I got here a little early, my husband, James, dropped me off." She smiled awkwardly and placed the menu down.

"Hi," Jason said, then added, "Merry Christmas."

"Merry Christmas," Kiana repeated. "It's great to see you again." As Kiana placed the folder on the table, Audrey gasped.

"So, this is it?" She looked up at Kiana.

"Yes," Kiana took a seat across from Audrey, closer to the window. Jason squeezed into the booth next to his friend. "So, are you ready?" Kiana opened the folder.

"I am," Audrey said, her voice shaky. "I must apologize, this time of year is tough for me. I still think about Anton every Christmas. I even told James, you know, I'd mentioned your investigation to him, though, of course, not all the details. He's a little worried about me. I'll need to text him once we're done."

"I'm sorry," Kiana said softly. Jason stayed quiet, waiting for Audrey to continue. He knew at moments like this, when people spoke of grief and pain, sometimes the best thing was to say absolutely nothing.

Audrey took a sip of her water, then drawing a sharp breath, turned to Kiana. "But please, continue. I know you've invested so much time to help me, and I appreciate it."

"Here is the latest information about Mary Ward. I got great help tracking her down."

"Are you sure it's her? The name is so common, I just didn't think it was possible to find her." Audrey's hand trembled slightly, as she shuffled the saltshaker to the window and back.

"Yes, it's definitely her. Everything checks out," Kiana said. "We were able to find her because of her father. His name was mentioned in one of the FBI documents, and he was affiliated with the church that Anton was frequenting."

"Oh, right." Audrey averted her eyes. "I should have thought of that."

"So, with the father's name, we were able to track her down through Ancestry.com. Their family tree was public, so it was relatively easy to do so with a paid subscription. And here is a print-out of the tree. As you can see, Mary Ward got married when she was twenty-two." Kiana pushed the piece of paper across the table to Audrey. "She changed her maiden name to Invernizzi."

"I see. Twenty-two, that's how old I was when Anton died." Tears welled up in Audrey's eyes. "You know, I haven't even told my husband the full story, not until very recently. I hid it until that awful documentary came out. Why did they have to drag Anton's name through the mud? He was just a kid. Just a young man, really. And so handsome, in his prime."

"Audrey, Mrs. Simmons," Jason said, "please, it's okay. We'll help you."

"I bet that woman, that Mary Ward, I bet she didn't even care about him." Audrey pressed a napkin to her eyes to wipe her tears. "She wasn't his fiancée, there was no way that could have been the truth. She lied, they all lied!"

"But now, you'll get to find out the truth," Kiana said. "Here's her information. She lives in L.A., still in the same area. And we even got her photos."

"How?"

"She has three children, and one of them is very active on Facebook. Lindsay Invernizzi." Kiana pushed another stack of papers towards Audrey. "All of her posts are public, and she seems to be close to her mother."

"So, this is her?" Audrey took the papers and examined them. The photos showed an older woman with cropped blonde hair, dressed in a beige dress and a matching cardigan, sitting near a fireplace, with three young children next to her. The woman's face was wide-set, with prominent cheekbones. She had bright blue eyes and was smiling broadly, revealing very white teeth. Audrey ran her finger along the woman's face, her lips curving down in distaste.

"Yes, that's her. Here is one more." Kiana moved another print-out on top of the pile. "This one is from Thanksgiving this year, I'm guessing." It showed the same woman with a tall, imposing man standing next to her, and the same three kids next to them. "I guess they like to go out to eat," Kiana noted, pointing to the Maggiano's logo displayed behind them.

"She looks happy," Audrey said gingerly. "And fulfilled. It looks like she's had a good life."

Kiana and Jason exchanged glances.

"Well, we don't really know what kind of life she's had. But she does seem to be close to her daughter and grandkids. Which is how we got all these photos," Kiana said quietly as she surveyed Audrey.

The slight furrow of Kiana's eyebrows revealed to Jason her unease. Kiana's facial expressions were too easy to read, and he started to worry she might throw Audrey off.

"It's interesting what you can find on social media," Jason said and immediately remembered Yuna and her posts. "I should remind my fiancée to be more careful."

"Fiancée? You have a fiancée?" Audrey pounced on the word.

"Yes, I just got engaged. In Korea," Jason said with pride in his voice. "Her name is Yuna. We'll be getting married in June."

"In Korea?" Audrey's small eyes gave Jason a careful look, then settled on Kiana. "And you know about this?"

"Of course," Kiana responded eagerly. "Jason and I are close friends. We picked out the ring together, for Yuna."

"Yes, Kiana will be coming to my wedding in Korea."

"I see." Audrey crinkled her nose. "I, I'm sorry, I just assumed the two of you, well, that maybe there was something. I guess one can never assume anything, least of all me." She pursed her lips.

"Oh, well, we do get along really well," Kiana said. "It's okay. My mom also thought maybe we had something going on. But being friends means so much to us, right, Jason?" Kiana looked over to her left, where Jason was sitting.

"Yes, absolutely!" Jason nodded. "Besides, in my culture, it's really important to marry a Korean. Makes so many things easier."

"Like what?" Audrey gave him a sad smile. "I'm just curious. Because I always thought, but, of course, maybe I'm just too idealistic." She crumpled up her napkin. "I always thought it didn't matter where the person came from. What mattered was love. Pure and simple. And you can't force love. You see, I fell in love with Anton, a defector from the USSR. You know what the USSR was back then? Worse than Russia is now. It was a country that wanted to annihilate ours. The villain. And yet, there I was. In love. I would have given anything for my Anton. Anything."

Silence fell over the table. Neither Kiana nor Jason responded to her words. Jason was trying to come up with a tactful way to explain to Audrey how little she understood of the Korean way of life, and how big the pressures were on him from his family, and how complicated finding a suitable match was in America.

He thought of telling Audrey about Gwen, and his naïve relationship that had ultimately broken his heart and had taught him the ways of the world.

Kiana was the first to break the silence.

"I have a few other photos of Mary, if you'd like to see them. And here is her contact information. I've got her address and also a few numbers. I think she's still got a landline, so this is the number."

"You have all that?" Audrey noticeably paled.

"Yes, of course. I've prepared everything for you."

"So, I can call her?"

"Yes, or email her. I've got her email as well. Email might be a good idea, to prepare her."

"Email?" Audrey blinked fast.

"Yes. At first, I thought you could reach out to her through Facebook, but then she might not even see the message unless you try to add her as a friend."

"I've got Facebook," Audrey said, and immediately clasped her heart. "Oh, this is a lot. Just a lot."

"I'm sorry. Would you like some more water?" Kiana asked, noting Audrey's empty glass, and gestured for the waitress to come over. The woman moved languidly and disappeared once Kiana asked for three waters. The waitress had the demeanor of a person who had much better things to do, but by some strange twist of fate, had to work at the Silver Line Diner on this late December morning.

"Thank you, sorry, I got so emotional," Audrey said, once the waitress reappeared with three large glasses of water, ice piled high in each one.

"My mom hates ice," Kiana noted, sipping her water. "She literally would make the waitress go back and bring her water without the ice. It's wild."

"My mom hates ice, too," Jason remembered suddenly. They rarely went out to eat in America, but when they did, his mom would never drink her water if there was even a tiny sliver of ice in it.

"Why is that?" Kiana asked. "I always thought it was a Russian thing. I mean, Russians are weird."

As she said this, Audrey noticeably tensed.

"It's because of digestion. You shouldn't put anything colder than room temperature into your body, because cold things take longer to digest," Jason said.

"Oh, that actually makes sense."

"Anton loved ice cream," Audrey noted solemnly. "He told me he'd never tried it as a child, and he could eat a whole bucket of ice cream here. He loved it. Especially chocolate."

"They definitely had ice cream in Russia," Kiana protested. "My mom told me. Even in the winter, they'd eat it. She had a whole explanation of how eating ice cream outside in the cold was fine, but not having ice in your water. But anyway, would you like to take this?" She put the papers back into the folder and closed it shut, sliding the documents across the table towards Audrey.

"I, I don't know," Audrey mumbled, averting her eyes. "Look, I really appreciate what you did, I really do. But seeing this woman, the woman who'd stolen my Anton from me, I don't think I can face her. I feel like it will destroy my memory of Anton. It's not what he would have wanted."

"You mean you won't contact her?" Kiana yelped. "At all?"

"I'm sorry." Audrey scratched her chin. "I'm just not sure it makes sense. I'm not ready. I need to tell James, he'll come get me now." Audrey reached into her purse and pulled out her mobile.

"But don't you want to know the truth?" Kiana pushed.

"Kiana," Jason said, and put his hand over hers in a gesture that was at once protective and signaling. "Let's talk later."

"But I've done all this work," Kiana said, pulling her hand out. "I was trying to help you."

"I'm grateful," Audrey said, looking up from her phone. "But I shouldn't have asked. I don't know what came over me. I'm not brave, you see. I'm just a regular person. And what would I even say to her? How would I even approach her? She might ridicule me for bringing up something that happened fifty years ago."

"Audrey, please, maybe you'll reconsider?" Jason said.

"You've mentioned how important this is to you. How much you care about Anton."

"I have thought about it since our last meeting. Every single day. I prayed you wouldn't find Mary. But I guess God doesn't listen to my prayers, not when they have to do with Anton." Audrey gave a rueful smile.

"I see. Well, if that's the case, maybe we should just make the best of it?" Jason said. "Why don't we order something? Would you like something to eat, Audrey?"

"Sure, why not. I'll just call James later. Let's place an order," Audrey said, noticeably perking up, now that the conversation had moved on.

"What would you like?" Jason turned to Kiana and tried to indicate with his eyes for her to snap out of her irritation. He could read her like an open book.

"Umm, let me take a look at the menu," Kiana said, rolling her eyes at Jason.

———

"Audrey, what if we were the ones to reach out to Mary?" Jason asked when they were waiting for their food to arrive.

"You? Both of you?"

"Yes, Kiana and I."

"You want to do that?" Audrey looked at each of them. Jason held the woman's gaze and hoped Kiana played along and didn't indicate her surprise at his suggestion. The idea had just occurred to him, and now he wondered why he hadn't thought of it sooner.

Of course, it should be someone else contacting Mary Ward. Of course, the whole situation is way too sensitive for Audrey. That should have been obvious from the start.

"I suppose it would be alright," Audrey said. She had straightened her shoulders and stopped fumbling with the silverware, which, Jason had realized, she'd been doing for several minutes, moving the knife and the fork from one side of the table to the other.

"Very well, then. We'll contact Mary on our own then."

"And then you'll just let me know what you find out? Is that right?"

Kiana gave him a curious look.

"Yes." Jason nodded.

Audrey had just finished eating her pie, when her phone pinged.

"It's James," she announced, opening the text message. "He's already arrived, I should go." She hastily stuffed her phone into her purse. "I'm sorry. I didn't realize he'd come back for me so soon. He told me he'd be over at Home Depot, but I guess he mustn't have found what he was looking for. I don't want to leave him waiting." She rose from her seat.

"Bye, Audrey," Jason and Kiana said in unison, then immediately yelled "Jjijjibbong" and "Jinx."

"Bye, you two," Audrey darted her eyes from Jason to Kiana, and took her exit, shaking her head.

CHAPTER

Thirty-Two

"WHY DID YOU PROMISE HER THAT?" Kiana asked, moving to a seat across from Jason. "It doesn't even sound like Audrey wants any real answers. Why should I be the one contacting Mary Invernizzi?"

"She does, couldn't you tell? She's just afraid to learn the truth."

"This is the problem with women." Kiana huffed. "This guy was clearly two-timing her, cheating on her with another girl, but Audrey doesn't want to know the truth. She's still pretending like Anton was this *perfect* man."

"If she didn't want to know the truth, she wouldn't have asked us to find Mary Ward, right?" Jason said.

"But the second we found Mary, she got scared. She told us herself she didn't want us to find the other woman. Was praying for us not to locate her. Because Mary Ward would compromise the memory of sweet Anton-the-innocent." Her brow furrowed, Kiana stared at Jason.

"So you don't want to contact Mary?"

"Not really. What would be the point?" Kiana threw her hands up in frustration. "No one needs this information. I spent all this time looking for her, reaching out to the group for help, and I now feel ridiculous. I should have said 'no' from the start. I've gotten my mom involved, thinking we could give this woman closure. Help her heal from trauma. But she doesn't want to heal. She just wants to keep living a lie."

"Kiana, please. I don't think it's like that."

"It *is* like that. It's all the women in the group. The wives. They don't want to know. They just pretend their husbands aren't actually cheating. And if they do cheat, it's the other woman's fault. Women are terrible to each other. Just terrible. Did you see how Audrey looked at Mary's photos? Like the other woman was the epitome of evil." Kiana bit her lip. "Anyway, I need to use the restroom." Abruptly, she rose from her seat, and walked off.

Jason had never seen Kiana communicate her opinions with such conviction. This was a new side of her, and it made him nervous. More than anything, Jason hated open confrontations. When he was young and their family prepared to move to America, his parents often argued. The subject was almost always about money. His mother accused his father of not caring enough for the family to keep his job after the Asian Financial Crisis had hit. It didn't matter that Korea's economy had tanked, that many families all around them experienced unprecedented economic hardship. Jason's mother blamed their financial problems on her husband.

"If you'd only done your part, been more pleasant to the big bosses," Jason's mother hissed back then. "You could have kept your job. You know how it is. They didn't fire everyone, did they? Only the likes of you, the ones who couldn't keep their mouths shut."

"Listen, I don't kiss up to people," Jason's father would respond. "You know I don't do that."

"Well, look how far your principles got you. Look where we are now. We're penniless. And no savings either. We've got to move all across the world now to America, so that Jun could have a chance. We're pretty much finished in Korea."

"At least we've got options. And maybe Korea isn't the right place for Jun anyway, he's way too straightforward."

"That's because he's your son. Not a clever boy who respects hierarchy and knows to be careful around the higher-ups."

Jason's parents never raised their voices, but that didn't make their arguments any less terrifying. He wondered who was right, his father, who maintained the belief that morality would ultimately prevail, or his mother, who wanted survival and money at any cost. The arguments about money got worse in America, and each time Jason heard his parents bickering, he blamed himself. After all, he'd heard his mother mention the move to America had been motivated by his future, and nothing else. Leaving for college had given Jason an escape, and he clutched onto it, embracing independence at just nineteen.

When, three years later, his parents' inheritance following his uncle's death prompted their move back to Korea, part of the reason Jason stayed behind was to avoid being around them and their arguments.

Now, waiting for Kiana to come back, Jason was paralyzed. A familiar feeling of panic spread through his body, his hands jittering slightly. She appeared suddenly, standing next to him.

"Ready?" she asked.

"Yes," Jason rose from his seat, struggling for words, and followed her out of the diner.

It wasn't until after they'd gotten into his car, that he forced himself to speak.

"Listen, let's just forget the whole thing," he muttered, snapping his seatbelt on. "I don't want to fight. It's not worth it."

"I'm not fighting." Kiana turned to face him with surprise.

"I'm just kind of frustrated, that's all. Like the whole thing, it's as if I've got nothing better to do than to chase down some woman from Audrey's past."

"Kiana, that's not at all how–"

"Well, that's how I feel, you know. Like basically, you're about to get married and have this wonderful life. Audrey also has this great life if she could just let go of the past. Everyone is so worried about hurting her feelings. But everyone assumes I've got nothing else to do, because I'm single. Charlie has moved away, you might move too if Yuna hates it here, and then I might not even get to see Percy," Kiana huffed. "At least, at the rate things are going. Wouldn't you give up if you were in my place?"

"I don't know," Jason spoke carefully. The jitter in his hands had subsided. He paused, putting the car in 'drive'. "Why don't we just put the whole thing on hold?"

"Can we do that?" Kiana asked, her voice upbeat.

"I don't see why not." They were now standing at the red light, which, Jason remembered, took forever to turn green.

He turned to surreptitiously survey Kiana's face and was pacified to see her expression change to normal. He let out a sigh of relief.

The light turned green, and he took his foot off the brake.

CHAPTER
Thirty-Three

JASON SNAPPED a photo of Percy and hit 'send'. Three dots appeared, and his heart leaped. A response arrived in seconds. Jason opened Kiana's message.

Cute.

He stared at the screen for a moment, expecting something else. But to no avail. With a sigh, he pulled on his running shoes and headed for Roosevelt Island.

This was the longest the two of them had gone without communicating since they first met each other in July. Kiana no longer came by to have coffee with Jason on Saturday mornings after her workout, and didn't ask him about wedding preparations.

At first, Jason was concerned, but he knew that in America, people gave each other space, and no one seemed to think twice about it. The memory of the last time Kiana had disappeared flashed in his mind, but something told Jason things were different now. Kiana wasn't in trouble. She was simply busy doing something else.

Jason's attention had almost entirely turned to Yuna and

the upcoming nuptials. The wedding date was set for June 15th, 2023. It would be on Thursday, as a compromise: made more affordable because of the weekday, but to be set at the glamorous Shilla hotel, which was legendary in Korea. It was named after the ancient Shilla dynasty and established over the historic state guesthouse site. Yuna and Jason's wedding would take place in the grand ballroom, which could accommodate 300 guests.

The negotiations over the wedding and its location had been handled by their parents, and the two families informed Jason and Yuna only after reaching an agreement. Yuna would apply for her fiancée visa at the American embassy in Seoul the day after the wedding, and then join Jason in America.

———

Percy's tail flicked into the video, as she jumped onto the couch back, appearing right behind Jason's head. He'd just settled into a call with Yuna.

"Is that the cat?" His fiancée asked unnecessarily.

"Percy, say hi to Yuna." Jason reached out to nudge her closer. "I am planning on extending the lease on the apartment."

"How long is the lease for?" Yuna asked, her voice suddenly tense.

"If I renew for a year, I get a better rate," Jason said. "I got a good deal when I moved in, so that's why I got a two-bedroom apartment, but that was still during Covid, and no one wanted to live in apartment buildings. But now, rents are crazy expensive. They're raising them ten percent each year. But they are offering me a discount if I renew early."

"Well, maybe we can find a place together," Yuna said. "So that it's special. I'd like to live in a place that I selected."

"Sure," Jason, feeling the tips of his fingers grow cold. He didn't want to confront Yuna, but moving out would complicate things. He knew it would be extremely challenging to find a place as convenient to the metro, with the same amenities as his current apartment. Not to mention the affordability.

"You don't sound too happy about it," Yuna said. "But I get it, change is hard, but it'll be so worth it. And we'll be together. I'll be there to support you, Jamie." Since the proposal, Yuna had started using the name Jamie, insisting it suited Jason better, though acknowledging it would take Jason some time to get used to his new name.

"Alright, alright," Jason said, eager to pacify his future wife.

"You aren't getting cold feet, are you?" Yuna asked.

Percy arched her back and jumped off the couch. "No, of course not." Jason chuckled. "No way you're getting rid of me that easily."

Percy let out a loud meow and walked over to her bowl. When Jason didn't immediately react, she meowed again, louder now, and looked at him expectantly.

"Listen, I've gotta go feed Percy," Jason said. "Can I call you right back?"

"You're literally going to hang up on me because of a cat?"

"Well, we can speak, but I've gotta feed her. She's hungry. Let me just turn the camera off."

"She's manipulating you, Jason," Yuna said. "You really shouldn't fall for that. You're just too nice and you assume everyone has good intentions."

'She's a cat, Yuna."

He walked over to the pantry and got out a can of wet food and cracked it open. Jason ran his hand between Percy's ears, as the cat ate hungrily.

"Hopeless." Yuna let out a sigh. "Oh, by the way," she said, the pitch of her voice much higher than usual, "I wanted to ask. Is the cat going back to her owner anytime soon?"

"Umm." Jason felt his cheeks flush red, and was grateful the conversation wasn't on video. "I'm not sure what's going on with her owner, really. She has a sublet staying in the apartment, and I guess the earliest she'd be back in DC would be in August."

"So, if I move to DC in July, and we move out, what'll happen to the cat?" Yuna asked, maintaining the same high pitch in her voice.

"Well, I was actually hoping to keep Percy. Didn't you mention you thought cats were cute?" Jason said, recalling Yuna's gushing over Percy when they were in New York.

"I mean, I don't really mind cats," his fiancée uttered. "But I'm going to be settling in a new country. I'm not sure taking care of a cat is what I want to be dealing with."

"I wouldn't expect you to take care of Percy," Jason countered.

"Jamie, this cat literally just interrupted our call. And I have all these friends who have dogs. All they do is take care of their dogs. I want us to have a real marriage. Not some kind of weird relationship where we are constantly distracted by things. Don't you see? I love you so much."

"I love you, too," Jason said. He felt a dull headache coming on, and remembered he hadn't made his morning espresso yet. "Yuna, let's talk later? I'll call you tomorrow morning your time, alright?"

"Love you," Yuna said and made kissing noises through the phone.

Jason hung up without reciprocating. He was in a bad mood, and he didn't know why. Usually, conversations with Yuna made his day, but he took a look at Percy and frowned. He had not thought of the consequences of keeping her. Instead, had got the impression keeping the cat, and an adorable one at that, would be fine with his new wife, who hadn't, until now, expressed any preference otherwise. Now,

Jason blamed himself for not discussing it further with Yuna, for not preparing her, and for assuming she would accommodate his pet.

Of course, I get it, she's never had cats, Jason thought, squatting next to Percy and running his hand through Percy's soft fur. *This is all my fault. What do I do with you, little girl?*

He got up, and immediately pain shot through his temple. Jason walked to the espresso machine, reached into his cabinet and only then realized he was out of espresso grounds. He stared at the empty container in resignation.

Never before had he run out. He'd always been so careful to keep his pantry stocked, but in the last month, he'd been too busy with the wedding to pay attention. Then Jason remembered how Kiana had brought him over espresso grounds a few times. How, during their weekly tradition to drink espresso together on Saturday mornings, she'd made sure to supply the coffee grounds after finding out his favorite brand, and he groaned. The last thing Jason wanted to do was to go outside, but he needed his caffeine fix.

Jason got dressed, put on his jacket and wrapped himself in a thick scarf. It was his second winter in DC, and he'd realized the DC winters were even worse than its summers. It was the humidity that made the temperature feel so much worse.

DC had been built on a swamp, Jason had read somewhere, but that explanation did little to alleviate his suffering. After zipping up his jacket, Jason checked himself in the mirror. The weather app said it was 20F outside, which in DC would feel like 10F, and he reached for a hat, put it on, then pulled it off after glancing one more time in the mirror.

Jason walked to the elevators. He pressed the button and waited. The elevator took an unusually long time. The doors opened and he was about to step inside, when he saw Kiana. Her cheeks were flushed red, and she had a headband on, as if she'd just come from the gym.

"Hey," Jason said, stepping back.

"Hi!" Kiana said brightly. She looked happy, genuinely at peace with the world. This was markedly different from the way she looked the last time they'd seen each other.

"What are you doing here?"

"I've gotta check on Charlie's apartment," Kiana said. "The subletter hasn't paid the January rent, it's kinda weird, so Charlie is worried something's up. Have you seen anyone going in and out of 805, by the way?"

"Not really," Jason said. His headache was getting worse, and now it felt like it was drilling into his temple. "Umm, listen, I really need some caffeine," he mumbled. "Do you want to come with me? It's good to see you, by the way."

"Right now? But I was just about to check out Charlie's place."

"Come on, I'll help you do it later," Jason said. "Please?"

"Haven't you had your espresso yet?" Kiana gave him a concerned look.

"Nope. I forgot to make one this morning and then realized I was out of espresso grounds, so gotta go buy one, like, right now. Gotta get my fix."

"Sorry. Alright, let's go," Kiana scoffed, pulling out a hat out of her pocket. She put it on and, turning to Jason, asked, "Where's your hat, Jason? It's freezing out."

"I'm not a hat person," Jason said, pressing the elevator button.

"That's ridiculous. And you're a doctor, of all people, you should know it's important to wear hats. We lose most of the heat through the head," Kiana said, but Jason interrupted her.

"Where have you been? Were you ever going to call?"

"I can ask you the same thing." Kiana shrugged. "I guess I was just busy. Lots of stuff going on at work. We've got the whole 'return to office' stuff happening, all these companies trying to get their employees to show up, but no one wants to do that. Everyone loves working from home. So much drama."

"I know. Well, I never got to work from home." Jason laughed. "Not sure how it would even work."

"You were on the frontlines, of course," Kiana said, as they exited the elevator. "I worked from home for three months, and that was about it. In June 2020 we went back, because it's corporate real estate. Companies aren't just going to justify paying that kind of money if their buildings sit empty. And we can't exactly promote real estate while sitting at home, right?"

They walked out, the cold air hitting them at once.

"Brutal, isn't it?" Jason tugged at his sleeves in a vain attempt to pull them over his hands to protect them from the freezing air.

"I don't mind the cold," Kiana said. "Just gotta dress for the weather." She zipped up her jacket and pulled on the hood over her hat, so that it fell right over her forehead.

"That's because you're Russian."

"Ha, I've never heard that joke before." Kiana laughed. "Let's run. We're about to walk through the wind tunnel." As she said this, a blast of cold air hit them so hard, Kiana cried out and Jason felt as if it was about to burn his face. "Ahh!" Kiana grabbed his hand, and they ran. They crossed the parking lot, then the Plaza and within seconds were on the other side of Clarendon Boulevard, running towards the coffee shop closest to Jason's apartment building. Without discussing it, the two of them were heading to the same destination, as if a telepathic force had connected them and been established without their knowledge.

"This is crazy!" Kiana yelped, jerking the coffee shop door open.

"It is!" Jason laughed, rushing after her inside.

The cold air, the short run with Kiana, felt so exhilarating, that Jason had almost forgotten about his headache and caffeine deprivation.

The café, despite it being Saturday, was nearly empty. An aloof-looking barista greeted them, and they placed their orders: Jason, a double espresso, and Kiana, an herbal tea. When Jason gave her a strange look, she shrugged and said, "I'm cutting out caffeine. And sugar."

"Why?"

"Caffeine was making me very jittery. So, I decided to stop. And sugar's just evil."

"Stop, like, completely?"

"Yep, I've weaned myself off caffeine. It was my New Year's resolution. And with sugar, it's actually a lack of other nutrients if you're craving it. So I've been taking supplements."

"You never told me that." Jason looked at Kiana in surprise.

"I decided to do it right after that Silver Line Diner visit. To take control of my life and to get healthy."

"Good for you."

"Thank you. It takes three weeks to turn something into a habit, and it was exactly three weeks ago that I started," Kiana said proudly. "I'm off caffeine, almost no added sugar, and I'm exercising five times a week, too."

"Great job. You look really good," Jason said and noticed Kiana's cheeks, already flushed from the cold, were now a deep shade of crimson.

"Thanks." Kiana smiled, her eyes sparkling. "I've been applying the 'drain the bucket' theory in dating, too," she said, lowering her voice. "It's been working!"

"Really?"

"Yes. I've been blocking guys left and right. Not giving them a second chance, like I used to. There's a whole language filter in the method, so I've been using that, too. If the guys use directives, I block them right away. Or if there's the 'I'm the prize' language."

"What does that mean?"

"So, if a guy has a dating profile where he's basically bragging about himself, then I just block him and move on."

"So, has anyone met the criteria?" Jason asked, ignoring the signs of a headache that had found its way back now that he was indoors. "I mean, with the blocking and everything."

"So far, just one guy. He seems very sweet. Though, I gotta say, he's really not my type."

"But you like him, right?"

"Well, we haven't met in person yet," Kiana said. "I've been taking it slowly, that's also what the method recommends, and I'm waiting for him to make the first move. But he hasn't so far."

"I see," Jason said, deciding not to press the issue.

"But in the 'drain the bucket' method, the women say it takes time to like someone. Most of the success stories say they all didn't feel much attraction to their 'drops'. Not right away. But it came once they got to know them as actual people. And that basically, the immediate attraction is just trauma. Trauma makes us like men that are bad for us."

"Really?" Jason took a sip of his espresso. Relief flooded his body, as the pulsing in his temple subsided. "I don't think I could wean myself off caffeine," he said, savoring the beverage.

"You're an addict. I love my tea now." Kiana stirred the cup with the orange liquid in it. "Turmeric is a fantastic antioxidant." She took a sip, immediately wrinkling her nose. "Umm, it's a little bitter, but it's really good for you."

"Don't you want to have it with honey or something?"

"No, I'm good. How's the wedding planning going?"

"We've set the date, June 15th," Jason said. "Will you come?"

"Yes, absolutely. I'll get my ticket soon. I've already told my boss I'll be taking time off in June, but didn't tell him exactly the date. He said he's fine with it, and he suggested I check out some buildings in Seoul." Catching Jason's curious look, Kiana responded, "he was joking, of course."

"Oh, I hope so."

"So, are you ready? When will Yuna move here?"

"Right after the wedding." Jason swallowed hard. "Listen, I gotta ask you something."

"What is it?"

"It's about Percy." Jason averted his eyes. "Yuna doesn't want her to stay."

"What?" Kiana stared at Jason. "But you love Percy. Have you told her that? Wait, is she allergic to cats?"

"No. She just said, she wants to focus on our relationship."

"What does that mean?"

"I'm not sure, exactly. I guess she doesn't want a cat around?"

"Did you tell her you've always wanted a cat? And how is Percy is short for Persimmon? And how you've bonded with her already?"

"I did." Jason confirmed, though he no longer remembered what exactly he'd told Yuna about Percy. All of it had blurred together, and the only thing that remained was a sense of loss. A sense of something terrible that would happen once he gave Percy away. "I don't know what to do," he said, his voice nearly a whisper. "I feel ridiculous even questioning this. A marriage is much more important than a cat. Right?"

"You should just talk to Yuna. Explain to her how important Percy is to you. And I'm sure once they meet, she'll fall in love with the cat, too. Percy is impossible not to love."

"And what if it doesn't happen? Yuna actually asked me to give Percy back."

"Well, if that happens, I guess you've got to see what kind of person Yuna actually is." Kiana took another sip of her tea.

"What are you saying?"

"I'm saying, maybe you should get to know her more before getting married."

"How? I mean, we're compatible, the algorithm says we're the *perfect* fit. And our parents, our dads, they worked for the same company. Even in terms of background, it's all a match."

"So, if there's nothing that bothers you, just give away Percy and make Yuna happy." Kiana narrowed her eyes. "But I'll tell you, as someone who's been married and divorced, if you accept being treated like this now, it's not going to get better. There are always signs we choose to ignore."

"Kiana, come on," Jason pleaded.

"A woman who would force you to abandon a pet can't be a good person. You've gotta know that, right?"

"Yes, you're right." Jason drew a sharp breath, and then mentioned something else he'd been too embarrassed to bring up to anyone else. "Yuna also got this idea I should change my name."

"What?" Kiana nearly jumped out of her seat. A bit of the turmeric tea spilled on the table, and she wiped it with a napkin.

"Yuna wants me to be a big-name doctor, and she thinks Jason Lee doesn't sound good. She wants me to change my name. To Jamie, like the guy from *Outlander*."

"Jason, that is the dumbest and the most offensive thing I've ever heard. When did she tell you that?"

"You mean the first time?"

"She's said it more than once?"

"Yeah. She's actually been calling me Jamie. So I'll get used to it."

"This is crazy. It's insanely rude, and also, who does she think she is?" Kiana's face took on the belligerent expression Jason remembered from their last meeting at the Silver Line Diner. He balked.

"Well, technically, Jason isn't my actual name. I chose it for myself, but my real name is Jun."

"You never told me that." Kiana crossed her arms.

"That's my Korean given name. But in America, I can't exactly be called Jun, so I picked Jason. So, in theory–"

"In theory, Yuna is out of line. You've been calling yourself Jason for over twenty years, right?"

"Right."

"You're a grown man, right?"

"Right."

"Tell her she can't call you some random name because of a TV show. That's ridiculous."

———

After sitting in the coffee shop with Kiana, Jason accompanied her to apartment 805. They knocked on the door together, waited for several minutes, knocked again. Finally, they were rewarded for their patience, when a sleepy-looking tiny blonde dressed in pajamas opened the door and, twisting her hair in a bun, asked them who they were.

"Jessica, I'm here to represent Charlotte, your landlord. She's been trying to get in touch with you," Kiana said.

"Oh, hi, I was traveling for the holidays," the blonde said. "I'll make sure to send her the money right away."

"Listen," Kiana said, "could you do it right now?"

"Right now?" The blonde ran her hand through her hair and let the bun out. "I can't, like, right this moment."

"That's what Charlotte asked. She told me to check on you and to tell you if you didn't do it, she will be filing an eviction notice."

"Oh, I mean, seriously?" The girl rolled her eyes, then, noticing Jason, said, "I've seen you somewhere. Alright, fine, I'll send the transfer right now." She reached for her phone and started clicking away.

"And also, Charlotte mentioned the February payment is due within the first five days of the month," Kiana said as she and Jason walked away from the apartment. There was no answer, except for the door to 805 slamming shut.

"So, do you want to come over? Say hi to Percy?"

"Just to say hi to Percy," Kiana agreed, smirking.

Both knew what this meant: whatever rift had formed between them after the diner incident had now closed.

WHAT KIANA POINTED out to Jason wasn't a surprise: deep-down he knew Yuna had crossed the line months ago. When they first saw each other in New York and she'd asked him to change his name. She didn't even suggest it, she'd almost demanded it.

Why did I ignore it? Why didn't I say something to her then?

But Jason knew the answer: he'd been too attracted to Yuna to care. He was tired of waiting, tired of being alone, he wanted to finally find the woman who would be his wife, and Yuna was perfect. Korean, but also with experience in America. A woman who was beautiful, cultured, well-mannered. Who spoke perfect English. On paper, Yuna was great. And in person, she was even better. So he chose to ignore a comment, which he wrote off as not serious.

Still, Kiana hinted at something ominous. Yuna's request to get rid of Percy meant there were potentially other character flaws, and now Jason paced his living room, thinking. *Is there a way to postpone the wedding? To get to know Yuna better?*

The wedding planning had gone too far. His parents were about to make a deposit on the rental of the Shilla Hotel ballroom. A rental, Jason knew, would cost them a hundred and twenty thousand dollars, once the total for the food, the flowers, and decorations was added.

What if Kiana is wrong? She didn't know the Korean culture. Yuna knew his real name couldn't have been Jason, which was something he'd never mentioned to Kiana.

He and Yuna shared a common culture. They would raise children together, speak Korean to them, feed them Korean food, teach them their culture and, most importantly, take them to Korea, where the kids would feel right at home.

Only the realization hit him: he, Jason Lee, Jun Lee, no longer felt at home in Korea. He remembered walking through his childhood neighborhood, feeling like an outsider.

Korea wasn't home. America was *his* home. The imperfect, strange country he'd come to love was now home. He looked Korean, he spoke Korean, but inside, his mentality was that of a different person. Unlike his parents, Jason could not move back to Korea and fit in there. He'd been gone for too long, had missed crucial parts of the Korean upbringing: had not served in the military. He could never practice his profession in Korea.

Jason sighed and sat down on his couch. He turned on a random episode of *Law & Order* to calm his nerves. In the middle of it, he sat upright, remembering his first date with Yuna. How she'd asked him about trauma, and they shared a moment.

Yuna told me that watching true crime and crime shows meant you'd grown up around arguments. Jason remembered the intense sense of connection he'd felt to her then. *She's probably just as traumatized as I am. I'm just being dramatic,* Jason reassured himself. *And Kiana hasn't ever met Yuna. I'm not going to implode my relationship and my future happiness for nothing.* Jason threw a guilty look at Percy and continued watching the show.

Two episodes later, and a bowl of ramen with kimchi

consumed in a hurry over the kitchen counter, Jason checked the time. It was seven pm, which meant it was nine in the morning in Korea, with the time difference being fourteen hours in the winter. Normally, Yuna liked to sleep in on Sundays, so Jason waited thirty minutes, then decided to call her anyway. Her voice was the only thing that could make him feel better. He needed to see her beautiful face. Her smile. Her lovely brown eyes. Jason's mood lifted in anticipation. He dialed her number. To his relief, seconds later, he heard Yuna's sleepy voice:

"Hey, Jamie."

"Hey, Yuna, can I ask you something?"

"Sure!" Yuna croaked. "What is it? I love you."

"I love you, too," Jason said. "Do you think you can call me Jason? Or Jun? I'm not sure I like Jamie."

"Oh, honey, come on? Jamie is cute."

"Please?"

"Alright, of course. It's not a big deal, honey."

"Thanks," Jason said, feeling reassured. "How are you?"

"Just waking up. I thought you'd call later."

"I just wanted to talk to you, that's all," Jason said. He realized he sounded needy and hated the feeling.

"Jamie, I mean, Jun," Yuna snickered, "I wanted to tell you something. Remember when we spoke about our finances at the sit-down, and we calculated everything. I realized we missed one thing."

"What thing? Is it a bag or something?"

"No, no, it's not that. I actually have this financial obligation. And I'll need to keep it once we're married," Yuna said. She'd switched on her camera, and Jason could see her face, still a little puffy from sleep, but beautiful. Her hair was down, and lay in thick locks on her shoulders. He couldn't wait to make her his wife.

"I miss you," Jason said. He wanted Yuna next to him. Wanted to make love to her.

"I miss you too," Yuna noted and blew him a kiss. "So, are you okay with the finances then?"

"What finances?" Jason asked, his mind not focused on the conversation.

"The obligation. It's not that big of a deal, but you know how I'm really close with my mom, right?"

"Sure."

"And my mom loves golf. I told you, right? She goes three times a year to Vietnam, and the golf courses, well, it's an expensive hobby. But it makes my mom really happy. So, my sister and I, it's not just me, you see, we both pay for my mom to golf."

"Alright," Jason frowned. "So how much is it? Like a couple of thousand a year?"

"Umm, well, I pay thirty percent of my salary right now," Yuna noted with a cute smile. "And I'm hoping to keep that, but to make it thirty percent of both of our salaries. So Mom could go to better resorts, you know?"

"Wait, what?" Jason stared at the screen, dumbstruck. "Thirty percent of my salary?"

"Well, it will be our money, right, honey?"

"But how are we supposed to live, Yuna?"

"I'll get a job right away, as soon as I'm in America. And then, I mean, my mom isn't asking for much, it's just a certain lifestyle she wants to maintain, Jason." Yuna pronounced his name bitterly, as if she were swearing.

"That doesn't make any sense," Jason said. "What if I say 'no'?"

"I guess it means you aren't serious about me." The corners of Yuna's mouth turned downward. "Aren't serious about us."

"You know I'm still paying off student loans, right?"

"Yeah," Yuna said nonchalantly.

"If I start spending thirty percent of my income to support

your mother's golf, I won't be able to put money away for a down payment."

"I thought your parents were helping. Didn't you agree on the size of the house, too?" Yuna pouted.

"My parents are only helping with the wedding," Jason said. "Look, I gotta go."

"You're going? But I thought we'd talk. And you woke me up so early. You aren't mad, are you?"

"Let's just talk later," Jason said and hung up.

He was about to toss the phone down on the couch in disgust, but stopped, noticing Percy, who was staring at him unblinkingly.

Jason placed the phone in the back pocket of his jeans instead.

"Oh, Percy," Jason said, running his fingers through her fur. "You are the cat that saved her owner, do you know that?"

With a sigh, he took his phone back out and called his mother. She picked up on the first ring.

"Jun, what's going on?"

"Eomma, I have a question."

"What is it? Is it related to the hotel? Did you hear from Yuna?"

"Listen, it's not the hotel. It's about Yuna, though. I'm not sure whether I can go through with this."

"What?" Jason's mother let out a scream so loud, he moved the receiver away from his ear.

"Yuna just called, and she asked me to pay for her mother's golf hobby."

"So, she asked to add to the negotiated list of presents? Is that all? Jun, this isn't quite a normal request, but it's within reason, of course."

"No, she asked me to contribute thirty percent of my annual salary to her mother's golfing in Vietnam. Or wherever she wants to go."

"What?" Another loud scream.

"Yes. I didn't go to podiatry school for this, Eomma. It isn't right. I mean, I guess there are traditions, and all that, and the Korean way of life, but no one had told me I'd have to do this. I want to get married, to have a family, to pay for whatever we need. But this isn't part of the deal."

"This isn't the Korean way of life, Jun." His mother's voice dropped. "Let me talk to your father. Please don't do anything. I think we can fix this."

"Alright," Jason said and hung up.

He sat on his couch, staring at the black TV screen in front of him, thinking. Did he want his mother to 'fix this'? Did he want to go through with the wedding? With marrying Yuna? What if she took back the request? What if Yuna stopped calling him Jamie forever? What if Yuna accepted Percy and let the cat stay? Would it make things right?

Jason already knew the answer.

CHAPTER
Thirty~Five

STANDING IN THE SHOWER, with the warm water pouring over him until it went cold, Jason thought of what he had lost. Ending the engagement hit him much harder than he'd expected. Losing Yuna cut like a knife, because of what she represented. He'd built up an image of his ex-fiancée as his perfect woman. His soulmate. Yuna was the epitome of everything he'd been told he would want in a wife: beautiful, educated, Korean, but exposed to America, cultured, funny, and he'd embraced that image wholeheartedly. It was as if Jason had lost his future. A happy, promising life that was within reach vanished in an instant.

He gnawed at himself for not recognizing the signs of Yuna's connection to her mother that would trump everything else.

She'd mentioned they were very close, he now remembered. *And the multiple golfing trips to Vietnam.*

The image of Yuna and her mother, guffawing, mocking him, swirled in his mind, as he went over the engagement and its ultimate unraveling. Why did he choose to ignore the signs? How did he let the situation get out of hand? How had he not noticed in Yuna the lack of love? The lack of reciprocity of feelings.

The second he'd made up his mind to make her his wife, things changed. Whatever she wanted was more important than anything else. He was willing to change, had even set up an Instagram account, though he'd resisted it for years, had entertained changing his name, had considered giving up his cat, only for her. Now he realized, nothing he would ever do would ever compare to the relationship with her mother. For Yuna, he, Jason, was just another step, possibly, just a ticket to America.

————

"Her mother called me, you know." He slid his elbows across the table and leaned on his hands, half-afraid to meet Kiana's eyes. From where he was sitting, he could just see Percy, sitting on the windowsill, frozen in observation.

"Her mother? Your future mother-in-law?" Kiana hoisted herself up on a stool.

"Yes, my *former* future mother-in-law. I'm starting to think she was kind of like yours. The Russian one, the one you couldn't say 'no' to." Jason forced a smile. Ever since his engagement to Yuna had ended, he'd been in a somber mood. He wasn't sure what was worse, his own disappointment or the fact that his mother was heartbroken over his lack of prospects and her own unfulfilled dream of grandchildren.

"So, what did she call you for? Was she trying to fix things?"

"No, she actually called to shame me into submission."

"I do recognize the style," Kiana said, her eyes unblinking.

"So I get this call, and it's a Korean number, so I pick it up, thinking it might be the hotel, you know, the wedding venue. Or who knows? Only this strange voice asks me, 'Is this Jun?'

I respond, 'Yes, it's Jun'. She says, 'This is Yuna's mother. I'd like to tell you that you're making a big mistake.'"

"No way! She actually said that?"

"Yes, then she continued speaking, and it was all about her lifestyle, how it took her years to get to that point and she wasn't about to give it up for a lowlife like me, and how I needed to man up and live up to the expectations. And how I wasn't a real doctor, because I only knew how to treat feet."

"Oh, that's low."

"I thought so, too. But in a way, it made things easier. Because by the time she was done, I told her to never speak to me again and hung up. And that was it. Then I called Yuna and told her the same thing."

"What? That's it?"

"Yes, that's it."

"And you told your parents?"

"I did. I called my mom before, just to check to make sure this whole extra request wasn't a normal thing. Because, I guess in Korea we've got some traditions, so I was thinking maybe I'd missed something. But no, it wasn't a tradition."

"So that's it? Yuna basically upended your wedding because of her mother?"

"That's an interesting way of looking at it. But I guess you're right."

"That's wild. Absolutely wild." Kiana shook her head. "I didn't expect this to happen. I really did not." She scanned Jason's face as if looking for a clue. "I thought it was all going to work out for you. But you seem so calm. Like you aren't heartbroken."

"I think I'm just too angry to be heartbroken right now." Jason dug his nails into the palms of his hands to stop himself from screaming.

"I think if she hadn't said anything about Percy, you would have gone along with it, Jason." Kiana furrowed her brow and gave him a critical look.

At the mention of her name, Percy jumped down from the windowsill and sauntered to the kitchen, positioning herself right next to her bowls.

"No, absolutely not. I wouldn't have agreed to the thirty percent! No way."

"Well, she may have brought it down to fifteen?" Kiana shrugged.

"Wait, you think it was a negotiating tactic? Is that what was happening?"

"I think it was some kind of manipulation. She started off high on purpose, and then she'd force you to settle for fifteen, or twenty, I don't know. Regardless, it's absurd, this whole thing. I'm glad you got out."

"You might be right. I guess you've gotta be a woman to understand another woman. I just give up."

"You give up?"

"Yep, I'm done. It's over, Kiana."

"Oh, you sound like me. You need to stop."

"Stop what? I'm just done. I told my mom, too. Warned her not to try and match me with anyone. I need a break. After this experience, I'm just so burned out." Jason rubbed his neck. "At least my dad's on my side. He flipped out, actually. And that helped. My mom was hesitating, well, because she really wants those grandkids. Not my dad though, as soon as he heard about this whole situation with the surprise request, he told me to get out."

"If you need a shoulder to cry on, you know where to find me," Kiana said. "You're an incredible guy, Jason. Handsome, a doctor, smart, funny, just all-around great, and you deserve the best."

"I don't feel so incredible. Dave once told me he thought I'd be single forever," Jason said.

"He said what?" Kiana nearly jumped out of her seat. "That's crazy. You're just a little insecure and way too trusting." She stared at him, as if verifying her assessment. "I think that's the only thing preventing you from being successful with women. If you wanted to, you'd have a line forming outside of your door tomorrow."

"But I don't want that. You don't have to say this just to make me feel better. And have you seen yourself in the mirror?"

"What? Is there something on my face?" Kiana started patting down her cheek, then moved to her forehead.

"No, I mean, you're a beautiful woman," Jason said, his voice soft.

"Alright, let's just have a pity party, shall we?" Kiana ran her hand through her hair. "I guess I'm not bad-looking, or whatever, but it doesn't seem to make a difference. Guess what happened to that guy? The 'drop' man?"

"What?" Jason rolled his shoulders back, rising from his seat. "I think Percy wants a treat." He walked over to the refrigerator to grab a slice of turkey for the cat, who devoured it straight away, then licked her lips in satisfaction.

"So we met. His name is Travis, by the way. And he lives in Leesburg, and actually works in Ashburn, so it's not really that far. So we met once, in Tyson's. And then the next time we're supposed to meet, I suggested he take the metro."

"Okay," Jason laughed, "I can see how that can go south pretty quickly."

"Why? I mean, what's wrong with the metro? We all take the metro, you do, I do, but anyway. Not Travis. So the metro idea sends him into a panic. Like a real panic. I can tell, though we were just texting. And then he tells me he'll 'think about it.' And we leave it at that."

Kiana rose from her seat and walked over to the couch, where Jason joined her.

"Alright." A smirk appeared on Jason's face.

"And then, the next day, he tells me he 'can't bring himself to leave Leesburg. And the mountains are so beautiful, and Arlington is such a dense, soulless place."

"Oh, God. So is that all?"

"Well, then he tells me about his ex-girlfriend, and how he isn't emotionally available, and how she'd messed him up. All of it, I would say, probably could have been summarized to say, he didn't like me enough to bother." A rueful smile crossed Kiana's face.

"Come on."

"It's true. So the whole 'drain the bucket' method is basically useless. Because I wasted all that time, like a month, more or less, blocking losers and whatever, and I ended up with this one 'drop' who ended up also being a loser. So here I am, with a terrible outcome."

"I'd say something to make you feel better, but I'm feeling pretty awful myself," Jason responded.

"I know." Kiana pulled up her legs and hugged her knees. Percy, who'd been grooming herself after eating the treat, jumped up and settled next to her, curling into a ball.

"You know what would be good?" Jason said. "I was thinking of going somewhere. Like a change of scenery. Maybe for Easter? Dr. McGrath won't mind. Now that I'm not going to Korea to get married, I can definitely take a week off."

"Really? Like where?"

"Well, not Korea, that's for sure," Jason scoffed. "Maybe Florida? I've never been to Florida."

"Florida is nice, but lots of college kids go there for spring break, so going there around Easter isn't the best," Kiana responded quickly. "You should go to Arizona or New Mexico. I mean, if you're looking for a nice place to visit."

"Would you like to come along?"

"Me? Like going on a trip together?"

"Yeah, why not? As friends," Jason added quickly. "We get

along really well, it'll be fun. And better than sitting here sulking."

"That's actually a really good idea," Kiana agreed. "You know what? I was actually thinking of visiting Charlie. She'd invited me to come up and see her in L.A., so I was planning on going in April." Kiana stopped speaking and stared at Jason, as if processing the idea.

"What is it? You know you don't blink when you're thinking."

"Oh, really?" Kiana responded. "That's interesting. Why don't we both go to L.A. then?"

"Are you sure?"

"Yes, I'm sure. I'll ask Charlie. I think they've got a few spare bedrooms, and her dad is doing much better. Besides, you've adopted Percy, so she owes you."

"And speaking of Percy, what do we do with her if we both go?"

"We can get a cat sitter, probably."

"Someone good that we trust though, right?" Jason said. His mood had brightened up markedly since earlier in the conversation. "So, when would you like to go?"

"I'll ask Charlie first, see if it'll work, and then we can decide on the time," Kiana said. "But it'll be good to go soon, right?"

"Yes, the sooner, the better." Jason nodded. "And you know what? I just got another idea."

"What is it?" Kiana opened her eyes wide.

"But please don't be mad," Jason said. "Remember Audrey?"

"How can I forget?" Kiana said and then shook her head. "No, come on, Jason."

"I mean, if we're in L.A. together. Isn't that where Mary Invernizzi lives?"

"So you want us to do what, exactly?"

"We can just stop by her house while we're there."

"Like, show up at her house, unannounced?"

"Yes." Jason nodded eagerly. "I think it'll be fun."

"Or it will land us in jail super fast. Trespassing, I think it's called."

"Kiana, don't be so dramatic. We can contact her beforehand, too. And you won't be investigating this by yourself. We'll do it together. What do you say?"

CHAPTER
Thirty-Six

AS SOON AS Kiana left his apartment, Jason started having doubts about the trip. Traveling all the way to L.A., the spontaneity, the novelty of it, felt daunting. He wondered why he'd mentioned the investigation of Anton Konovalov to Kiana. Especially since the key person involved, Audrey Simmons, had clearly told them she was not interested in the outcome.

Clearing up the dishes from the table, Jason was absorbed in thought. The trip to L.A. was just postponing the sad reality of facing his failed love life. The trip was just a distraction, nothing else. Percy pawed her toy, a tiny mouse, which made a squeaking noise, and reminded Jason of the additional complication the trip presented: finding a cat sitter.

Maybe we should bring Percy to Charlie and leave the cat there? Jason considered for a brief second, but then, throwing one look at Percy, shook his head. He couldn't part with his cat, not now.

There was no denying: Jason was back where he'd started. Lonely and with no prospects. He was about to turn on the TV to get his usual dosage of *Law & Order*, when he noticed his phone flashing. It was a text message from his mother:

Jun, call me.

Jason checked the time: it was the middle of the night in Korea. Adrenaline rushed through his veins: there must be an emergency.

Immediately, he picked up his phone and called her.

"Eomma, what's wrong?"

"Jun!" His mother's voice was urgent. "I need to talk to you."

"Did something happen?"

"I couldn't sleep. I was up all night, and I just went online. I got a ticket and I am coming to see you."

"What?"

"Aren't you glad? Jun, I am so worried about you. I know this breakup must have crushed you. So I've come up with the best idea."

"Eomma, please, I'll be fine." Jason blinked fast, frantically searching for the right words to stop his mother from flying to America to see him. "You don't need to come here."

"I've already gotten the tickets. I arrive on April 15th. It's right after Easter, so tickets were less expensive. I'll make you all your favorite foods, make sure you are settled in your apartment, and then we'll go to church together and find you a nice girl."

"Eomma, please, I don't think it's a good idea. I'm not ready to date right now," Jason said, and immediately realized it was exactly the wrong thing to say.

"There's no time to waste. Now, I haven't yet told your father, he's still asleep, but as soon as he wakes up, I'll tell him the good news. I'm going back to bed now."

"Good night, Eomma," Jason said, but his mother had already hung up.

———

The conversation with his mother jerked Jason back to reality and snapped him out of wallowing in self-pity. He needed to tell Kiana about his mother's arrival, because now a trip to L.A. couldn't happen. He picked up the phone and called his friend.

"Hey, sorry, I can't do L.A.," Jason blurted out.

"Why? What's wrong? I was just about to get in touch with Charlie." She sounded breathless.

"Is this a good time? What are you up to?" Jason asked. Kiana rarely sat around in her apartment, she was almost always doing something.

"Just reorganizing my place a bit. I've decluttered so much during Covid, now I can't find anything and I am starting to think I may have given away some stuff I actually needed," Kiana said. "It was all this Marie Kondo insanity, sparking joy, whatever."

"I see." Jason drew in a breath. "Listen, my mom just called. She's coming here. She said she wants to take care of me and to take me to church."

"Are you religious? You've never told me that."

"I'm not, not really. My mom is, though, and I used to go to church, but that's not why she's coming. She wants to match me with someone from church."

"Just tell her you aren't ready to be set up yet." In the background, Jason heard the sound of something being moved, and then a clanking noise. "Ouch, these hangers just fell on top of my head," Kiana yelped. "That doesn't spark any joy."

"You're just saying that because you've never met my mother," Jason said. "I can never say 'no' to her."

"Well, maybe you need to start. It's called 'having boundaries,' Jason."

"We don't have that concept in Korea. Not with the older generation."

————

"Jun!" Jason's mother rushed to hug him. She emerged from customs with fresh makeup on, her hair neatly done, not a sign of having just spent fourteen hours on an airplane. Jason, who'd been waiting right outside of the arrivals door with a large bouquet, handed her the flowers.

"You're so sweet, you shouldn't have."

She pushed her cart to him. Jason saw three matching suitcases, two large ones and a carry-on, stacked on top of each other. "I brought you a few things," his mother said, business-like. "So you can finally set up your apartment. And a few presents for your uncle Henry and the rest of the family."

His mother's two-week visit included a trip to see their family in New Jersey, which would free Jason from at least some of the responsibility of entertaining his mother for a part of the time.

"Thank you, Eomma," Jason said, walking with his mother to the parking lot. He was pushing the surprisingly heavy cart in front of him.

"Eomma, how did you manage with the luggage? It's so heavy," Jason asked.

"This very nice young man helped me with the suitcases," his mother said. "He was sitting next to me during the flight, and then we spoke. I got his information. He's a banker, Jun, and I think he might be a good connection for you to have. I am worried you don't have any friends here yet. This young man recommended a church to me, I wrote down the address, and we can go tomorrow."

"Eomma, I was thinking, maybe we go sightseeing first?" Jason said. "I wanted to show you around Washington, maybe go to a museum?"

Jason thought of the visit to the National Gallery of Art with Kiana, the lunch the two of them had, the bitter-sweet memory of how hopeful he'd been at that time, his mind filled with dreams of finding his great love in Korea.

"Sight-seeing isn't really my thing, Jun, I came to help you. There is no time to waste."

"But maybe we can just spend time together, Eomma?" Jason tried to steer the conversation away from the topic of marriage.

"Jun, this is exactly the reason you're still single at thirty-seven. I'm not going to be around forever. Every day I cry thinking about my son, who is lonely and will never give me grandchildren." His mother wrung her hands.

"Eomma," Jason started to say, but felt bile rising in his throat. He knew, no matter what he said, his mother's counter-argument would make it so much worse. On the way from the airport to his apartment, he stayed quiet, listening to his mother recount in excruciating detail the return of the wedding gifts following Jason's failed engagement.

"Eomma, I have to tell you, I have a cat," Jason said, opening the door to the apartment. Percy greeted them at the door with a loud meow.

Jason knew his mother would not approve, but Kiana's words about boundaries had struck a chord. He decided he didn't want to hide the little cat, who had become an important part of his life, from his mother.

"A cat? You're a grown man, living with a cat?" After taking off her shoes, his mother placed her handbag on the kitchen counter. Percy approached, smelling her feet, but Jason's mother pushed the cat away. "Where can I wash my hands?"

"Please, Eomma, here." He led her to the guest bathroom. "And this is where you will stay." He pointed into the guest bedroom. "I've been keeping it just for you and dad." Prior to his mother's arrival, Jason had cleaned the bedroom, ironed the sheets to make sure they met his mother's high standards, and bought a set of new towels for the guest bathroom. The bedroom smelled fresh and, Jason was sure, would make his mother happy.

"Alright, thank you," his mother said, following him into the guest bedroom. She examined the room, then ran her hands on the bedspread. "Jun," she scoffed, staring at her fingers, "take a look at this." She gave him a grave stare.

"What is it, Eomma?" Jason walked over to her.

"It's cat hair. How do you expect me to sleep here? This disgusting animal has been shedding all over the bedspread. It is unhygienic."

"Eomma, I'm sorry." Jason swallowed hard.

"I never expected my son to become a *goyangi jipsa!*"

Jason had heard the expression before. A *goyangi jipsa* or 'a cat butler' was a reference to pet owners catering to their feline 'bosses'. Normally, it was a playful reference, but his mother made it sound ominous and dismissive.

"Where did this cat come from?" His mother continued her attack.

"It was my neighbor's," Jason said. "It's her cat, and then I helped to take care of it, and here we are."

His mother observed him, her eyes narrowed.

"It was her, wasn't it? That woman, the one who'd helped you pick out the presents."

"Eomma, I've told you, Kiana and I are just friends."

"Jun, I know a few things about how the world works. Men and women cannot be *just* friends. Tell me the truth, is she the reason you broke it off with Yuna?"

"Of course not." Though immediately, Kiana's face flashed in his mind, the vivid memory of his initial attraction to the woman who had become a close friend and confidante. Jason had worked hard on ignoring the pull Kiana had on him.

Is Eomma right? Jason brushed the idea aside.

"I'll make sure Percy doesn't come into your room, okay? And I'll get you a new set of sheets."

"Jun, I worry about you. This cat is just a distraction, it's not going to solve your problem." The tone of his mother's voice was softer now, and Jason, emboldened, moved to change the subject.

"Come on, let me get you something to eat. You must be so tired and hungry. I know I am when I first land in DC." Jason led his mother to the kitchen and demonstrated the Pajeon he had prepared after practicing and watching a cooking show.

"You did this yourself? What is happening, the world is truly upside down?" His mother stared at the scallion pancakes in consternation, her forehead creased.

"See, Eomma, you don't have to worry about me. I'll be just fine." Jason took out a pan to heat up the dish.

———

The following morning, after Jason got out of the shower, he found his mother sitting on the couch, watching Percy play with her toy mouse. A slight smile crossed his mother's face, as the cat moved the mouse expertly on the floor. Noticing Jason, his mother straightened up, then commented:

"Well, at least this cat is well behaved."

"She is, Eomma," Jason said proudly.

"I suppose they can be pretty cute," Jason's mother added, rising from the couch. "But we didn't finish speaking last night. What about finding you a wife?"

"Eomma, you told me yourself, if it isn't meant to be, it won't happen. Let me make you an espresso." Jason made a move to the kitchen.

"Jun..." His mother shook her head and dropped her arms in resignation.

"I am so glad to see you. I love you," Jason said. "And I'll be alright."

His mother did not answer, but surveyed his face, her expression focused. Never to give up easily, he knew she was mulling over his words, planning her next move.

"I love you, too, Jun," she said after a long pause. "But this," she took a look around his apartment, "is not what your life should be. You should have a home, filled with children. You shouldn't be cooking your own food, Jun. You're a doctor."

"Eomma." Jason tried to stop her, but she put up her hand, gesturing for him to stop speaking.

"I know it's hard, Jun, I know. But please, give the Kayeon dating app another chance. Let's try again in the summer. What do you say?"

"Again?" Jason shook his head.

"Just one more time. How about that? When you're ready."

CHAPTER
Thirty-Seven

THREE MONTHS later

"I can't believe we're actually doing this," Kiana told Jason as they settled into their seats on a United flight from Dulles International Airport to Los Angeles. The flight was only half-booked, and they had a whole row to themselves, leaving the middle seat between them empty.

"I'm glad it's actually happening," Jason said, "aren't you?"

"Yes, of course. And it's good we're going over the summer. That way, you've had time to get over the breakup."

"That's true. I feel so much better." Jason nodded. "I didn't even realize how sad I was until after my mom left."

"So, are you going to start looking at Kayeon app again?" Kiana asked, fixing her eyes on him. Jason swallowed hard. Though he'd gotten over the breakup with Yuna, the idea of going through the same process, of planning blind dates in Seoul, made him queasy.

"I don't think so, not yet," Jason responded. "But my mother refuses to take 'no' for an answer.

"I might get on the apps again," Kiana said half under her breath, fumbling with her purse.

"Really?"

"Yes, after we get back from L.A. I've been reading a lot about dating, and I found this book about attachment styles. I think I have the 'avoidant style' in dating."

"What's that?" Jason raised his eyebrows.

Kiana never ceased to surprise him: she never gave up. Whereas Jason's attitude had been to sulk and regroup, to retreat from any more pain, Kiana was always all action. After unsuccessfully applying the 'drop in the bucket' method, she had been busy attending singles events in the DC area, and going to dance classes once a week in the hope of meeting a potential match in person. So far, her efforts had not yielded any serious prospects, but it wasn't for a lack of trying.

"I think I pick men who aren't ready for emotional intimacy." Kiana stared at him, wide-eyed. "I spent all week reading about this, and it fits. It's because I don't feel comfortable getting close to anyone. I really value independence, so I end up attracting men who don't want a relationship."

"You've just described me." Jason shrugged. "Does this mean I'm also avoidant?"

"Maybe so. That's probably why we get along so well. You and I." She looked at him carefully, her eyes glistening.

Jason looked away.

"I'll have to read more about it," he said, pulling up the blind. Bright afternoon light beamed through the window. "This way, we can see the sunset."

"How cool!" Kiana leaned across the seats to look out of the window, and Jason caught a whiff of her perfume. It wasn't a smell he recognized, and he wondered when she'd changed it. "You know, for some reason, I'm kind of nervous about meeting Mary Invernizzi," Kiana shared, shifting back into her seat.

"Here, show me the messages," Jason said, and Kiana, for the third time that evening, opened her phone and showed him the exchange.

A month prior to the trip, Kiana had written to Mary Invernizzi through Facebook Messenger. Kiana had decided that was the surer way to reach the woman, after finding her account through her daughter's friends list, which was public. Mary, posting under the alias 'Mary Nizzi', spent a lot of time on Facebook, judging by her regular posts and updates.

Kiana and Jason discussed the content of the message together and drafted and re-drafted it, to a point Jason had memorized it by heart.

Dear Mary, my name is Kiana Nasiri, and I am writing to inquire if you'd be available to speak with me and my friend, Jason Lee. Both of us will be in Los Angeles the week of July 12th, and we'd like to use the opportunity to meet with you. We wanted to ask you a few questions about Anton Konovalov and the nature of your relationship.

We appreciate your time.

A response from Mary came the following day, much faster than Kiana anticipated.

Dear Kiana, thank you for reaching out. I've been waiting for something like this to happen. Please call me, and we can take it from there.

The two of them spoke on Facebook Messenger the next day. Mary agreed to meet Kiana and Jason at her house. Ahead of the meeting, Mary requested copies of their driver's licenses and assurances no part of their conversation would be recorded, but was otherwise friendly and forthcoming.

"You know, Jason," Kiana said, taking her phone back, "it's just strange, don't you think?"

"What is?"

"Like, it just seems so easy. As if it was all meant to

happen quickly. I just wonder why didn't Audrey ever do it? She's had fifty years to get in touch with Mary Ward, and she never did."

"It's like you said, I don't think Audrey wants to know the truth." Jason sighed.

"That's for sure. Here," Kiana took out her lunch bag, "I brought us some food for the flight, help yourself."

"Really?" Jason gave Kiana a curious stare. "Thank you."

"Yes, I figured, I've been on this whole clean eating kick, and my mom always packed food for us if we ever traveled anywhere. So, here we are." Kiana unzipped the bag. Jason saw beef jerky, cut vegetables and several pieces of fruit.

———

The moment Jason saw Charlie emerge from her car and rush to hug Kiana, he realized he never thought of Charlie as an actual person. He'd only pictured her as an extension of Kiana. She turned out to be a petite woman of indeterminate age. Her dyed jet-black hair was tied in a ponytail. She wore black yoga pants and a white t-shirt. The most striking feature were her eyes, they were clever and scrutinizing.

"It's so great to meet you, Jason." Charlie extended her hand to him. "I think the car should fit your luggage, Kiana said you guys travel light," she gave the two of them an assessing stare, as she pointed to her white Mercedes convertible.

"We do," Kiana and Jason said in unison, then immediately added 'jinx' and 'jjijjibbong'. Charlie raised her eyebrows.

"I can't believe it's been a whole year!" she said, turning to embrace Kiana, while Jason stuffed their suitcases in the trunk.

"Girl! Are you ever coming back?" Kiana shook her head at Charlie in mock admonishment. "I'm so glad to see you!"

"Well, I kinda like being back home," Charlie noted, opening the driver's side door. "And thank you, by the way," she turned to Jason, "for adopting my cat."

"Of course." Jason smiled.

"I hope you're okay sitting in the back," Charlie said, "it's a little tight, but you'll have the full seat to yourself."

"No worries, thank you for picking up us." Jason climbed in.

They rode with the top down, the voices of the two women drowned out by the wind. Jason took in the cloudless sky, the bright sun, the palm trees and contemplated the strange turn of events his life had taken.

Over the past year, instead of getting married and settling down with his wife, he had become a cat owner, made friends with a stranger he met in an elevator, and had become so immersed in investigating a cold case murder, that he was about to meet with one of the leads.

A row of one-story sprawling houses drew his eye. The exterior of the ranch-style home felt eerily similar to the homes in Palisades Park, New Jersey. On his daily walk home from school, he dreamed to one day live in a house like this with his parents rather than a dark and small apartment. Those homes were similar to the Brady Bunch house he saw on TV, and symbolized the epitome of the American dream.

"So, here we are, this is where I grew up." Charlie led them into her house.

The second Jason stepped inside, he was transported to that very dream. Charlie showed them the living room, and Jason took in the checkered couches, the low glass coffee table and an old TV that looked straight out of the eighties.

"My dad refuses to redecorate," Charlie said, "and I don't want to rock the boat. Anyway, let me show you to your bedroom." Jason assumed she was speaking to Kiana, but then, having noticed his confusion, Charlie added, "I figured, the two of you would be comfortable there. And it's very private."

She led them to a large room, all the way in the back of the house, as Jason wondered how he could have missed the crucial fact that he and Kiana would be sharing a bedroom.

"It's just that the only other spare bedroom is being used for storage, and the living room couch is not a great option, because my dad usually stays up until three in the morning. His whole sleep schedule is completely off, he is a total night owl. So this room is the best solution if you want to get any rest," Charlie clarified.

"It's not a big deal, I can sleep on the floor," Jason offered.

"No, no, that would be silly, it's a big bed, plenty of space for both of us," Kiana noted with a smile. "I'll let you settle in, Jason, while I go catch up with Charlie."

Before Jason could argue, Kiana moved her suitcase to the door and followed her friend out of the bedroom, leaving him alone. Jason sat on the bed, pondering what to do next. The first thought that crossed his mind was to get a hotel room, only to realize it might seem rude to do so.

Besides, Kiana and I are just friends, and friends can share a bed, Jason thought, rising from the bed to get a fresh change of clothes from his suitcase, then headed out to meet the two friends in the living room.

That night, as Jason got into bed and wished Kiana good night, he wondered where his life had made the wrong turn. He was lying next to a beautiful woman, with no possibility of romance, bottling up whatever desires he had for the sake of their friendship. It was not how Jason had pictured his life as he neared forty. He let out a sigh, and turned to the wall, rolling himself to the farthest edge of the bed, as far away from Kiana as possible, willing himself to sleep.

———

Two days later, Kiana and Jason set out to visit Mary Invernizzi in Old Town Pasadena. Driving over there from Charlotte's, Kiana admired the neighborhoods they passed on the way.

"Jason, this is beautiful. Just look at the view. I want to live here!" she said over and over again. Until they saw a 'For Sale' sign and Kiana pulled up the listing on her phone, only to learn the house was listed for $2 million. "Well, never mind, I guess prices here are even higher than in Arlington." She sighed.

"Yeah, and people complain about DC real estate being unaffordable," Jason said, pulling up to the curb.

They parked on a shaded street and sat in the car, chatting, until it was time to go in.

"In Korea, if you're on time, you're late," he told Kiana, who complained about leaving Charlie's too early. "And besides, with traffic here, we've got to make sure we build in extra time."

At exactly 11am, they rang the doorbell.

Mary Invernizzi was instantly recognizable, thanks to all the photos posted on Facebook. She was a tall, imposing woman with striking blue eyes. Her light blonde shoulder-length hair was cut in a bob, with bangs brushed to the side, revealing a high forehead. Mary wore a beige turtleneck with a long, flowing skirt.

"Well, hello there," she said, smiling at the two of them, as she opened the door. "I'm pleased to meet you, Kiana." There was a slight lilt in her voice. "And you must be Jason. Please come in."

She led them to the living room, which was decorated with dozens of Pueblo pottery pieces. There were matching plates hanging on the wall, large vases standing in each corner and next to the couches, and a carpet with the same, brown, white and black geometric design.

"Mrs. Invernizzi…" Kiana started to say, when the three of them sat down.

"Please call me Mary. And help yourselves." Mary pointed to a pitcher and a bowl of cashews that stood in the middle of the coffee table. "I just made lemonade this morning. It's lavender, sweetened with honey, my favorite," Mary smiled.

Jason fidgeted uneasily in his seat. Something about Mary was too zen. Too sweet for a woman who was about to reveal key information about a murder she may have witnessed fifty years prior.

"So, I suppose you want to know about Anton?" Mary turned to Kiana, entirely ignoring Jason, though the two of them were sitting side by side. "As I told you, I've been waiting for this conversation for over fifty years. Ever since Christmas 1972, the day of the phone call."

"What phone call?" Kiana swallowed hard.

"When Audrey Simmons called Anton to wish him a Merry Christmas. I'd been the one to pick up the phone. Anton was staying with us. We'd planned this as a family trip, a ski vacation, and it was his first time skiing in America. He was very fit, of course, so physically strong, but he'd never been skiing here before. He'd only done cross-country skiing in Russia," she cleared her throat, "and so, he was very excited to go."

"How did the two of you meet?"

"I met Anton right after he defected. My father was very active in the Evangelical Church, and after Anton landed in Canada, somehow the Church found him, or he found the Church, and right away, my father became Anton's mentor."

"I see. So you met him *before* Audrey?"

"Yes. I believe so. We met about a month after he landed in Canada. Right away, at least for me, it was love. Anton spoke so little English back then, but we found a way to communicate. I actually helped him learn English. He was a fast learner. And I was the one helping him write his book."

"Really? I was wondering about that. How Anton had been able to write a book so soon after landing in America."

"Oh, yes, I'd read so much as a child, and had always dreamed of being a writer myself one day. So when the idea of Anton's memoir came up, I jumped on it. We spent days sitting together, typing it out. And I finished it posthumously," Mary said. "Of course, my role in the memoir was never acknowledged." She adjusted the collar of her turtleneck.

"Mary, was everything he said true? In the book?"

"I can't answer that." A rueful smile crossed Mary's face. "For Anton, as I've now realized, truth was a foreign concept."

"You were fifteen years old when you first met him?"

"Yes." Mary nodded solemnly. "Fifteen, going on thirty. At least that's how my parents must have seen it. I was head over heels in love with Anton. Very headstrong. I was sure he was the one. But with me being underage, my parents did their best to separate us. So they shipped Anton off to Washington, DC, hoping we'd forget each other."

"And that's where he met Audrey?"

"I guess so." Mary's nostrils flared.

"Were you engaged to Anton?"

"Yes. We got engaged after a year of being apart. He came back to see me regularly. He was in DC for work reasons, or so my parents claimed, to promote his book before it was published, things like that, but our agreement was that he would always come back to California and he would stay at our house for the holidays. And that, as soon as I turned eighteen, we would get married."

"Did you know Anton had another relationship with a woman who was also his fiancée?"

"I found out on Christmas Eve. When Audrey Simmons called him. I'd picked up the receiver in another room. Once I realized it was another woman calling him, I kept on listening. I heard everything. Their entire conversation." Mary clenched her fists and the knuckles turned white from the pressure.

"So you knew he was cheating on you?" Kiana pressed on. Jason bulked at her directness and wondered whether that was a good idea. He suspected Mary was getting increasingly uncomfortable with the conversation, but, to his surprise, she responded.

"I did. I heard everything. It was awful. It broke me. I remember heaving in the corner, unable to speak. Until that moment, I trusted him completely. My first love, the man I was sure I would one day marry, who was about to publish his autobiography with *my* help. Only to hear him speaking to another woman, telling her he loved her. That she was pure and sweet, that she was his princess. I was crushed."

"Wow." Kiana moved her hand to her mouth. "That sounds awful. And you were so young!"

"Yes," Mary, encouraged by Kiana's compassionate response, continued speaking. "Anton hadn't realized I'd heard his conversation. He'd been speaking in the bedroom, with the door shut, and the other phone was in the master bathroom."

"Did you confront him?"

"Not right away. Before he hung up, I left the lodge and ran outside. I wanted to come up with a plan. You see, Anton was staying with us for nearly two weeks, and I couldn't let on. Because then my parents would have known Anton and I had been intimate." Mary sighed. "Little did I know, he'd be dead just a few days later."

"What happened next?" Kiana shifted in her seat.

"I was heartbroken. But I forced myself to return to the cottage and to act like nothing happened. It was killing me inside, but that was the only way for me to survive that trip."

"And then? You never asked him about the other woman?"

"I did. Two days later, I'd mustered up the courage to confront him. I waited until the two of us were alone in the cottage." Mary wrung her hands. "I asked him about the woman who'd called him. He tensed. Then he told me she was a colleague in Washington, that she was checking up on him because of an assignment. He was a really good liar, Anton. If I hadn't heard their conversation, I would have been sure he was telling the truth."

"And that was all? You didn't press the issue?"

"I started crying. I was so, so sad. He tried to comfort me." Mary's body language stiffened. She uncrossed her arms and pulled at the collar of her turtleneck, as if struggling for air.

"It was my fault Anton killed himself." Mary's voice was hoarse, as she uttered those words.

The room fell into silence. Jason noticed Kiana gripping the edge of the sofa.

"We were sitting together, right after I'd asked him about the call. Asked him to prove to me he really loved me," Mary continued speaking. "He'd just gotten this gun, and he said he'd show me how to play the Russian Roulette, that he wasn't afraid to die. He said that God was on his side, and he would prove to me he loved me. Next thing... the gunshot. And he was gone. Just like that, right next to me."

Kiana gasped. "That's how it happened?"

"I've never told anyone." Mary's shoulders slumped.

"That's horrible." Kiana rushed over and sat next to the woman. "I'm so sorry. Sorry this happened to you."

"I've lived with the guilt for fifty years. Never told the whole story to anyone, not even to my father. I don't even know what he thought, maybe that I'd killed Anton. My father protected me, he told the authorities I'd walked in after the accident, but the truth is," Mary rubbed her neck. "I was *there* when it happened. If it weren't for me, Anton would have lived."

The three of them sat in silence, and then Jason said, "If I may, I don't think it's your fault. For a person to play the Russian Roulette, to take a risk that high, they had to have a certain predisposition."

"That's what I've read somewhere, too." Mary nodded, giving Jason a curious stare, as if noticing him for the first time. "But the memory still haunts me to this day. That scene replayed in my head thousands of times. Each time, I try to stop him, plead with him not to do it. I only wish I'd never confronted him in the first place."

"What made you decide to tell us?" Kiana asked.

"I needed to do tell someone. Been praying for this to happen. Anton still comes to me in my dreams. I dreamed of him, I think it was about a year ago. He asked me to share the truth with someone. And here we are. I believe in things like that. I believe the dead never really leave us. Maybe now that I've shared his story, Anton will leave me alone." Mary drew a sharp breath.

Neither Jason nor Kiana said anything, but sat quietly, waiting for Mary to speak again. The woman shifted in her seat, then took a long, slow drink of lemonade.

"Well, thank you for coming to see me," Mary said and rose from her seat. "And thank you for trying to get to the bottom of Anton's story." Her lips curled into a sorrowful smile.

"Thank you very much." Kiana shook Mary's hand and followed Jason out. "You really helped us."

CHAPTER
Thirty-Eight

WITHOUT A WORD, Jason and Kiana got into the car. It was as if both of them were concerned Mary Ward would overhear them.

"So, what did you think?" Kiana said once Jason started the car.

"What a horrible story." He glanced at her. "And what a terrible thing to live with for fifty years."

"How awful that she still blames herself for his death." Kiana took a deep breath. "Just imagine, Anton Konovalov made two women agonize over him for half a century."

"It's a tragic death, regardless." Jason put the car in 'drive'.

"I think we have to tell Audrey about the Russian Roulette," Kiana said. "She'd want to know the full story, don't you think?'

"Yes, absolutely."

"But I guess the rest of it makes sense, with the FBI testimony. All that nonsense, how one document mentioned Mary was in the room, another said she wasn't. And how Anton was confused by a gun. I mean, the guy'd served in the military. I don't think he'd be confused by a gun."

"It does make sense." Jason cleared his throat, steering the car. "So, do you think we should tell Audrey the truth about Anton's relationship with Mary?"

"Yes, we have to. She needs to know the full story," Kiana said emphatically. "And it's not like it never happens now. I'll tell Audrey about Ross, or even about that movie, 'Mrs. Wilson'. I think it's important for her not to keep idolizing Anton."

"It might be too late for that." Jason noted with a sigh.

"It's never too late to know the truth," Kiana said and Jason turned to look at her. She met his gaze. Looking into Kiana's eyes, Jason felt a spark. A flash of their connection. A mutual understanding of a bond that existed between the two of them.

This has to be more than friendship, the thought occurred to him. But then, Kiana looked away, and the certainty was gone.

"Now, where are we going?" she asked.

"No idea. I just wanted to get out of there. Let me check the directions." He pulled over and took out his phone.

———

"So, this is kind of perfect. Five hours, and we'll be home," Kiana said, stuffing her bag under her seat. Their flight back to Washington left on time. It would land at nine in the evening.

Just like on the flight to L.A., the two of them occupied a three-seat row together. This time, however, Kiana sat by the window.

"Yep. This was a good trip. And it was great meeting Charlie."

"It was. And solving a cold case." Kiana clapped.

"I still can't get over it. Did we actually do it?" Jason

looked at Kiana and extended his hand. "Nice doing business with you, Sherlock."

"Thanks, Watson," Kiana responded, shaking it. "You don't mind being Watson, do you?"

"No. You did all the crime solving. You were the one who found Mary Ward. And then you got her to meet with us. How did you actually get her to agree to meet you in person? I never asked."

"When we had our call on Facebook messenger, I told her I was interested in romance. Basically, about the 'Is This Your Man?' Facebook group. And how, if the group had been around in the seventies, she and Audrey both would have known sooner about each other."

"That was so clever."

"Thank you." Kiana flashed him a grateful smile. "I also shared with her my own experience with Ross. How he'd been two-timing me. It's always easier to get people to open up, when you have something in common." Jason didn't respond, careful to avoid the sensitive topic, but then Kiana flipped on the display. "Oh! They have *True Detective*. I heard it's great," she exclaimed, reaching into the pocket in front of her and fished out the headphone set.

"Yeah, yeah, I was thinking I'm going to watch *The Godfather*." Jason scrolled on his own screen.

"Totally, yeah, I mean we, uh, I'm exhausted. So, some downtime would be good, right?"

"I can't wait to get home," Kiana said an hour before landing. "I'm in the middle of Episode Three, but even that can't stop me from rushing off this plane as soon as we land. Are you still watching *The Godfather*? Which one?"

"The second one. It's my favorite. I can watch it over and over."

The PA system interrupted their conversation.

"Folks, this is your captain speaking. We're just about 200 miles northwest of Washington, and there're some strong storms coming through. We're going to be in a holding pattern here until the storms clear. We've got plenty of fuel, so we're in good shape, folks. I should have more information for you at the top of the hour."

"Oh, no, Jason." Kiana gave Jason a pleading look. "Top of the hour? This sucks."

"It's not a big deal, just another, umm," Jason checked his watch, "forty-five minutes before we're able to land."

"Yeah. I just feel kind of nervous."

"It's because you're watching this creepy show, Kiana. You should stop. *True Detective* is so dark."

"Said the man watching *The Godfather*," Kiana giggled and put her headphones back on.

The plane went quiet after the captain's update. Even the usual rustling of bags and the occasional conversations stopped. The PA system turned on at nine, and the captain, his voice a little less perky, made another announcement:

"Alright, folks, this is your captain speaking. Some pretty strong storms are still happening around the Washington, DC airspace. There's a ground stop in DC for another hour, so we'll be flying this plane over to BWI. We should be landing there in about an hour, folks."

"BWI?" Kiana turned to Jason.

"We can take an Uber from there, not a big deal, or even a train," Jason said, remembering his Amtrak ride and the rowdy neighbors on the train up to New York. "I guess an Uber will take up about an hour if there's no traffic. Good we didn't drive to the airport, right? It was great to take the metro, wasn't it?"

"Yes! Absolutely." Kiana nodded. "I should have told Travis about it."

"Your 'drop in a bucket' guy who refused to take the metro?"

"Yep, the one and only. It's not like I'm bitter about it or anything." Kiana smirked. "Alright, I better hurry up. I'm in the middle of an episode and I want to finish before we land."

————

The plane descended in jerking motions, moving roughly through the air. It landed with a thumping noise, diving forward, and as soon as it was moving on stable ground, the passengers clapped. Kiana clapped as well, and Jason, looking over at her, also joined.

"Are you crying?" he asked, noticing Kiana wiping her eyes.

"I am," she said. "For some reason, I was really scared. I'm glad we're safe now."

"Don't worry. Everything will be alright." Jason placed his hand on top of hers. Kiana didn't pull hers away. A feeling of calm spread through his body. He did not want to be anywhere else in the world. Only next to Kiana. The cabin lights turned off, and the plane sat on the tarmac, but neither Kiana nor Jason noticed.

The moment of quiet contemplation was interrupted by the PA.

"Well, folks, just going to be staying here for a little while. We're trying to figure out what's going on over here at BWI to get the airport to unload our plane."

A murmur ran through the airplane. They had been sitting on the tarmac for ten minutes now, and it was getting hot, stiflingly so.

"Jason, did you hear that?" Kiana turned to him, her forehead creased with worry. "He just said they might not unload our plane."

"I heard." Jason tried to read the expression on her face.

Did she feel anything? Normally, Jason could read her like an open book, but now, when it came to how she felt towards him, he was at a loss.

"Folks, please remain seated," the PA system announcement came on. "Our flight attendants are bringing out water for the babies and the little ones. Please remain seated, folks. We know it's hot in economy. Please turn your vents on, folks. I repeat, please turn all the vents on."

"Oh, gosh, this is bad," Kiana said, looking over to the aisle, as the flight attendant walked to the front of the plane, carrying a tray with cups of water. Jason reached to turn on the three vents above them. He moved his hand up and down, feeling air flow.

"This feels a little better," he said, only half-believing his own words. But he wanted to reassure Kiana. Wanted her to feel comfortable. "They'll unload the plane in no time. You'll see."

In response, Kiana looked down at her phone. "Look, it's already past ten. We were supposed to have landed over an hour ago. We're just sitting here, and then we'll still have to take an Uber."

"Try to sleep, maybe?" Jason offered. "Or, if you still have the show? Watch that, just get your mind off this situation."

"Alright, I'll watch the show. Maybe I'll finish another episode." Kiana pulled her headphones back on.

Jason turned on his movie back on, but found that he couldn't concentrate. His mind wandered. He closed his eyes and drifted into an uneasy sleep. The PA announcement woke him up.

"Folks, this is your captain speaking. Your crew has clocked out for the day. This is per FAA regulations, so we're waiting for another crew to get over here so we can get you back to Dulles."

"Wait, what?" Kiana turned to Jason. "What does it mean, they have clocked out?"

"I guess they can't fly anymore, because they've exceeded the number of hours they can fly in a day? It's a safety thi–"

"This is crazy. We're on a plane full of people. Like, 200 passengers. Lots of little kids, even babies." She pointed to the front of the plane. "They're not unloading the plane and not letting us out of here? This is really cruel, you know that?"

"I know. But they'll sort it out. Don't worry. We'll make it home soon."

Eyes wide, she stared at him.

"Okay, Episode Five now."

CHAPTER
Thirty-Nine

IT WAS ALMOST two in the morning when their flight finally landed at Dulles, and after three when the taxi stopped in front of Kiana's building to drop her off before continuing to Jason's place. He stretched, as he set foot on the pavement, getting out of the cab, so he could help Kiana with her suitcase.

"I'll see you tomorrow," Jason said, "Get some rest, alright?"

"You, too," Kiana responded. "This wasn't too bad, was it?"

"No, not at all. Come here," Jason said and hugged his friend. As he did so, he caught a whiff of her new perfume. He inhaled deeply, having gotten used to the smell during the trip to L.A. Light and airy, pleasant, but also fresh. It was filled with hope.

The taxi driver, who'd gotten out to get something out of the trunk, got back into the car and slammed the door shut, breaking the magic of the moment. Jason forced himself to let Kiana out of his grasp and stepped back.

"Good night, Jason," Kiana said, looking at him carefully.

"Good night," Jason squeezed out, getting into the back seat of the cab.

He'd just spent a week in Kiana's company, and the last thing he wanted was to let her go. As they rode away, he turned to look at his friend.

I wonder if she feels the same way. I should have asked her to come with me, I should have done something. Jason gnawed at himself, but the risk of losing such a great friendship was too big. *What if she'd said no, what if she doesn't feel the same way? We shared a bed at Charlie's and nothing happened,* Jason thought gingerly.

The realization of how he felt towards Kiana had hit Jason with full force on the flight back from L.A.

Up until that point, his feelings for her were bottled up. Neatly stored and carefully ignored.

Jason had told himself nothing romantic was ever possible, that he and Kiana were too different, that both of them had been too traumatized, and that their friendship had been too important. And she'd said it herself. Jason had mulled over the 'avoidant' attachment style, and had even looked it up on his phone, while Kiana was catching up with Charlie.

While they were sitting on the tarmac, waiting for the pilot to provide them with an update, Jason felt surprisingly at peace with the world. The stress, the hot airplane, nothing bothered him.

Because I was next to Kiana, he understood with sudden clarity. *I love her, I am in love with Kiana.*

Jason walked into his apartment, and was immediately greeted by Percy's indignant meows. He picked the cat up.

"How have you been, little girl? You look alright, did the cat sitter take good care of you?" He kissed his cat on the nose. Percy wiggled out of his grasp and ran to the food bowl. "Alright, let's make sure you have a good dinner, shall we?" Then, checking the clock, sighed, and said, "Or breakfast."

———

That night, Jason could barely sleep. He dreamed of Kiana, who was slipping away from him. One moment, she was next to him, and the next, she moved further and further into the distance, and all that remained was a sense of loss. One second, he was holding her hand, and the next, she was absorbed into a dark void.

Tossing and turning, Jason forced himself to stay in bed until nine, then shuffled into the kitchen, feeling groggy.

Percy was waiting for him there. She examined him, meowed, and rubbed against his legs. Jason could tell, Percy wasn't hungry, he'd fed her just six hours prior, and her dry food bowl was still full, but he fed her anyway, disregarding all the cat rearing advice he'd perused since getting Percy.

It's been a year, Jason thought, staring at the cat, who had become a part of his life. By July, if things with Yuna had gone according to plan, Jason would have been married. And yet, there he was, single, and pining for Kiana.

Kiana.

Jason made himself an espresso and sat down at the kitchen counter, thinking, *Is this what life would be? Always waiting, guessing?* "It's never too late to know the truth," he suddenly remembered Kiana's words. *I need to know the answer,* Jason pushed his chair back. The revelation struck him: he needed to see Kiana right away.

Jason got ready and left his apartment. He walked through Clarendon to Trader Joe's, thinking over the next steps. He'd given himself time to mull over his decision on purpose, but, by the time he stopped by the flower buckets at the entrance to the store, his resolve had only gotten stronger.

Carefully, he picked out a bouquet of roses. A soft shade of pink, with multilayered petals. He surveyed the bouquet, counted the roses. There were twelve of them. He picked out another bouquet, identical, to the first one. After paying for the flowers, Jason took one rose out and handed it to a forlorn-looking woman who had just walked into the store. Her face lit up and she thanked him profusely.

Twenty-three, like the year, he thought, walking to Kiana's apartment. His hands felt clammy, and his heart was beating fast, when, minutes later, he stood in front of the familiar door with the 2023C and knocked.

Kiana opened the door.

"Jason!" she exclaimed, then, seeing the bouquet, raised her eyebrows. "Is everything okay?"

"No," he said, then immediately corrected himself. "Yes. These are for you." He handed her the flowers, awkwardly and blushed.

"For me? Thank you." Kiana stepped back, rubbing her eyes. "I just woke up."

"I," Jason leaned on the doorway, "I don't want to be friends."

"You don't?" Kiana stared at him, blinking fast. "Would you like to come in?"

Jason did.

"No. I can't be friends with you, Kiana. I'm attracted to you," he said, once he was inside. "I've always been attracted to you," Jason muttered, as paralyzing fear spread through his body.

"You are? But, you've never told me. You've never showed it." Kiana's eyes filled with tears.

"Kiana, I have to know," Jason forced himself to continue speaking. "I came to ask you," he stuttered. "Would you like to go on a date with me?"

"A date? Are you asking me out?" Kiana pulled her hair back. Normally, Jason could read her facial expressions like an open book, but again, he was stumped.

I am about to lose her forever, the thought flashed in his mind. *She's about to reject me and it'll be all over.*

"Yes, that's why I'm here."

"But I'm not Korean, Jason. I thought you only wanted to be with a Korean woman. I'm not looking for a fling."

"I'm not looking for a fling, either." Jason gave her a serious look.

"Oh, Jason." She shook her head. "But what about our friendship? Aren't you afraid we'll ruin it?"

"What I'm afraid of is that you find someone else and I'll lose you forever. Will you give us a chance?"

"But you know me, Jason. I'm avoidant, and I'm divorced, and just look at me," Kiana said. Tears were now streaming down her face. "And your family, and you've told me yourself, there are so many expectations."

"I don't care about any of it. Last night, when we were on that plane, you know what I realized? Even if the plane crashed, it would have been okay. Because you were next to me. All I want is to have you by my side. Just you." He spoke confidently now, as the lines of Kiana's face softened. "I know it's taken me way too long, but I kept thinking it over and over. It was always you. Only you."

"Only me?"

"Yes." He nodded. "I should have never gone to Korea last year. I should have fought for you."

"Oh, Jason," Kiana said, gazing into his eyes. "I never thought you had any feelings for me. So whenever I started to feel anything for you, I just tried to run away from it."

"I'm in love with you, Kiana," Jason said. When she didn't answer, he peered at her. "Please don't run away. Are those happy tears you are crying?"

"Yes, definitely happy tears. If you hadn't said anything, I would have never known." She shook her head in disbelief.

"You couldn't tell?"

"No. Never. How could I? We just spent a whole week sharing a bed, and nothing. I just figured it wasn't meant to be."

"I think it is, Kiana. Will you please give us a chance?"

She nodded, and he continued, "I know we haven't had our first date yet, but, I really want to kiss you right now." He gently brushed his hand against her cheek. Kiana smiled.

For the first time, finally, he reached for her lips.

———

The following morning, when Jason got to the office, Betsy greeted him with a broad grin.

"How was your vacation, Dr. Lee?" she asked, tilting her head. "Now, don't tell me, I think it went very well, right?"

"I had a great time," Jason said curtly, trying his best to avoid eye contact.

"Cassie, Cassie, come here, take a look at Jason," Betsie called into the PT space. It was before seven in the morning, but Cassie padded into the reception area with surprising speed.

"Welcome back, Jason," Cassie said, then, turning to Betsie, noted, "I see what you mean. He looks different."

With the two women staring at him intently, Jason started to back out of the reception area.

"Did you get those fillers again? Is that it?" Cassie asked first.

"No, not those." He shook his head, taking another step back into the safety of his office.

"Then it must be an enzyme treatment. Is that what you had done in L.A.?" Betsy pressed.

"Oh it's not the fillers, Betsy. I think he's in love," Cassie said.

"No way!" Betsy clapped. "Is that so? Jason, tell us, please."

Immediately, Jason's cheeks flushed red, and Cassie, encouraged, continued, "Am I right, Doc? Am I right?"

Despite himself, Jason could barely suppress a happy smile.

$$Epilogue$$

SIX MONTHS later

"Do you think she'll accept the invitation?" Kiana asked, scanning Jason's face for a reaction.

"I'm sure she will," he said, taking her hand into his and bringing it to his lips. "Should we tell her before or after you think?"

"Let's do it after."

Kiana's engagement ring sparkled brightly in the ray of light. Following his eyes, she noted, "I still can't get used to it. It's so beautiful."

He kissed her hand again.

Their meeting with Audrey Simmons was taking place many months after the L.A. trip. Though she welcomed the meeting, Audrey kept postponing it on the account of being busy with her grandchildren. And so, it was the week of Christmas the three of them reassembled at their usual location, the Silver Line Diner in Tyson's corner.

Audrey was already waiting for them inside, a serving of apple pie in front of her. She looked at them expectantly, then fixed her small, clever eyes on Jason. He couldn't help but reflect on how much his life had changed since their first meeting at this very location.

"It's good to see you," Audrey said, and the three of them exchanged pleasantries.

"Audrey, we wanted to tell you what we'd found out in L.A. We met with Mary Ward," Jason said, expecting Audrey to balk at him, but the woman simply nodded, indicating for him to continue speaking.

"It's thanks to Kiana. She did all the research and arranged for the meeting. If it weren't for her, I don't think we would have had a chance with Mary. But in the end, Mary Invernizzi really opened up to us."

"I see," Audrey noted solemnly. She dug her fork into the dessert, then placed a small piece of the pie into her mouth, chewing in silence.

"She really did." Kiana said.

"So, this is it, isn't it?" Audrey hummed, placing her fork down on the table. "I suppose it's time to face the facts. What did she tell you?" She brushed a piece of invisible lint off her shirt, her discomfort palpable.

"Audrey, I'm sorry," Kiana said. "But Anton *was* cheating on you. Actually, he was cheating on Mary with you, because by the time he came to Washington, DC, he was already engaged to her."

Audrey gasped. "What?"

"This isn't the reason we wanted to see you," Jason noted.

"My Anton? But how is that possible?" She drummed her fingers on the table.

"What Mary told us checks out. She told us they started dating shortly after he arrived in Canada. When he traveled to Washington and met you, they were already engaged," Kiana explained. "I'm sorry to be the one to tell you this."

Audrey bit her lip.

"We learned about Anton's death, and you might be interested in how it happened. Mary told us she was there."

"She killed him? But we must report it to the police!" Audrey exclaimed, pulling out her mobile.

"She didn't kill him, but he played the Russian Roulette because of her. She'd learned about you and dared him to prove he loved her."

"What?" Audrey's mouth gaped open. She then shook her head, as if dispelling a vision. "It all makes sense, Anton was like that, so spontaneous, so daring. I can completely see it happening."

"So, you think it's true then?" Kiana leaned forward, careful to conceal her left hand.

"I do, I do. This is the only explanation that actually makes any sense. A suicide doesn't and I never believed Anton would have done it. But this, yes, a dare, that's exactly like Anton." Audrey spoke of her former lover as if he were still alive. The way she was reminiscing about him sent a shiver down Jason's spine.

"This is a lot," Audrey said after a pause. Suddenly, her eyes sparkled. "I've noticed something," she said, her eyes darting from Jason to Kiana and back, her expression suddenly mischievous.

"You have?" Jason frowned.

"The two of you." Audrey smiled. "Was I right about the two of you? Something's changed, hasn't it?"

"It did." Jason nodded and threw a look full of love at Kiana. She met his gaze. They exchanged a light kiss.

"I'm so happy for the two of you," Audrey said. "What a gorgeous couple you are. Inside and out. What you have done for me, I'm incredibly grateful. It's very hard when you find out someone you've put up on a pedestal is not the person you've thought they were. But you've been open with me about Anton and I appreciate it."

At that moment, her mobile pinged. Audrey looked at it, and her expression brightened. "It's James! He's on his way to pick me up. We are going on a getaway for New Year's, just the two of us. I'm grateful to both of you for another reason. You know, these past months, I've been reflecting on my life. How I've been pining for a lost love all these years. I realized it's time I give my marriage and my James my whole heart." Tears welled up in her eyes, and Audrey pulled out a tissue.

Jason and Kiana were silent, giving her a moment. After Audrey recomposed herself, the two of them exchanged a quick glance.

Then Jason said, "Audrey, there's something else we wanted to tell you." He looked over at Kiana, and she continued, "We would like to invite you, you and James, to our wedding. It'll be in March, at the Meadowlark Gardens."

"Really? Oh, how lovely!" Audrey exclaimed. "Will it be at the Korean Bell Garden?" Her eyes glistened with what Jason assumed were happy tears, as she looked at him, then Kiana.

"Yes. It was Kiana's idea. It's like having a little piece of Korea right here." He looked over at his fiancée with undisguised admiration.

"James and I will be there. Thank you for extending the invitation in person." Audrey smiled.

"If it weren't for you and the investigation, we probably wouldn't have gotten together," Jason said. "And what you said to me before, about love. You're our fairy godmother, Audrey. You and Percy."

"Who is Percy?" Audrey raised her eyebrows.

"A cat," Jason and Kiana responded in unison.

"Jinx," Kiana exclaimed, looking over at Jason, while he yelped, "Jjijjibbong."

He leaned over to Kiana and kissed her on the cheek.

The End

———

Thank you for reading 'Matched in Seoul, Found in Love'.

If you enjoyed my second novel, I would love your honest review on Amazon and Goodreads. Why am I asking for reviews? For an indie author like myself, each review means I can get more books to other readers who enjoy stories written in the contemporary fiction genre. This is why every single review means a huge amount to me.

Thank you for your support. And above all, happy reading.

Acknowledgments

Whether you believe everything in life is predestined or happens by chance, this book would never have happened without a happy coincidence that led me to Korea. I discovered this amazing country bit by bit, slowly falling in love with its history, its people, and the culture. And as I got to know its people more, I made friends and learned their stories. Some of them seemed so fantastical and intriguing, I couldn't help but think they would make a great book.

First and foremost, to mention Kevin Kim, who has so generously shared with me his stories and has been my primary advisor and sounding board about this book. It would not have happened without him. Kevin, thank you for patiently answering my many questions and not only sharing information, but also explaining the reasons behind the various traditions.

I would also like to thank Hyoung Sun Ryu for introducing me to modern Korean literature and for advising me on many cultural aspects that were crucial to the book. Sharing our love of literature has been incredible, and I am especially grateful to Sun for reviewing the early version of the book.

The final person I'd like to thank is Dr. Chang Yong Kim for sharing with me his professional journey and the information about the podiatry practice. Without him, Jason's story would not have been the same.

About the Author

Alex Alvin grew up fascinated by how history and current events connect through stories of love. That fascination has translated into Alex's books that explore how world events impact people and their fates. Creating historically accurate books, where these stories come to life, is Alex's passion.

If you'd like to keep in touch, please subscribe to my newsletter. Or you can find me at any of the social media sites below.

facebook.com/AlexAlvinAuthor

instagram.com/alexalvinauthor

bookbub.com/authors/alex-alvin

amazon.com/author/alexalvin